MW01147811

One Love

Bill Holmes

Xpress Yourself Publishing

Xpress Yourself Publishing, LLC
P.O. Box 1615
Upper Marlboro, MD 20773

www.xpressyourselfpublishing.org

This is a work of fiction. All of the characters, incidents, and dialogue, except for incidental references to public figures, products, or services, are imaginary and are not intended to refer to any persons, living or dead, or to disparage any company's products or services.

For information about special discounts for bulk purchases, please contact Xpress Yourself Publishing Special Sales: 1-301-404-5615 or info@xpressyourselfpublishing.org.

Manufacturered in the United States of America

ISBN 0-9722990-4-1

Dedication

This book is dedicated to my parents, William L. Holmes, Sr. and Sandra Baytops. Thanks for always being supportive of all my creative endeavors and for giving me the courage to dream big dreams that exceeded my imagination.

Also, I would like to give a special dedication to my brother and friend, Gene Roberson. You, Kenny and Marv laid the foundation for many artists in Philly, including yours truly, to hone their skills and to pursue their craft at Buttamilk. *One Love* would not be possible without your experience, humor and insight.

Acknowledgments

To God, You are and will always be the foundation of my strength; Uva, all dream, some conceptualize, few like us, mi amiga, realize. Thank you for all of your assistance and the use of your poem *Strange Fruit*; Janet Benton, your writing courses assisted me in the transition from writing poetry to writing fiction; my brother, Mike Holmes, and my entire family, thanks for all the love and support over the years; Jessica Tilles, my publisher, thank you for all the opportunities and for joining the Xpress Yourself Publishing family; John Wooden, thank you so much for your excellent and punctual editorial services; Tonya Marie Evans-Walls, thanks for your legal assistance; Drs. Phillip L. Benditt, MD and Steven B. Nagelberg, MD, thanks for your medical advice; Tanya Dinkins-Williams, Deon Browning and Osay Karume, you are my dearest friends and will always have a place in my heart; Kim Davis, Mel Young, Bernard Collins, Aisha Harrington, Rita Caldwell, Aranna Haywardo, Sandra Walls, Kerie Grey, Stephanie Lee, Rhonda Byrd, Rhonda Karim and Dough and Ebony Cradle, thanks for your feedback, friendship, suggestions and enthusiasm to read more.

A special acknowledgment to the following authors whose works inspired me to keep writing and dreaming: Tracy Price-Thompson, Marcus Major, Nicole Bailey-Williams, Eric Jerome Dickey, Colin Channer, Diane McKinney-Whetstone and Timmothy McCann.

A special acknowledgment of thanks to the following artists and individuals for allowing me to use their names and/or likeness in the novel: Gene Roberson, Warren Oree and the Arpeggio Jazz Ensemble, Lamont "NAPALM" Dixon, Lamar Redcross, Koko Darling, Aziza Kineth, J. Michael Harrison and the Twin Poets.

Most importantly, I need to give thanks and praise to everybody

One Love

Chapter One
Chris

This was the fifth time this month I had seen her aboard the R3 Regional Rail at the Lansdowne Station. I didn't know who she was, but every time I saw her, the more I came to the conclusion I knew her from someplace. Our paths had crossed before, but I had no idea where and when.

She always looked sharp going to work, and today was no exception. The one thing about her, which always turned me on, was the confidence in her stride. There was something so commanding about the way she walked, like Maxine Shaw from *Living Single*. I wasn't sure if she was an attorney, but she had that elegant, classy beauty like Vanessa L. Williams. The linen khaki business suit she was sportin' on this humid June morning worked well against her cinnamon complexion. Her auburn shoulder length hair she usually wore down was pinned up.

Uh oh, she must have realized I'd been checking her out because she made eye contact with me. The quizzical look on her face told me she thought she might know me, too. But she wasn't certain either. She sat down in the empty seat across the aisle from me, next to the balding white guy sleeping against the window.

"Hi," I said.

"Good morning," she replied.

She pulled out her BlackBerry and I went back to writing in my journal. I had enough problems with women. I was already going to catch all sorts of hell from my girlfriend, Veronica, when I got to work this morning. It wasn't cool to leave her high and dry the way

I did after our argument Friday night. To make matters worse, I hadn't called her all weekend. She was going to be pissed off big time.

Ronnie and I had hooked up three months earlier. We met for the first time when she came into my department one day to deliver a file to my supervisor regarding a bankruptcy case. Pretty soon, when we ran into each other in the elevator and the break room, we were exchanging small talk. Small talk led to us having lunch, and then, before you know it, we were dating.

I don't know when and how our relationship went from sugar to shit. Why was I still involved with her? My heart wasn't there. I was much more consumed with trying to complete my new book of poetry and a spoken word CD project. But I couldn't do either. I had the worse case of writer's block and no matter how hard I tried, no fresh ideas were coming to me.

Pete, the R3 conductor, made his way into the car. "Next stop, University City. Please have all tickets and passes out for final inspection."

I retrieved my pass from my wallet while Pete made his way down the aisle making small talk with the passengers.

Pete extended his fist towards me. "What's up, Poet?"

I gave him some dap. "Nothin' to it. How about yourself?"

"Just another day, another dollar."

"I hear you, brah," I said. "Just trying to get some creativity flowing before I get to work."

"No doubt, Poet. I'll talk to you later."

"Later," I said, watching Pete depart towards the rear of the car.

As I placed my wallet back into my suit jacket, I noticed the sistah sitting across from me was staring in my direction. She exchanged a friendly smile and went back to messing around with her BlackBerry.

"Excuse me, Miss?" I asked.

"Yes, can I help you?" she replied.

"Please forgive me for saying this, but you look familiar."

"Is that a line you say to every lady you meet on the train?"

"No, it's not like that at all. I know I've seen you somewhere before and I feel embarrassed because I don't know where."

"Relax, I'm joking with you. Honestly, I was thinking the same thing when I saw you."

"Okay, I see where you're coming from."

She chuckled. "What's your name?"

I extended my hand to shake hers. "Chris Harrington."

She took my hand into a firm, but gentle shake. "Nice to meet you, Chris."

"And yours?"

"Regina Simmons."

"Pleasure meeting you, Regina." Hmmm, now why did her name sound so familiar?

Pete came walking down the aisle when the R3 came to a stop at University City. I stood up from my seat to let the passenger sitting to my left get off the train with the departing commuters. As I sat back down, Regina gestured to me with her eyes to slide over to the next seat while grabbing her belongings to sit by my side before any new passengers came aboard. After the train pulled away from the platform, Pete came through the doors and walked down the aisle, announcing to everyone that the next stop would be 30th Street Station.

"So, Chris, you're a poet?" Regina inquired.

"Check you out, girl. Got your nose all up in the Kool Aid and don't know the flavor of the punch?"

She laughed. "You got me. I like poetry and I think poets are cool. Do you mind if I take a peek?" She pointed to my journal.

"I'm not finished with this piece yet, and uncomfortable sharing incomplete poems."

"Well, you don't have to share that poem. Why don't you recite something from the top of your head?"

I laughed and she gave me a *what's-so-funny* look.

"Well, I'm kinda on the bit of the shy side and..."

"You're not a poet, Chris; you're a playa. I see the game you and your buddy, Pete, are trying to run aboard this train to the ladies."

"You're funny, Regina. Are you always this comical first thing in the morning?"

"No, not really. I'm a riot at the office after my third cup."

"You drink three cups of coffee? Damn, that's a lot of caffeine."

"Some people are addicted to smoking and to drugs. I'm addicted to..." Regina paused. She had noticed the male passenger sitting in front of us eavesdropping in on our conversation. He turned his head towards the right and stopped typing on his laptop. She cleared her throat loudly while bulging her eyes wide open.

"Would you please mind your damn business?" she told him.

No, she didn't do that. He turned his head around and did so without uttering a word in response. I couldn't help cracking up. Neither could she.

"Anyway, back to you, Chris, before we were so *rudely interrupted*. How do I know you're a poet and not a playa?"

I handed her my journal. "Would you like to read what I wrote so far?"

"No, that's okay. How about I give you a topic and you recite the first thing which comes into your head."

"Bet!" I returned, full of confidence.

"Okay. Azaleas."

"Azaleas?" Damn, this was going to be a tough one. I stroked my goatee and thought for a deep moment. Why the hell did she pick that word? Regina stared at me. I took a deep breath and responded to her request.

Azaleas bloom
beneath the sunrise
that welcomes the arrival
and the promise of a new day
when divine intervention flows
from the tree of Life

into the ties that bind us
in the joy of friendship.

Regina smiled. "It was beautiful and deep."

"Thanks."

"You've got some skills, Chris, but I think Pete is wrong about calling you a poet. You're more like a poet-in-training because you hesitated for a good minute before you finally got your words together."

"Damn, Regina, I prove my lyrical talent and creative skills and now you gonna bust my stones!"

"Now I know you're a poet because *'you are 'sensitive about yo' stuff'!"*

"Okay, Erykah Badu!"

Regina laughed and twirled the silver dolphin pendant hanging around her neck.

"Your pendant is lovely. Where did you get it from?"

"Thank you. I bought this last summer at a marketplace in Ocho Rios, Jamaica."

"Really? I went to Montego Bay last summer in June. First time there and had a ball."

"Me, too. My girlfriends and I went there for our annual All-Girls Getaway the entire week before Labor Day. We've done it every year for the past four years. Pick a destination, pack our things and head off to the islands for some fun in the sun. It was a week to remember."

"I bet it was."

"And what are you trying to imply?"

"Nothing. Nothing at all."

Regina shook her index finger. "Yeah, right! You don't get off that easy, Chris."

"I'm just making an observation about what you said."

"So, you're making an observation about my girlfriends and I being in Jamaica for an annual getaway from the stress and the men in our lives?" She paused for a moment. "Wait a minute, aren't they one and the same?"

I waved my hands. "Ouch!"

As the train came to a complete stop, the next wave of commuters made their departure. I was known for putting my foot in my mouth from time to time and not wanting this to be one of those times, I silently prayed while waiting for Regina's response.

She playfully rolled her eyes at me and murmured, "Hmmm."

"I felt the same way when I went to Jamaica alone."

"You went to Jamaica by yourself? Yeah, right!"

"I did go to Jamaica by myself...for a personal retreat."

"I bet it was."

"And just what are you trying to imply?"

"I can't imagine going away by myself to another country, not unless I was trying to hook up with an exotic, Caribbean lover, like Terry McMillan's character in *How Stella Got Her Groove Back.* Were you looking to get your groove back with a fine Jamaican sistah, my brotha?" Regina asked, raising her eyebrows.

"Isn't it a little too early in the morning for your mind to be in the gutter, Ms. Simmons?"

Regina released a soft laughter that was a sweet melody to my ears. I told myself to relax because...one, I had a girlfriend, although things were rocky, though it's always nice to keep our options open, and two, the shape of her full lips accentuated by her red lipstick and perfect white teeth was making my dick hard.

Once again, Pete made his way through the doors as the train left 30th Street Station. He announced that Suburban Station would be our next step. Regina placed her briefcase in the empty space between us.

"Are you getting off here?" she asked.

"No, not until Market East at the Gallery."

Regina stood up in the aisle, placed her purse over her left shoulder and grabbed the briefcase with her right hand. "Well, it was nice to meet you, Mr. Harrington. I hope you have a good day."

"You, too. Don't work too hard."

"I'll try not to."

"Hope to see you around."

"Maybe…we'll see, Chris. You never know," she teased, flashing her gorgeous smile. "Take care of yourself."

"You do the same," I said.

Regina made her way to the front of the car, turned around and waved goodbye. I still couldn't remember where I'd seen her prior to today, but so much about her was familiar, especially her smile. Her identity would probably come to me later on, and I had a feeling our paths would cross again, at the very least on the R3 train.

Chapter Two
Chris

The entrance to the Internal Audit Department, with its gloomy, gray sign affixed to the white wall to the right of the door, had intimidated many employees of Aurora Mutual Savings Bank when they stepped off the elevator and onto the fifth floor. For me, the department was simply a place I could call a job for the time being. Work was the last place I wanted to be today, but there was no way to avoid the inevitable showdown with Ronnie.

There were a lot of employees who were on pins and needles ever since rumors about a possible merger with a larger bank began circulating the office when the annual statement revealed unsatisfactory results to the Board of Directors. Although I was concerned like anyone else, I was confident in my performance since my annual evaluations were usually rated four on a one to five scale, with one being, "Falls Below Expectations" and five being, "Significantly Exceeds Expectations." However, there were a few strikes against me. I didn't have an advanced degree or professional certification beyond my Bachelor's; I was a black male in a predominately white industry; and I was losing my enthusiasm for working in Corporate America.

I walked down the narrow corridor with the drab yellow walls and saw Mary, the departmental secretary, filing away audit binders in the adjacent office room and singing to herself.

"Good morning, Chris. How was your weekend?"

"It was alright, Mary."

"That's nice. Veronica Taylor from the Mortgage Services Department came by earlier to see you. She asked me to tell you to please call her."

"Thanks," I said. Shit. I knew our conversation wasn't going to be as pretty as the one I'd had with Regina. I picked up my gym bag and went to my cubicle, while some of my co-workers sat at theirs and pretended to be working.

I sat down at my desk and stared at the audit work lying on my desk. Then, I glanced over at the black phone resting beside the computer monitor. The red message light was blinking and I hesitantly pressed the voicemail button to listen to the one message as I prayed it was not from Ronnie. To my relief, it was my half-brother, Sam, saying hello and reminding me about our father's upcoming retirement dinner. Sam and I had the same father and were almost ten years apart. We've had an on-again/off-again relationship while growing up. Then again, I've always had the same rapport with my father. We barely spoke to each other as adults since our relationship went downhill after my parents separated when I was nine years old.

One Friday afternoon, after coming home from school, I saw this ugly, green station wagon sitting in the driveway. Dad's clothes and some of our personal belongings, including my parents' record player and album collection, along with the color TV I got for my last birthday, were in the back seat. I walked through the front door and saw my dad and an unfamiliar woman carrying boxes downstairs. He told me to have a seat on the living room sofa, not bothering to introduce me to the stranger. She didn't even say hello. A year later, she would become my stepmother. Dad picked up the telephone, called Mom at work and told her, "I'm out of your life forever." Years later, when I was much older, Mom told me her response was, "Nigger, you've been out of my life for years." Dad then told her he had gathered his belongings, forwarded his mail to my grandmother's house in South Philly and that her son was home from school. Mom dropped everything she was doing at work and rushed home as fast as she could. By the time she arrived, the strange woman and the station wagon were gone.

My parents had the nastiest argument I'd ever witnessed and it brought tears to my eyes. Even though Mom told me to go upstairs, I could still hear the yelling and the cursing. I cried uncontrollably, wondering what I had done to make Dad leave our family. I wished it was only a nightmare. Unfortunately, it wasn't. After the arguing stopped, a car pulled up to our house, the front door slammed and then there was silence. Looking out the bedroom window, I saw Dad get inside the passenger side of the station wagon right before the car pulled off.

Later, Mom walked up the stairs and knocked on my bedroom door. Sitting on my bed beside me, she put her arm around me and rubbed my head. I stared at her soft face, mascara smeared from the tears she had cried. Mom said, "Everything is going to be alright, Chris. Sometimes people do crazy things we don't understand and they don't get along, but it doesn't mean they love you any less. No matter where your father is going, he still loves you and don't you stop loving him either." Six months later, my parents' divorce was official.

"Hey, Chris," a female voice said, startling me.

I drew a heavy sigh of relief when I saw April Williams standing beside my cubicle. "Hey, April. How are you doing this morning?"

April was the administrative assistant who was a temp in the Marketing Department. We had met at a poetry reading several months earlier and since then, she had come to work at Aurora.

"I'm fine, thanks. I mean, it's Monday and I'd rather be home, but you know how it is."

"I hear you," I replied.

"How was your weekend?" April asked.

"Good. And yours?"

"It was okay, nothing to complain about."

"I see somebody got her hair braided. It looks real nice."

"Thanks," she said, combing her fingers through the freshly-done braids. "How's the new book and CD coming along?"

"So far, so good. I have two more tracks to finish on the CD and maybe another poem or two to write and it's a done deal."

"You know I want my copy to be personally autographed, just in case you blow up and become rich and famous."

"Yeah, right, April. We'll see about the rich and famous part."

"No, it's going to happen. Trust me. By the way, are you coming out to Brave New World tonight for the Po/Jazz Series?"

Just then, I heard the front door open and someone walking into my department.

"Damn!" I said, snapping my fingers. "I forgot tonight was Po/Jazz."

"You know you have to represent Chris and do a little sumthin' sumthin' on the mic tonight. Please?" she begged.

Out of the corner of my eye, I saw Ronnie standing at Mary's desk. She was sporting a major *Poetic Justice* attitude this morning: long hair pulled back in a ponytail, arms crossed and dressed in an all-black wardrobe from her blouse to her shoes. I bit my bottom lip, not knowing what the hell she might do or say. Without saying a word, Ronnie turned around and went about her business.

"We'll see," I responded, exhaling a sigh of relief. "If I can get done what I need accomplished early enough with my boy, Gene, then I'll come out and support."

April tapped her fingers on my cubicle. "Well, I might be brave tonight and sign up for the open mic."

"Aw shit!" I exclaimed.

April hunched her shoulders and smiled. "Maybe, Chris, maybe. I'm feeling in the mood to read a new poem I wrote the other day."

"There's a first time for everything."

"I know, but I'm scared."

"Please! I still get scared every time I recite poetry. If I can do it, so can you."

"But you're good. Myself, I don't know."

"Don't underestimate yourself. I think you'll do fine. I like what you've shown me so far and I think it's good. However, nobody else will know unless you, pardon the cliché, let your light shine."

"Thanks, Chris, for the encouragement. Well, have a good day, and I hope to see you tonight." April smiled, while walking away from my cubicle.

I got up to get a cup of water from the water cooler. Empty. Little trifling things like that really irked my nerves, just like someone being too lazy to replenish paper in the copier after they used it to run a large job. After replacing the empty bottle with a new one, I came back to my desk and stood over my chair. The telephone rang with one beep, which indicated it was an internal call. I stared at the phone until I decided to pick it up after the third ring.

"Audit, Chris speaking."

"I would like to see you in the stairwell. Now!"

"Good morning to you, too, Veronica."

"I apologize. Good morning. I want to see you in the stairwell. Right now!"

"I'm sorry, but now is not a good time."

"Fine! Then I will come back upstairs and say what I have to say in front of your entire department! I don't give a shit!"

"Okay, I'll be in the stairwell in two minutes."

I shook my head, left the Internal Audit Department and went to the bathroom down the hallway before meeting with Veronica. Mother Nature had a funny way of calling every time I found myself nervous or excited. I washed my hands and stared at my reflection in the mirror, while listening to the theme from *The Good, The Bad, and The Ugly* play inside my head. After slowly counting to ten, I left the bathroom and made my way down the hallway.

Standing in front of the stairwell for another ten seconds, I recalled the entire incident in my mind from Friday night. Ronnie's former co-worker, Renee, had invited us to happy hour at Savannah. She told me she despised "that cute fucking bitch" and wanted to rub shit in her face now that she was making more money at Aurora. Although I suspected she also planned to include her new boyfriend in the equation, I told her she was being petty and I didn't think it was a good idea. She kept whining about me not caring and being supportive of her needs. We argued throughout the day and after work when I tried to convince her to forget about the happy hour.

I said, "Honey, let it go! You don't need to prove anything to Renee. Okay? Why don't we either go to the movies or to dinner?" Before I could say another word, Ronnie replied, "I bet if I were one of your tacky poetry groupie bitches, you'd go the extra mile!" After hearing her comment, I left work, went to the Gallery and caught the next R3 train without her.

Our usual meeting place was right between the third and fourth floors. The dimly lit, dusty stairwell seemed cold and eerie, but today, there was also a feeling of hostility present as the sound of Ronnie's footsteps grew near. When I saw her, I could see the anger written across her pecan face, etched into her raging brown eyes and tightly held lips.

"Good morning, Ronnie. How are..."

"Don't give me that good morning shit! Who the fuck do you think you are, Mr. Harrington? First, you walk away from me in the middle of an argument! Second, you never bothered to call me at all any time this weekend to see if I made it home safe! And this morning, I came into your office at eight thirty to speak with you and you weren't there. You didn't call me when you arrived at work, but I did see you took time out to speak with the phony, high maintenance bitch that's temping in the Marketing Department!"

"First, I apologize for walking away... "

"You had no right to leave me the way you did. You hurt my feelings," she interjected.

"I know, Ronnie, and I'm sorry. There's no excuse for what I did."

"You're damn right, because you really didn't give a fuck about my well being!"

I sighed. "If you'd let me explain..."

"There is no explanation for what you did, considering the fact you never bothered to call me the entire weekend."

No matter how hard I tried, there was no way I was going to get a word in our conversation. Once Ronnie got her neck rolling and her hands up in my face, forget about it. I waited for her to finish telling me about myself before I finally told her how I was fed up with her silly accusations and that I wasn't cheating on her.

Ever since she first saw me recite a love poem I dedicated to her and the positive reaction I received afterwards from the females, girlfriend kept bombarding me with insults and nasty remarks about my writing and poetry. I hadn't been to a poetry reading in over a month because she wanted us to spend some time together. At first, I wasn't with that, but then agreed with her because I could be insensitive at times and get self-absorbed when it came to my writing. However, we'd been hanging with each other too much at work five days a week and on weekends. I suggested that maybe we might need a little personal time for ourselves.

"What you just said was totally bullshit! You're just being selfish as hell!"

"Ronnie, that's ridiculous!" I replied, widening my eyes. I couldn't believe she had the nerve to make such a hypocritical statement. "Speaking of ridiculous, what you said about April Williams justifies my first point. She's someone I met at a poetry reading at Gloria's Gourmet Seafood Restaurant and who happens to be an aspiring poet. April came to work here several weeks ago and remembered me. We were talking about the Po/Jazz Series at Brave New World tonight. She asked me if I was coming out tonight and I told her, I had other plans."

"I bet you do! You know damn well she has eyes for you! And you love soaking up all the attention she gives you, don't you? I can hear her now…'Oh, Chris, you are such a good poet. Can you please critique my poetry for me? I wrote this poem especially for you!' I bet she'd love to stroke your Longfellow, wouldn't she? And you know you love to flirt with her, don't you? You don't fool me for one minute dressed in your favorite navy blue, double-breasted suit, trying to pimp her like a fake P. Diddy."

"You know something, Ronnie? You might need to seek counseling for your insecurities."

"What did you say?"

"You heard me! It's not even nine o'clock. I can't handle all this melodramatic bullshit first thing in the morning. Goodbye." I began to walk up the stairs to the fifth floor as Ronnie stood in the stairwell motionless. I turned around and looked back at her standing there in complete silence and looking at me with an expressionless face.

Once I made my way back to my cubicle, I thought about cleaning up the work paper comments to take my mind off of what just happened, but instead, I picked up the phone to leave a message with Gene, a friend of mine on the Philly poetry scene.

Gene was the former host of Buttamilk, a weekly venue at the North Star Bar in North Philly, which featured poetry, comedy and R&B music that was on the love jones tip before the movie came out. He invited me over to his apartment to record some poetry for a demo he was putting together in his makeshift home studio. When I told him my plans to write a poetry book, he suggested I have a complimentary CD to go along with the book. We'd been working together for the past six months and it was nothing but smooth sailing until I hit my creative snag six weeks ago. I recovered and went back into the studio with Gene last week. Although he felt everything was good with what we had, it didn't feel complete to me.

"Peace and blessings. You have reached the Roberson residence. Please leave a brief message and we'll get right back to you."

"Hey, Gene, this is Chris. Just giving you a call to say what's up and..."

"Cool C in the place to be! What's goin' on, man?" Gene interrupted.

"Wassup, Gene? Whatcha doin' home at this hour?"

"Nothin' much. Took the day off from work to parlay with the Misses. We're havin' breakfast and then we're gonna be headed out to the doctor's office to do this ultrasound thing."

I rested the receiver between my left shoulder and ear. "Sounds good. How's Kymm doing?"

"She's doing well. Getting excited about being a mom, even though she hasn't started to show yet."

"Tell her I said hi."

"No problem, Cool C. Kymm, Cool C says hi. She says hey. So what's goin' on with you?"

"Nothin, my brotha, just the usual. If it's not work, then it's the woman, but I'll be alright. Things can't get any worse."

"Oh shit! That doesn't sound good."

I massaged my temple with my index finger. "Not really, brah. I'll fill you in on the details later. Are we still on tonight?"

"Yeah, what's up?"

"I forgot tonight is Po/Jazz night."

"Word? You know we gotta show face."

"Are you sure, Gene? What about studio time?"

"Nah, don't even worry about it. We can always reschedule studio time on the weekend. You never know what cats might be up in there and we can always hit folks up with promo CDs."

"I was thinking the same thing. Hold on for a moment. I have another caller on the line."

"No problem, Cool C. Let me finish eating breakfast so Kymm and I can roll on out of here. Hit me back on my cell to let me know what time you'll swing by. Aight man?"

"Aight."

"Peace."

I pressed the button to answer the call on the other line. "Audit, Chris speaking."

"Hello, Chris, it's me," Ronnie said.

"Hey."

"I'm sorry, honey. I wasn't listening to you when I should have been. It's wrong for me to say these things, but I don't want to lose you. Can you forgive me?"

"If you can forgive me for my behavior, then I can forgive you, too."

"Chris, we need to sit down and talk."

"I agree. I'm going to Po/Jazz tonight, but can I call you when I come home this evening?"

Ronnie deeply sighed. "Do you have to go to Po/Jazz tonight?"

"Why do you have to say it like that?"

"I'm sorry but poetry ain't my thing!"

"What did you say? Since when did you all of a sudden not like poetry?"

Now, why did I have to go and say that? Ronnie cursed me out by telling me how I'm wasting my time going around to these poetry venues and how my efforts would never amount to anything. She repeated the same accusations of me cheating on her and berated Gene for being unfaithful to his wife. Ronnie had never even met Gene and only knew him based upon the things I'd told her. I sat there in complete shock, devastated by her nasty comments. I had to ask myself was my mental sanity and emotional stability worth this sacrifice?

I rubbed my head in frustration. "I don't know what else to say to you, Ronnie, but…"

"You don't have to say anything else, Chris," Ronnie interrupted. "Just get together with your buddy tonight. I hope you two have a good time with your fucking poetry groupies! Goodbye!"

Chapter Three
Regina

Marcia popped into my cubicle for the third time in the last fifteen minutes. "How are you coming with the financials, Regina?" she asked.

"Almost there. Five more minutes," I said nonchalantly. Not wanting to see the pitiful, desperate look on her face, I kept my eyes glued to my PC monitor.

"Okay, let me know ASAP because there may be another change in the expenses."

I clenched my teeth and asked the Lord to forgive me for rolling my eyes and for what I was thinking the moment those words escaped her lips. Throughout the morning, I kept murmuring aloud, "I love my job, I love my job."

I spent most of my morning revising the financial statements for my boss, Marcia, before her meeting this afternoon at three o'clock. I had to get a grip because I was already on my fifth cup of coffee and about to lose it. I couldn't let this crap get the best of me. I kept trying to convince myself that this too shall pass and I would leave work by one thirty. I refused to reschedule another doctor's appointment for these fools.

I let the phone ring twice and concentrated on finishing the financials for the next ten minutes. Printing two copies, I scrutinized the numbers one last time and walked over to Marcia's office. All I saw, though, was the usual clutter of spreadsheets, flowcharts and superseded copies of financial statements she scattered across her desk. So I sat the statements on her chair with a Post It note attached to the front page.

On Marcia's desk was a picture of herself and her husband, Phil, taken on their five-year anniversary. It made me laugh. She was sitting in a chair wearing a Donna Karan black dress that accentuated her hourglass figure. Phil stood by her side, all five feet two of his pudgy frame, sporting an overexcited grin on his face and appearing dapper in an olive suit. She had a pretentious smile, which clearly said, "I married you for your family's wealth along with your six-figure salary." Damn gold-digger!

After leaving Marcia's office, I returned to my cubicle and listened to my messages.

"Hello, this message is for Regina Simmons in the Accounting Department. This is Carl at the front desk in the lobby. You have a delivery waiting for you downstairs. Could you please give me a call when you have a moment? Thanks."

"Hey, Gigi, this is Cami. Just giving you a call since I haven't heard from you in a minute and you missed your second hair appointment. Only God knows what you're doing to that nappy head of yours, but if I find out you've been going to somebody else, I'll shave your head bald and then I'll kill you! So give me a call when you get the chance. Talk to ya soon."

Upon returning Carl's phone call, he informed me the delivery was a lovely bouquet of flowers along with a card, which arrived not too long ago. I asked him to put them aside until I was able to pick them up. Most likely, they were from Keith's sorry ass with another tired attempt to reconcile. Some men can't take a hint that when it's over, it's over. I was moving on with my life, so why couldn't he? Don't get me wrong, Keith had it goin' on: educated, employed, didn't live with his mama and knew how to cook something in the kitchen besides microwave popcorn. However, he was a self righteous and arrogant jerk who had no respect for me while we were dating. Keith would annoy me every time we went to the movies, dinner or a concert and he would attempt to glance at other women. This was the beginning of the end for me as far as our relationship was concerned. I had my suspicions whether or not Keith was cheating on me whenever he received phone calls in the middle of the night or his cell phone rang and he didn't answer them in my presence. The final straw for me was when he let one of his ex-girlfriends, who had marital problems, stay over at his apartment until "things got better." Not one to be anybody's fool, I realized it was time for me to permanently leave Keith's world.

For some strange reason, I couldn't get the guy I met aboard the R3 out of my mind. Chris Harrington. I knew I'd seen him before because his face was too familiar. "Mm hmmm," I sighed, thinking about how handsome he looked in that navy pinstripe suit. I closed my eyes and reminisced about his light brown eyes, trimmed goatee, luscious lips and broad shoulders. Lord, give me another chance to sit next to him again. I didn't know Chris from Adam, but I bet my last dollar he was already involved with someone special. The good ones usually were.

Next, I picked up the phone and decided to give Cami a call. She was my best friend, but I hadn't spoken to her in weeks. There was nothing we wouldn't do for one another. We had known each other since freshman year in high school when we tried out for the cheerleading squad. Cami was the funniest person I've ever met and she had a genuine heart, unlike some of our classmates that were into ass-kissing cliques. Although I barely cursed, I had my moments like anybody else when they became angry. Cami, on the other hand, could make Dave Chappelle blush with some of the things she said. I tolerated her profanity as best as I could, but I wouldn't allow her to use the words *nigga* or *bitch* to degrade our people.

We were roommates during our freshman year at Del State. That is, until Cami quit college to enroll in beauty school. Her parents were furious with her decision, but I supported her since life was too short to not chase after your dreams and tomorrow was not promised to anyone. Possessing a love for doing hair, Cami was always determined to own a beauty salon. I wouldn't trust another person to touch my scalp because my girl was talented with cutting and styling some hair. I smiled and recalled when Cami was beside herself and overcome with nothing but joy when she opened Camille's. She had fulfilled her dream and it was quite an accomplishment for her to achieve two months shy of her thirtieth birthday.

"Who dis?" Cami asked.

"Who dis? I see somebody's watched *Boyz N The Hood* recently, Ice Cube."

"I see you got jokes today, huh?"

"Always. I know your mama taught you better than to answer the phone like a chickenhead."

"Girl, please! I knew it was your triflin' ass callin' me. You know, they do have this invention called Caller ID. Besides, you might be my ruffneck on the side, hitting me up with my Monday afternoon booty call before the husband and kids get home."

"You better quit playin', girl, because Damon would go off if he heard you talking like that."

"Well, at least he would have some incentive to get off since he's been a little slow in that department for quite some time."

"Damn, you ain't right," I laughed.

"And you know this, hussy! But all jokes aside, things ain't bad between Damon and me. I'm in this till death do us part or until I kill the nigga."

"Excuse you!" I snapped.

"I'm sorry, my Afrocentric conscious sistah," Cami apologized sarcastically.

I shook my head and stared at the ceiling.

"So, how you've been, Gigi?"

"Copasetic. I'm trying to get out of here on time so I can make my doctor's appointment this afternoon, but the nuts in this insane asylum are driving me up the wall."

"You okay?"

"Yeah, I'm fine, but I've already rescheduled my appointment twice and I can't keep putting it off."

"Speaking of canceling appointments, I know how your doctor must feel since you've missed your last two hair appointments. You must be wearing either a wig or a baseball cap because you're probably lookin' like Raggedy Ann by now."

"You still ain't right. And for your information, I haven't been going to anyone else to get my hair done, because I've been doing it..." The receiver fell to the floor when my hands began to tremble.

"Gigi, are you there? Hello?"

I picked up the phone. "I'm here, girl. The phone fell out of my hand."

"Oh, okay. By the way, what are you doing tonight?"

"Nothing, what's up?"

"April, Darlene and I are going to a poetry reading at Brave New World. You should come out because you haven't hung with us in a minute. Besides, it's been a while since you've read poetry and sung anything."

"Let me think about it and get back to you."

"Alright, girl. Well, I'm not going to hold you any longer. If you decide to meet up with us, just let me know. Bye."

"I'll talk to you later."

After placing the receiver back on the hook, I stared at my hands for a good minute. It was the fourth time since Friday the trembling had occurred. The Tapazol prescribed to treat my Grave's Disease apparently wasn't working, at least that's what I suspected. I would have a better answer to my dilemma after my appointment with my new endocrinologist, Dr. Fitzpatrick.

Marcia knocked on the side of my cubicle. "Excuse me, Regina."

"Hi, Marcia." I turned towards her. "How do the financial statements look?"

"They look good. I only have one more change to the Administrative Expenses and that's it."

"No problem. I'll make the change, print off another copy and leave them with Annette to make copies for your meeting before I take off for my appointment."

"Okay, Regina." Satisfied with my response, she left my cubicle.

I watched her walk back to her office and prayed the Lord would give me the strength to get out of here on time before Marcia changed her mind again.

Chapter Four

Regina

The receptionist took my referral and five dollar co-pay.

"You can have a seat, Ms. Simmons, fill out the new patient questionnaire and the doctor will be with you shortly."

I thanked her and sat down in the empty waiting area. An endocrinologist's office was the last place I wanted to be. I wished I kept the card Keith sent to me because I needed a good laugh right about now, but I had decided to throw it in the nearest trash can along with those cheap, dilapidated flowers. If a man was going to be sincere about his apology, he should at least have the decency to send a lady fresh roses from a professional florist instead of choosing some mom-and-pop operation from the Yellow Pages.

As I completed the questionnaire, I thought about Cami's offer. It had been a long time since I hung out with my girlfriends. To finish school, I spent the last three months burying my nose in the books without a social life. April was good people, but I didn't know if I was in the mood to listen to Darlene run her big ass mouth about everything screwed up in her personal life. Nonetheless, I missed Cami and would love to see my girl again.

Also, the conversation I shared with Chris from this morning stirred my memories of singing and performing poetry. The feel good vibe at those gatherings at Del State and venues across Philly was nothing but love for the passion. The poets who would breathe life into their words were fierce, inspiring and encouraging.

Although I was fond of poetry and could hold my own in a cipher, singing was my first love. I inherited my singing voice from my grandmother. Nana was fond of Mahalia Jackson, Sarah Vaughn, Dinah Washington and Billie Holiday, and she could often be found in her own world crooning while she worked around the house. I loved to get up on stage, stand in the blinding spotlight and sing straight from my heart into the mic. To listen to the audience's applause was an unbelievable sensation.

I sighed. Yeah, those were the days…until I met Leon Willis and things fell apart from there.

I returned the questionnaire to the receptionist and sat back down, clasping my hands in prayer. I had to take my mind off my worries. I didn't feel like reading the three week old issues of *TIME*, *Newsweek*, *FORTUNE* and *Cosmopolitan*. And I wasn't in the mood to peruse through the variety of pamphlets about the thyroid, hypothyroidism, hyperthyroidism and Grave's Disease on display against the wall near the metal coat rack. Truth be told, I'm not fond of medical centers or hospitals due to some very bad past experiences.

My parents were killed in an automobile accident when I was seven years old. They were on their way to pick me up from my grandparents' one Sunday evening when they were caught in a head-on collision with a drunk driver. Daddy died at the scene and Mama was listed in critical yet stable condition. I'll never forget seeing her lying in that hospital bed with those tubes hooked up to her mouth and nose, bandages covering her head and arms, and cuts in her pretty face. Nana, Pop-Pop and I stood by her side praying for a miracle, but our prayers went unanswered. Mama died four days later. Nana tried to comfort me with her words, telling me my parents were in a better place in heaven where God would watch over their souls. I cried myself to sleep every night for several months, asking God why my parents had to die and begging Him to please bring them back to earth so we could be a family again.

After my parents' deaths, Nana and Pop Pop raised me. They provided for me and made sure I wouldn't go without the necessities for school, birthdays, holidays and family gatherings. While I was growing up, Nana and I had our confrontations, and they weren't pretty, but she was my heart and soul. Always was and always will be. I didn't like interacting much with my other relatives because the majority of them were alcoholics. To them, a celebration wouldn't be a celebration without the beer and corn liquor. My grandparents never drank much, but Pop-Pop was good for sneaking a taste every now and then.

The wooden door in the waiting area opened and the nurse came out to the reception area. She stood about my height, five feet four inches tall, and had sandy blonde hair with ice blue eyes. I would guess her age was somewhere in her mid to late forties.

"Hi, Ms. Simmons, my name is Carol. You can come with me."

I stood up, grabbing my purse in the process. "Thanks, Carol, and please call me Regina."

I followed Carol down the narrow corridor to the first examination room on my right. Upon entering, I sat my purse down on the strip of tissue paper covering the black examination table.

Carol placed the clipboard on the counter. "Dr. Fitzpatrick will be with you shortly, Regina. There's a gown on the back of the door you can change into and I'll shut the door to give you some privacy."

Before she left, I thanked her and then looked around the room, which was fully stocked with the typical medical equipment in every physician's office needed to examine patients: scale, blood pressure machine and ear thermometer. While concealing my bra and panties inside my folded clothes, I noticed there was a radio on the counter tuned to WJJZ, which was playing Chuck Mangione's *Feels So Good*. I hadn't heard that song in years and remembered it was Daddy's personal favorite. He wore out the album and the record player's needle repeatedly playing it over and over again. I'll never forget how pissed Mama was and the argument they had so many years ago. Every time I think about my father, I somehow think of Leon. He resembled a younger version of Daddy in his early twenties, at least as he looked at the time from a picture Nana had taken when Daddy graduated from Cheyney University. Leon had the same rich, chocolate brown skin, fine hair, handsome face with a well-trimmed mustache, and slanted caramel eyes that could work their magic on a sistah's heart, especially mine.

I was hanging out with Cami attending Buttamilk the first night I met Leon. Black folks were coming out in masses every week to support and throw down poetry on the mic, especially erotic poetry. I was never into erotica. Some of the men who read the stuff were a bunch of playas who thought they were God's gift to poetry. They used the art to their advantage and wouldn't give you the time of day unless you gave them your phone number. I could easily decipher the pretenders from the contenders by some of the crap spewing from their lips.

I was the featured performer for the evening and caught a glimpse of Leon sitting at the bar next to Cami drinking a Heineken, while I sang Sade's *No Ordinary Love*. Immediately hooked by his uncanny resemblance to Daddy, I almost forgot the lyrics when our eyes met during my performance. At the end of the night, Leon introduced himself and told me how much he enjoyed my song. We exchanged small talk for a few minutes before he left for the evening with his friends. I enjoyed our conversation immensely. He didn't try to press me for my phone number like most of the fools I met. I didn't think I would ever see him again. But something inside of me told me I wanted to. Sometimes, fate has a funny way of bringing people into your life for a reason, but always not for the best reasons.

Two soft knocks brought me back to the exam room.

"Excuse me, Regina," a deep masculine voice spoke from outside the door.

"Just a minute," I responded, checking my gown to make sure it was tightly secured in the back. "Okay, you can come in."

Dr. Fitzpatrick entered along with Carol. He stood about six feet four with a thick head of salt and pepper hair, looking like a younger version of Barry Bostwick from the TV show *Spin City*.

He introduced himself as we shook hands. "Hi, Regina, I'm Dr. Fitzpatrick. How are you doing today?"

"Just fine. And yourself?"

"Well, I could complain, but if I did, then who would bother to listen?"

I managed to crack a half-smile at his corny attempt. Carol, who stood off to the side of the room, let out a small chuckle.

"I was looking over the file your PCP faxed to us last week. It appears you were diagnosed with Grave's Disease back in 1997. Correct me if I'm wrong."

"Yes, I was."

"And how were you initially diagnosed?" he asked.

I sat back on the examination table and told Dr. Fitzpatrick about my diagnosis. He jotted the details on his clipboard while Carol stood in the background nodding at times. They both had an attentive look while I described my symptoms: the emotional problems such as irritability and anxiety; the physical discomfort of insomnia, random heart palpitations throughout the day, tremors in my hands, and brittle hair and fingernails.

I also told him about my unexpected pregnancy. My first endocrinologist, Dr. Lee, recommended two choices for treatment since I was pregnant, Tapazol or thyroid surgery. I couldn't elect to have radioactive iodine since I was pregnant and it could pass through the placenta, enter the baby's thyroid and destroy the fetus. Even if I hadn't been pregnant, I wouldn't have chosen the iodine for fear of not being able to have children in the future.

"And how did you manage with the Grave's Disease during your pregnancy?" he asked.

"Everything was…fine," I whispered, nodding my head. "I began taking Tapazol for one year. I stopped taking it when my health improved." Both Dr. Fitzpatrick and Carol seemed to notice the hesitation in my voice. I continued, telling him I was in remission with the Grave's Disease up until last winter when I began having heart palpitations and slight tremors in my hands. After Cami made a comment one day at the salon about my hair being brittle, I went back to Dr. Lee for an evaluation, but she was preparing to close her practice and relocate to California. The only thing she could do was prescribe another dose of Tapazol until I could find a new endocrinologist. She also recommended I have an ultrasound performed on my thyroid and a blood test.

"So, shall we get started with the tests?" he inquired.

"No problem."

Carol took my weight, temperature and blood pressure while Dr. Fitzpatrick recorded the observations. He then performed specific tests applicable for Grave's Disease: swallowing a cup of water to measure the size of my thyroid to check for enlargement, observing the trembling in my hands and running his fingers across my throat to check for any lumps. I slightly flinched when he meticulously touched my right thyroid.

"I'm sorry, Regina. Did that hurt?" he asked.

"No, but it felt weird."

He rubbed his chin and stared at the ultrasound with an unusual look on his face. I felt concerned because I could tell there was something he wanted to say to me in private. After the examination, I was left alone to put my clothes back on. Once dressed and while waiting for Carol to return for me, I decided to give Cami a call and leave a message on her cell phone to say I was interested in hooking up with her and the girls later at Brave New World.

Carol knocked on the door and led me to Dr. Fitzpatrick's office. When I entered, he was on the telephone, but gestured for me to have a seat. Carol shut the door and I sat down, patiently waiting for him to wrap up his business. I glanced around his tidy office at his medical degrees from Villanova University and the University of Pennsylvania and the various awards and certificates of achievement. Pictures of his family adorned his desk along with organized patients' files. This man could give Marcia some lessons about efficiency and responsibility.

"Sorry, Regina," Dr. Fitzpatrick said, hanging up the phone.

"It's alright," I responded. "So, what's going on with me?"

I sat back in my chair and listened to his diagnosis. According to the blood test, my immune system was no longer responding to the Tapazol. My body had developed an allergy to the medication. He told me there were only two forms of treatment for my condition:

thyroid surgery or radioactive iodine. My thyroid was not protruding, but he felt a small lump in my thyroid not detected in the ultrasound. It might indicate that goiter was in development. Once he had the second ultrasound, he could recommend what method of treatment I should undergo. He requested me to have the procedure done by the end of the week, if possible. He also wanted to have a follow-up appointment with me a week from this Friday to discuss the results.

I closed my eyes and thought about my options. If I had thyroid surgery, I could develop hypothyroidism and have to take medication for the rest of my life. Or, if I took the radioactive iodine, there was the possibility of not being able to conceive children.

"Are you alright?" he asked.

I opened my eyes and managed to crack a half-smile. "I'm okay. It's not like I haven't been down this road before."

"I do have one question I need to know for my medical records," he stated. I stared at him, waiting for his words. "Did you have any complications at childbirth due to the Grave's Disease?"

I shook my head in response and sat in total silence for a minute. I revealed to Dr. Fitzpatrick my decision to have an abortion two weeks before the end of my first trimester. He nodded, expressed his sympathy and said he would send his findings to Dr. Faison, my PCP, for her records. We both stood up, shook hands and I thanked him for his time as he escorted me to the waiting area.

Before leaving, I asked the receptionist if I could use the bathroom. She handed me the pink office key and told me where the ladies' room was located. I thanked her and walked through the empty hallway as fast as I could, trying not to reveal my emotions. I opened the door, went inside the stall and sat down on the toilet seat while the tears fell from my eyes.

Chapter Five

Chris

I pulled my Ford Explorer into the nearly full parking lot across the street from Brave New World. It looked like there was a good turnout for the monthly Po/Jazz series. The sun was setting in the sky over Philly, bringing another day to an end. Although the temperature on my dashboard monitor displayed seventy-five degrees, it felt twenty degrees hotter tonight.

Gene climbed out of the passenger side of my truck and closed the door. "Man, Cool C," he said, inhaling the smoke from the last of his Newport. "You weren't bullshittin' when you said things were crazy at work."

"Brah, bullshittin' ain't the word to describe what it was like trying to deal with Ronnie today," I replied, sitting my traveling bag on the ground.

"She got to go. I don't care how good the sex is between y'all. It ain't worth the headache."

"I hear you loud and clear," I said, closing the car door. "She called me before I left work today, cursing me out on my voicemail and saying, 'Maybe you and I do need some space after all! So you get yours tonight because I'm getting mine!'"

"That settles it, so don't even trip, Cool C."

"Still, I got to deal with her tomorrow..."

"Forget about tomorrow because tonight we're here to chill," Gene interrupted, putting out his cigarette.

Crossing Arch Street from the parking lot to the other side, we entered the front door of the VIP Room of Brave New World and paid for our admission. The ambience was dark and intimate, just right for the poetry crowd that frequented the monthly Po/Jazz Series. The long red couch, which stretched from the back to the front of the club with scented candles positioned along the top, had its share of couples, brothas and sistahs who came out to support friends, lovers or spouses who were reciting poetry.

I recognized a few faces, including tonight's featured poet, Lamont Dixon. The Arpeggio Jazz Ensemble, led by Warren Oree on upright bass, was performing at center stage. I almost had a big one like Fred Sanford when I heard Warren call out April's name. She got up from one of the tables in the front where she was sitting with her girlfriends. Good, we arrived just in time.

"Yo, Gene, check it out. That's my co-worker, April, I was telling you about," I said. Gene nodded in approval.

April had a lovely speaking voice. She introduced herself to the audience and said the title of her poem, *Masquerade.* She sounded great on the mic, but you could definitely tell she was nervous, stumbling over a few words. It was expected since she was a virgin on the mic. The audience gave her a nice round of applause, but I could see the disappointment on her face as she sat back down with her girlfriends who were giving her support.

"Give it up for Ms. April Williams," Warren announced. "We're going to bring our featured poet for the evening back up here and then we're going to take a brief intermission. Let's hear it for Lamont."

"Well, look who's in the place to be! Mr. Superstar himself, Chris Harrington!" a deep voice broadcasted from my left.

A nauseous feeling rose in my stomach as I turned towards the bar and saw the object of my disgust, Greg Quinones, aka The Gentleman Poet, sipping on a Heineken and standing to our left next to J. Michael Harrison, the radio host of WRTI's The Bridge. There were some conceited poets who thought they were all that and Greg was certainly the King of the Hill. He was a legend in his own mind and suffered from *Purple Rain* syndrome – translation:

like Prince, his poetry made absolutely no sense to anyone except himself.

I shook his hand. "What's goin' on? Lookin' fly as always."

"And did you expect anything less?" Greg snorted, showing off the Roc-A-Wear denim ensemble he was sporting for the evening.

"Okay, papi," I said.

"How's it goin', Mike?" I asked, shaking his hand.

"Not much, fellas. What's up with you?"

"Gene and I came out to support Po/Jazz," I responded.

"Anyway," Greg interjected. "I was telling Mike about the erotic poetry slam I'll be hosting next week at Club Mystique. It's gonna be off da hook!"

I tilted my head and stroked my goatee. "Really?"

Mike rolled his eyes up toward the ceiling in annoyance and murmured, "Oh, yeah."

Greg put his beer on the bar and handed Gene and myself flyers. "You might want to work on your technique and come on out, Chris, if you're up to par."

I briefly glanced at the flyer's heading: FREAKEASY EROTIC SLAM! I'd been to one of his poetry shows before to know there were two things this lounge lizard was about...one, how much money could he make off the front door, and two, which female would be his sexual conquest for the evening. I could tell by the look on Gene's face that our thoughts were in agreement.

"Sounds like it's gonna be too freaky," Gene said, placing the flyer on the bar. "Besides, we got studio time that night."

"Studio time?" Greg asked, displaying a perplexed look on his face.

I nodded and said, "Yeah, we do."

"By the way, how's the new project coming along?" Mike inquired.

"Nothin' but butter and gravy," Gene answered.

I reached into my traveling bag and handed him a CD. "Everything's going well," I added. "Check this out, Mike, and let us know what you think."

"Will do and maybe we can get you fellas on The Bridge in the future."

"That works for me," I said.

"Ahem!" Greg said, clearing his throat with his hand out.

"Oh, my bad," I added, giving Mr. Humility his copy. "Why don't you take a listen and see how it's *done*!"

Greg murmured something under his breath as he put the CD in his coat pocket.

"Excuse me, fellas, I gotta go to the bathroom," Gene announced while departing.

"Wait up, Gene," Greg said, picking up his beer and following him.

Some folks are a piece of work. Although Greg would never be the first to admit he was a fan of my work, I had no problem admitting I wasn't a fan of his.

"Excuse me, Mike, but I saw someone I know up front," I said, patting him on his shoulder. "It was good talking with you."

"Always a pleasure, man," Mike said. "I'm headed out after Lamont's performance, but definitely give me a call so you can come through soon."

I nodded and shook his hand before I made my way in the direction of April's table. Her chair was turned towards the stage and she watched on attentively as Lamont did his thing. The seat to her left was empty, so I sat down next to her without her noticing me. I held my index finger to my lips to signal her girlfriends not to give me away. The two sistahs waved hello and nodded in agreement.

"Excuse me, Ms. Williams, can I have your autograph?" I whispered while sliding my seat closer to hers.

After April reached over in excitement and gave me a hug, I sat back with the three ladies and listened to Lamont recite two poems that left the audience roaring with approval and yearning for more. Afterwards, the band took a brief intermission and Warren made his way over to the table to speak with April.

"You sounded real good tonight, April," Warren complimented.

"Thanks, but I wasn't feelin' it," April said.

"Trust me, you did fine. Keep comin' out."

I stood up, tapped Warren on the shoulder, and asked, "What's goin' on, playa?"

"Hey, man! Where you been?" Warren inquired, shaking my hand and giving me a hug.

"Been busy working on the new project."

"Sounds good. Listen, I've got to talk to a few people, but we'll rap at the end of the night. Okay?"

"Cool," I said, before he walked off towards the back.

I sat back down with April and her friends. "Congratulations, April, you were great."

April sighed. "Thanks, Chris. I needed the lift."

"Hello, ladies," I said to April's girlfriends.

"I'm sorry, Chris," April apologized. "Chris, this is Cami and Darlene. Cami and Darlene, this is Chris."

"Hey, Chris," Darlene replied, smacking her lips and toying with her ponytail extension. The stench of cigarette smoke was heavy on her breath. Her eyes glowed with lust. She had a pretty face for a full-figured sistah, but struck me as the phony type who thought highly of herself. I don't know who girlfriend was trying to impress dressed in a black bebe t-shirt that was too tight and unattractive for her husky frame.

"Hi, Chris," Cami said. "You look familiar. I think I've seen you before."

Cami was very attractive and had a laid back demeanor. She sported a white blouse and a New York Yankees baseball cap. I could definitely see her and April as girlfriends, but not Darlene.

"I don't know where," I replied. "Ah, am I taking anyone's seat?"

"We were waiting for our friend, Gigi, but I guess she's not coming," April said.

Darlene flipped her ponytail and hissed, "I told you she wasn't coming out tonight. She's probably too good to socialize with us ever since she got her Masters'. Go 'head and make yourself at home, Chris."

"Shut up, Darlene," Cami said. "She said she would be here."

"Actually, I'm here with my boy, Gene, who's around here somewhere. But I wanted to stop by and say hi..." A hard hand slap against my back caught me off guard.

"Oh my God! Is that you, Chris?" the female voice yelled from behind.

I didn't need to turn around to recognize who it was, but I did so anyway. Veronica. Still dressed in her all-black ensemble with her hair pulled back and holding a drink in hand. By the look of things and the smell of liquor on her breath, it appeared Ronnie had tossed down a few drinks since coming here straight from work. Damn, the freaks were out tonight.

I shook my head in disgust and asked, "How's it going?"

"I was sitting by the bar having a drink and watching the poetry. And guess who I saw strolling along?" Ronnie added, rubbing my right shoulder. "My co-worker, Chris Harrington. What's up, baby?"

"Nothin'," I said, trying to maintain my cool.

Ronnie pointed to April and yelled, "And I know you, too. You're the temp who works in the Marketing Department."

April sighed in embarrassment. "Yeah, up until this Friday."

"What?" I asked, not sure if I had heard her right. Cami and Darlene, who also appeared shocked at April's revelation, sat in total silence absorbing the conversation.

"No shit!" Ronnie yelled. "Damn, that's fucked up! Tomorrow, you need to march your pretty ass down to HR and tell them muthafuckas a thing or two! If you want, I got your back!"

Tired of listening to Ronnie's shit, I rose up from my seat and excused myself.

"You sit back down, Chris," Ronnie said, putting her hands on my shoulders. "I'm on my way home to get my freak on, if ya know what I mean. But I want you and your friends to have a good time tonight. I'll see you tomorrow at work. Give me a hug. C'mon, sweetie, don't be shy."

Ronnie sat her drink down on the table and gave me a tight, sloppy hug before I took my seat.

"That's more like it. See ya tomorrow. Bye, ladies," Ronnie said, waving her hand.

"Bye," April, Cami and Darlene said in unison.

Before walking off, Ronnie turned towards April and said, "And honey, if you need me, holla atcha gurl in Mortgage Services!"

She wasn't but five seconds out of sight when the ladies and I burst out in an uncontrollable laughter. After the hell she put me through this morning and seeing her make a fool of herself, I needed that laugh.

"Damn, that bitch was crazy drunk!" Darlene roared.

"They should let her get on the mic and speak her mind. She obviously likes you, Chris," Cami said.

"I guess you learn something new everyday," I replied, rubbing my hands together and ignoring Cami's comment. "I'm sorry to hear about your assignment ending, April."

"I'm okay. I found out this afternoon before I left work. Two weeks ago, my supervisor told me they were going to hire me as a permanent employee but to keep things quiet. Then he turns around and calls me in his office to tell me the bad news. After today, nothing surprises me anymore."

"Speaking of surprises," Darlene interjected. "I told y'all Gigi wasn't comin' out."

"You know something, Dar," a woman's voice called out from behind Darlene. "You're always good for talking about people behind their backs."

Everybody turned their head towards the voice. I could have closed my eyes and recognized her voice. She stood there dressed in a denim blue shirt with a WB logo and cartoon characters, blue jeans and black boots with matching purse. A silver dolphin pendant dangled against her neck.

"It's about time you got here, hussy," Cami said. "What took you so long?"

"Had to find a parking space and – you!" she said, looking at me.

"Well, Chris, you know everybody up in here," Darlene blurted.

There she was, Regina Simmons, the sistah from the R3 train with the cinnamon complexion skin and auburn shoulder-length hair pulled back in a ponytail. Gigi.

She chuckled, shook my hand and said, "Nice to see you again, Poet in Training."

"Likewise," I replied while smiling.

Darlene sucked her teeth and frowned. "I take it y'all know each other," she blurted

Regina put her hand on Darlene's shoulder and said sarcastically, "Girl, what a good observation. We can't get anything past you, huh?"

"Fuck you, Gigi," Darlene snapped, grabbing her purse and walking away from the table.

Whoa! I didn't expect Regina's joke to set her off like that. Maybe it was best that Darlene left because I could hear the disdain in their voices towards the other.

"Damnit, we can't go nowhere without the two of you going at it," Cami said.

"Forget her. I'm not in the mood to deal with her crap tonight," Regina responded, sitting down in the empty seat. "So, what's going on?"

"Well, since you were late as usual," April started before spending the next few moments filling Regina in on the details of her reading and on Veronica acting a drunk fool.

"So, you and Chris work together…it's a small world after all," Regina said. She filled Cami and April in on how we had met earlier that morning.

"Yeah, it's a small world," April said.

"Did you tell Chris you're a poet too, Gigi?" Cami added.

"No, she didn't," I said, glancing at Regina. That was very interesting indeed, especially considering our conversation from earlier. She bit her bottom lip, blushed and hunched her shoulders.

"Yeah, Gigi's the bomb!" Cami added.

Regina gave Cami a hard, penetrating, *you-talk-too-damn-much* look while Cami acknowledged it with a *what-the-hell-is-wrong-with-you, girl* glance.

The Arpeggio Jazz Ensemble made its way back to the center stage to begin the second set. Warren announced they were getting ready to start and would need the sign-up list from the back. However, Kia, his assistant working the entrance, couldn't locate it at the moment.

"Well, why don't we bring a special guest poet up to the stage?" Warren said. "He hasn't been up here in a while and he's sitting in the front. Give it up for Chris Harrington."

Oh, no he didn't! The audience clapped, the band played on and Regina, Cami and April cheered me on with, "Go, Chris!"

My eyes adjusted to the spotlight as I made my way onstage. While raising the mic, I searched the crowd for Gene. "Wassup, Po/Jazz? How's everybody doing tonight?" I asked, stalling for time. The audience responded back with a few acknowledgments. "It's been a while since I've done this and I might need some help tonight."

"Wassup, Chris!" Ronnie yelled from the back of the club. She was still here! Several people in the audience were amused by her drunk ass, including April, Cami and Regina.

I found Gene and waved to him to come up on stage with me. "I'm going to ask my partner in crime to join me, so everybody put your hands together and give him some love, y'all, Gene Roberson."

The audience clapped as Gene made his way to the stage. Warren brought another mic to the front for him to use. Once onstage, Gene flashed me a *let's rock this one, Cool C,* look as I nodded in the affirmative.

"We're going to do something we've been working on for a couple of weeks now," I said while they were setting up the mic.

I noticed Regina tapping Cami on the shoulder and pointing towards Gene. Cami nodded in approval, mouthing, "Yeah, Gigi, that's him."

"Wassup, Chris! Wassup, Gene!" Ronnie yelled from the bar.

"Hey, girlfriend!" I snapped. "Chill! Know when to say when!" Everybody was cracking up as Ronnie, feeling embarrassed, finally shut her mouth.

"This is a lil' something I wrote a few weeks ago and it's called *Sexy*. Y'all let me know what you think."

Gene began singing the chorus to Norman Connors' *You Are My Starship* in a deep baritone voice that elicited oohhs and aahhs from several females in the audience. The band started to play the music to the song while I took a deep breath and recited into the mic.

You don't need
to take your clothes off
to arouse my desires
because I adore the way
the prominent hue
of your mahogany skin
is accentuated by the flavor
of the tangerine sundress
you wear so well,
and reflects your self-esteem
like incandescent embers
drifting from burning flames
in an ambitious smile
with fearless eyes to match!

You see, that right there
is what turns me on:
your confidence,
yeah, your confidence;
the way you stand alone
like the brightest star
in the sky dancing
amongst the comets
and the constellations
along the stairway to Heaven!

And how you hold yourself
in the highest standards
as a woman, first and foremost,
proud and strong,
recognizing the natural power
of your femininity:
to be the very best
you can be
without
surrendering your soul
or compromising your integrity
to the promiscuous ways
of silver-tongued
devils disguised
as men who can
neither control nor conquer
your dreams,
your emotions,
your thoughts,
or your love!

The audience roared in approval. I gave Gene a hug and he whispered, "That was tight, Cool C." I had to agree with him because it felt damn good.

Several females stood up from their seats to give us a standing ovation, including April, Cami and Regina. I couldn't help letting out a few laughs when I saw the disgusted look on Ronnie's face. I shook my head and ran my index finger across the other and mouthed, "Shame on you, boo," before she grabbed her drink and stormed out of the VIP Room.

Chapter Six

Regina

Wow! I couldn't believe how great Chris was when he recited that poem. The words were so beautiful and vivid. He looked so comfortable and confident on stage. By taking a look around at several faces in the crowd, I could tell he had the audience's complete attention, including Cami's and April's. And don't get me started on the way his voice became sensual with every verse he spoke, causing the heat to rise from between my thighs. Lord, please forgive me because I might need a drink or two to cool myself off.

Chris also caught me by surprise by calling Gene up on stage to perform with him. At first, I didn't believe it was true, but when I saw him, I knew it was Gene Roberson. I hadn't seen him in years.

Before they began their performance, I whispered to Cami, "Do you remember him from back in the day? It's Gene from Buttamilk." She agreed by responding, "Yeah, Gigi, that's him!" This was indeed a welcome blast from the past. Gene was one of the few cool guys from the poetry circuit who never tried to push up on females. He was always the type of person who would give you the shirt off his back.

"Give it up for Chris and Gene," the emcee said. "That was real smooth, fellas. Love is definitely in the air tonight. All right now, do y'all have the sign-up list together? Let's have it so we can get the second half of the show on the road."

Chris and Gene made their way over to our table while several members of the audience congratulated them.

April stood up, giving Chris a hug. "Chris, that was beautiful!"

"Thanks, April. This is my friend, Gene, who's putting together my CD."

"Wassup, April?" Gene said. "You sounded real good tonight."

"Thanks," April replied.

"And let me introduce you to her girlfriends, Cami and Regina," Chris added.

Gene stared at me for a few seconds before he finally recognized me.

"Flipper?" Gene asked, staring at my face.

I nodded and smiled.

"Where have you been hiding? Girl, get over here and give me a hug."

"Flipper?" Chris, Cami and April said together in confusion.

I stood up and gave him a tight embrace. "What's up, Gene? It's good to see you again." I laughed and sat back down in my chair. Damn, I haven't heard that name in years. He used to call me Flipper because of my love for dolphins.

As Gene and Chris sat down on the empty couch next to our table, Cami and April turned their seats towards the right.

"Chris, you remember Flipper, don't you?" Gene asked. "C'mon now...this sistah used to be one of our Buttacups back in the day. Flipper could sing and recite poetry along with Jill Scott and Trapeta Mayson. Y'all must have crossed paths. When you were first coming out on the scene, Cool C, she was one of our featured performers at Buttamilk."

Chris and I stared at each other and then the proverbial light bulb went on in our heads. I had seen him at some Buttamilk functions, but never saw him reciting back then. Then again, I was infamous for leaving poetry readings early.

Chris laughed. "Damn, this *is* a small world."

"And, Gene, you remember my girlfriend, Cami, who would sometimes hang out with me?" I asked.

"Yeah, I remember you," Gene responded. "How ya doin', Cami?"

"I'm fine," Cami replied, shaking his hand. "It's good to see you again."

Gene and I sat there along with Chris, Cami and April, reminiscing about Buttamilk and playing catch up. We weren't paying attention to the poetry, but kept our conversation low and respectful of the artists. Gene filled me in about his marriage and his wife's pregnancy. He also told me how he was producing the CD portion for Chris's new project. Chris gave the three of us CD samplers and I could hear the passion he felt for his art in his voice. I had to admit there was a part of me that was a bit envious, seeing another person using their creative talents and doing something they loved.

"You okay, Gigi?" Cami asked.

I gave her a gentle slap on her thigh. "Copasetic."

When Cami's cell phone rang, she excused herself from our conversation and turned her chair in the opposite direction. April got up from her seat to go to the bathroom and I sat between Chris and Gene as the three of us began watching the rest of the Po/Jazz show. At times, I found myself taking glances of Chris instead of listening to the poets. If I was not mistaken, I could have sworn Chris took a few glances at me, too. We did make eye contact once and exchanged somewhat slightly flirtatious smiles. As I turned my head to my left to avoid blushing, I noticed Dar approaching the table with an orange flyer and a chapbook in her hand.

"Girl, where have you been all this time?" Cami asked after finishing her phone call.

"Let me tell y'all," Dar started, plopping down in an empty chair. "I went to the bathroom and then stepped outside for a smoke. I met this fine, sexy brotha outside having a smoke, too. He's a poet and was telling me all about this poetry reading he's gonna be hosting next week up on South Street at Club Mystique. He gave me a flyer and I bought a copy of his book. I was reading a couple of poems and his shit is *bangin'*!"

Chris and Gene chuckled, giving each other a look as if they were onto an inside joke.

"Could I take a peek?" I asked out of curiosity.

"Hell no!" Dar snapped.

"Hell no! Listen to the playa hater in you. Meow!" I replied, waving my hand in the air like a cat using its claw.

Dar stood up, put her hands on her hips and blurted, "You know something, bitch, you startin' to get on my last fuckin' nerve!"

"Who do you think you are calling somebody a bitch?" I responded, standing up and rolling my neck.

"Clear your seats, fellas," Cami interjected. "It's about to get ugly up in here."

"It's cool, Cami," I said, not giving Dar the verbal exchange she wanted ever since I arrived. "I'm going to get a drink. Anybody want anything?"

Everybody shook their head and I grabbed my purse, proceeding to the bar. As I walked away, I could see Dar rolling her eyes at me. I ignored her childish behavior as best as I could, but it wasn't easy.

From the first day we met, we got along like matches and gasoline. She had insecurities due to her weight, dark skin complexion and pitiful love life. Dar enjoyed tearing down other people's accomplishments with her smart ass mouth to build up her low self-esteem. Often, I was the target of her verbal assaults since I was a size eight, had light brown skin and a steady boyfriend up until six weeks ago. However, I wasn't about to be her scapegoat and had no problem letting her know. Cami tolerated her because Damon, Cami's husband, was Dar's older brother. He asked Cami to socialize with his sister because she didn't have many friends. If that wasn't a prime example of love for better or worse on my best friend's part, I didn't know what was. Myself, I would have sent baby sister to psychotherapy and enrolled her in a few anger management classes.

"Could I have a Merlot?" I asked the female bartender.

As she went down to the opposite end of the bar, I stared at my reflection in the mirror recalling my appointment with Dr. Fitzpatrick from earlier this afternoon. I rubbed my hand across my right thyroid to feel the small lump Dr. Fitzpatrick found. Although it wasn't painful, its presence alone was enough to scare me. Why didn't the previous ultrasound pick this up? Was it cancerous or not? I would have to wait until next week to find out the answers after my next ultrasound.

"Excuse me, Miss," a deep voice whispered into my ear with the foulest breath I ever smelled. "Could I buy you a glass of milk since it obviously does your body good?"

"What the – " I said, turning around.

I was so caught up in my thoughts, I didn't notice this lummox creep behind me. He stood about the same height as Dr. Fitzpatrick, had a butterscotch complexion, straight hair and was dressed in black Roc-A-Wear from head to toe. His features suggested he was half Black/half Latino. My Playa Alert Warning System was screaming run for cover!

"And how are you on this lovely evening?" he asked.

"I'm fine."

"Yes, you are."

"That will be seven dollars, Miss," the bartender interjected, placing my drink on the counter.

I gave her a ten dollar bill, thanked her and told her to keep the change. Picking up my drink, I took a sip. This was going to be a good one.

"If you don't mind me asking, what's your name?" Count Stankula politely inquired with his sour breath that reeked of fried onions and cigarettes.

"Candice," I lied. "But my girlfriends call me Candy."

"Oh, so sweet," he said, doing his best Larry Blackman impersonation. "My name is Greg, but everyone calls me The Gentleman Poet."

I sipped my Merlot and held my breath. My nostrils were screaming for an oxygen mask. "Scared of you," I added.

"And you should be."

I stood there like a fool and listened to this hustler run his game. He boasted about how great he was compared to some of the clowns who came out to read on open mics. He gave me an orange flyer about his poetry reading at Club Mystique next week. Looks like I met Dar's knight in shining armor. He also tried to sell me his poetry chapbook called *Velvet Lullabies: For Mature Audiences Only.* I glanced through some of his work and the titles alone were hilarious: *Knee Deep On Bended Knees, If These Sheets Could Speak, How Many Licks, Skin On Skin,* and the best of them all, *Sixty-Nine Degrees Of Separation.*

I handed Greg his poetry chapbook, declining his offer.

Not to be deterred, he leaned over and whispered in my right ear, "Some people can only appreciate poetry when it's spoken, Candy, as opposed to being read."

I couldn't believe the garbage he called a poem was spewing from his lips. I've had my encounters with knuckleheads at poetry readings, but this fool was definitely the worst. Talk about bold and brazen. If his breath wasn't humming like a broken air conditioner emanating mildew in the summer, I would've been on the floor laughing hysterically. Now, I got the joke Chris and Gene were keeping to themselves.

Greg stood erect with a sinister grin on his face. "Well, what do you think?"

I laughed. "I think you need some breath mints because you are full of crap," I said, waving my hand in his face. "Step aside, son."

I walked away from the bar to rejoin my friends. April had returned from the bathroom and the girls were getting ready to leave. By the looks of things, so were Chris and Gene.

"What's up?" I asked.

"We were waiting for you to come back, Gigi," Cami responded. "I've got to get out of here because I need to open up the shop early tomorrow morning to do some inventory."

"Yeah, I've got to get home, too," April said. "But I'm not in any rush to go to work tomorrow."

"I heard that one," Chris said. "Gene and I were about to bounce, too."

"Well, when in Rome," I sighed, finishing my drink as everybody said their goodbyes, gathered their things and headed out the door together.

Wanting to share something with me, Cami decided to ride in my car. The drive wasn't out of my way since she lived not too far from me in Wynnefield. "So, what's up?" I asked after buckling up in my Mitsubishi Galant.

Cami sat down, shut her door and fastened her seat belt. "You tell me?"

"I'm copasetic. And yourself?"

"Don't give me that copasetic shit, hussy. I've been cutting, styling and pressing your hair for almost seventeen years to know when something's bothering you. I noticed it when you gave me that ugly look after I told Chris you were a poet."

Damn, she had me. I took my car keys out the ignition and sat them on my lap.

"What's up, Gigi?"

"I was thinking about how much fun I used to have at poetry readings. Sometimes I wonder what my life would have been like if I were still out there. That's all."

"It was a special time in your life. I was there, ya know. Why did you step away from it?"

"I had my reasons. I made my choices, although some were not so good."

"You can't keep beating yourself up for what you did," she added, squeezing my hand. "I never had one, but I know it's – "

"I understand what you're trying to say," I interjected. "You don't know what I've been through. No matter how deep you think the past is buried, it finds a way to resurface...especially something like that."

Outside of Drs. Faison, Lee and Fitzpatrick, Cami was the only person who knew I had an abortion. I never told my grandparents or any of my relatives. She tried to convince me not to go through with the procedure, but I wasn't trying to hear it. Since Leon didn't want to assume his responsibilities for making a baby, I wasn't about to go down that route alone. I had enough promiscuous cousins having babies every nine months from some of the sorriest black men I've ever met. Sometimes I wanted to slap some common sense into their heads after listening to their baby-daddy drama.

"You're right. I don't know what you've been through. But I do know you've got to keep living. Turn the negative experience into something positive. Get back out there and do your thing again, Gigi."

"Okay, Obi-Wan," I chuckled. "Girl, I'm thirty-three years old. I can't pick up from where I left off six years ago."

"So what if you're thirty-three? Do you think I let my age stop me from owning my own beauty salon? No, because I had a goal and kept on going until I accomplished it. It's not too late."

"After today, it just might be," I said, then placed my hand over my lips.

"What did you mean by that?"

"Nothing, Cami, just forget it."

Cami grabbed my hand tightly. "What happened at your doctor's appointment today? Gigi, talk to me. Is everything okay?"

Not wanting her to have a panic attack, I tried to calm Cami down and assure her everything was fine, but she wasn't buying it. She knew me too well. With no other choice, I confessed everything that transpired. Although Cami was aware I was diagnosed with Grave's Disease and had been in remission, she didn't know about the symptoms I'd been experiencing the past few months and now the discovery of the lump. Afterwards, she sat in silence, absorbing all of the information.

"Well, aren't you going to say anything?" I asked.

"I don't believe you've been keeping that from me all this time. I thought we were close?"

I crossed my fingers. "We are."

"Then why haven't you said anything until now?"

"At the time, it was manageable. I was going to tell you, but there was so much going on the last few months with Keith, work, moving and finishing grad school. My mind wasn't right and I didn't know what to do."

"What you should have done is tell me! That's what friends are for: to give each other support and comfort at all times. We've known each other for half of our lives. You've always been there for me, so what makes you think I wouldn't do the same for you?"

"I know and I'm sorry."

"How many times have I been there for you? Whether it was being the sister you always wanted, the girlfriend to discuss your relationship problems or the hairstylist to hook up your hair."

"Okay, point taken! Damn!"

She pointed her finger. "See, that's your problem. You're too hardheaded, hussy. Always have been. Ain't nothing changed about you."

I waved my hand in the air, dismissing her comments. "Whatever."

"You know I'm right. Just like you know those black-eyed peas in the back of your kitchen need touchin' up, Raggedy Ann," Cami said, poking my neck with her index finger.

No, she didn't just go there. Two could play this game.

"Look who's talking, Kissy Reynolds," I retorted, snatching her baseball cap off her head.

Cami snatched the cap from my hands. "Hey! Give me that back!"

She put it back on to disguise her short natural, which was in need of a haircut. She stared at me and murmured, "You ain't right."

"No, but if you're nappy and you know it, comb your head," I sang, clapping my hands twice to the beat.

She pursed her lips and widened her eyes. "Now it's on, hussy!" Cami yelled.

We sat back and took jabs at each other. It had been a long time since we played the dozens. No subject was off limits, except for mothers and grandmothers. We went for a couple of rounds until our sides were in pain from laughter. It felt good to use humor as a means to alleviate our problems. After we were finished acting silly,

Cami and I held each other for a good minute prior to me driving her home.

Before exiting my car, she whispered, "Everything's gonna be alright, Gigi. Trust me."

I was grateful for her friendship and support. No matter what choice I would have to make, I knew I could always count on her to be there for me.

Chapter 7
Chris

The morale at Aurora was at an all-time low since the announcement was made that American Sentinel National Bank had purchased our financial institution. Fiction became fact when the memo from the President's office announcing the Board's approval of American Sentinel's acquisition of Aurora was distributed. A company-wide evaluation would be conducted for every employee's job performance to determine what areas would be recommended for change and/or implemented to increase efficiency and serve our customers better. We all felt the same - you could pour twenty-five gallons of maple syrup on a pile of cow shit and it still wouldn't smell or look like pancakes. In other words, it was apparent layoffs were coming.

I tried my best to focus on work, but I wasn't feeling it today. The prospect of hunting for a new job wasn't very appealing. I wasn't certain to what extent my department would be involved in American Sentinel's evaluation, but no one was above review.

"Here are the copies from the mortgage audit you requested, Chris," Mary said, placing them on my desk.

"Thanks, Mary."

"You look a bit troubled. Is everything okay?"

"I'm fine, just have a lot on my mind regarding the purchase."

"You're not alone. We're all in the same boat. I have faith that everything will be fine. You hang in there."

I nodded and gave Mary a smile. I always admired her for her positive outlook – never allowing anyone or anything to get the best of her.

"If you ever need someone to talk to, please don't hesitate."

"Thanks again."

While perusing through the copies, it dawned on me that I hadn't heard anything from Ronnie for the past two days since her Po/Jazz attempt to embarrass me blew up in her face. Not that I was interested in seeing her, but eventually our paths would have to cross. My telephone rang and I picked up the receiver.

"Audit, Chris speaking."

"What's up, Chris?"

I sucked my teeth when I recognized the voice of my half-brother, Sam, on the other line.

"Hello? Chris?"

"How are you doing, Sam?"

"Damn, big bro, you don't have to sound so enthusiastic."

"Sorry, you caught me at a bad time. I apologize."

"It's cool. Besides, I know how moody you can be," Sam snorted.

"Can I put you on hold for a minute?" I asked, hanging up the phone.

The last thing I needed right now was to listen to his smart-ass comments. The phone rang again. However, I took my time answering it.

"Yes?"

"You know that was pretty fucked up."

"Sam, what's up? How you livin', baby bro?"

"Ha ha! Very funny."

"So, what do you want?"

"Why do you think I always want something? Can't I just call my brother and say hi?"

I lowered my voice so my co-workers wouldn't overhear my conversation. "Cut the bullshit, Sam. You only speak to me for two reasons. You either want something from me or you want to stick your nose in my business."

"Damn! That hurts, Chris. I tried to be courteous to you and reach out to you since we're brothers. I know we didn't always get along when we were growing up, but we're still family, ya know?"

"Look, spare me the lame we're brothers/we're still family tirade. Okay?"

"Alright, I'll get to the point. I wanted to know if you're still coming to Dad's retirement party."

I sighed. "I haven't decided."

"C'mon, man, that's our father you're talking about."

"Mm hmmm."

"He's retiring from work and this is a special occasion."

"Mm hmmm."

"It would mean a lot to Dad if you would come out."

I laughed. "Ha! Are you serious?"

"Hell, yeah! Why can't you forgive and just move on?"

I couldn't believe Sam came at me with this Mother Love bullshit. I reminded him that Dad and I had sporadically spoken to each other over the past few years since he decided not to attend my graduation from Lincoln University. I was hurt because I couldn't believe how spiteful he could be. I never asked him for one dollar and worked my way through college without his help. I also managed to graduate in four years with a 3.4 GPA. I invited him there for us to have the chance to reconcile after the falling out we had in my senior year at high school. In his warped mind, since I didn't need his assistance because I was an emancipated minor, he felt there was no need for him to be at my graduation. I also reminded Sam about the beginning of my falling out with Dad after I went out for the track team in the tenth grade.

My goal was to build a better relationship with Dad. He was a track star in both high school and college and took pride in his accomplishments. Most times, his pride went to his head. I knew he only expressed interest in his children's activities if they ran track, and just as I thought, he began to pay attention to me when I did.

Although I was a decent long distance runner, my heart wasn't in it. The training took its toll on my body. The butterflies in my stomach forced me to vomit uncontrollably before races. My hamstring muscles and ankles would ache for days.

I'll never forget the last race I competed in. Dad helped train me for a week before the race. We went out to the track every day in addition to practice. I felt confident going into the race, but the butterflies were kicking in big time. I gave it my best, but it wasn't enough. Our team lost the event and the coach came down on me hard for not giving my all. I was disappointed in myself. To make matters worse, Dad came down on me harder even though he hadn't attended the race. I'll never forget the stinging remarks he made about me not having enough desire to win. The worst of them all was, "You're a quitter, Chris. You'll never amount to anything in life." Afterwards, I never ran again. That day, I also decided to prove him wrong, because, other than track, I wasn't a quitter.

"I'm sorry, Sam, but I just can't do so."

"Look, I know we have our issues with Dad, but he *is* our father."

I sat back and listened to my brother argue his position. It sounded so sincere and reasonable, but my mind was made up. He knew firsthand how stubborn I could be. After all, I did inherit that trait from Dad.

While Sam was talking, Ronnie came into our department, giving me a nasty look before going over to Mary's desk to talk with her. I rolled my eyes to let her know how excited I was to see her, too. It appeared girlfriend finally gathered her bearings together from the hangover she must have had.

"Just think it over for a few days, Chris, and let me know."

"We'll see."

"It's all I ask. Later."

"Peace," I said, hanging up the phone.

Ronnie walked over to my cubicle. "Excuse me, but I'd like to know if I could have a word with you in private?"

I put my head in my hands and shook it in disbelief on how many beer cans this knucklehead was short of a six pack.

"Actually, I'm quite busy right now," I responded, not feeling comfortable with having another confrontation alone with her on the stairwell. Besides, Ronnie was liable to go postal, and if anything crazy was going to go down between us, I'd rather it happen in the open with plenty of witnesses.

"Well, I wanted to come by to tell you how much I enjoyed your performance the other night."

"Thanks."

"There was this young lady sitting next to me and she said, 'Oh, he sounds so sexy. Do you think he has a girlfriend?'"

Normally, I would have walked away from this situation and not given this pathetic conversation any thought. However, my ego wouldn't allow her to think she could get away with this psychodrama anytime and anyplace she desired.

"Did you get her phone number?" I joked.

She shook her head. "No, I didn't. Besides, she wasn't your type anyway."

"She couldn't be that bad. After all, you should have met the last sistah I dated. Talk about someone who wasn't my type."

"Yeah, right!" Ronnie replied, pressing her lips together.

"Can I help you with something?" I asked, trying to get her to reveal the purpose behind this discussion.

"I've said everything I wanted to say to you."

"Bye!"

As Ronnie began to walk away, she stopped and turned around. "Oh, I almost forgot. I received a phone call yesterday from an old friend of mine who wants to take me to dinner this Friday at the Chart House."

"Really?" I could tell she was lying by the fake gleam in her eyes and the way her voice cracked.

"Oh, yeah! His name is Allen and he operates his own consulting company. He has a townhouse in Chestnut Hill, drives a Lexus and owns several rental properties in Germantown and North Philly."

"Congratulations. I hope dinner turns out well."

She reached out, touching my arm. "Oh, I'm sure it will."

"But take it easy on the brotha at the Chart House, would ya? It sounds like Alex has a lot of bills on his plate."

"That's Al-len," she enunciated.

"Whatever," I said, giving her the verbal cue that the conversation was officially over.

The train was running twelve minutes behind schedule and I was growing impatient standing on the platform. After the R3 train finally arrived at the Market East Station, I sat down in the first available empty seat to enjoy the ride home. Right now, I wanted to collapse on my living room sofa for the rest of the night. I called Gene on my cell phone asking if we could reschedule studio time again. He was cool with my request since he had some last minute errands he needed to run. I was grateful because my concentration wouldn't be where it should have been if I went into the studio. I needed a mental break from all of the drama that went down this past week. Friday couldn't arrive soon enough for me.

I attempted to write something in my journal, but it was no good. I threw it down on the empty seat next to me in frustration as the passengers at Suburban Station made their way aboard the train.

"Excuse me," a female voice said. "I was wondering if I didn't need to take my clothes off to arouse your desires."

What the fuck, I thought. I looked up and saw Regina standing in the aisle. She was holding my journal and wore a friendly smile on her angelic face.

I smiled. "Hey, Regina. How are you doing?"

She sat down next to me and handed me my journal. "Just fine, Sir. And yourself?"

"Cool."

"That's good. I wanted to tell you how much I really enjoyed your poem the other night at Po/Jazz. It was so refreshing to hear you share your thoughts about what you admire in a woman. And the line about you admiring her confidence and the way she conducts herself was beautiful. It's been a long time since I've heard a man express sensitivity in his words."

I chuckled. "Thanks." It looked like I had an attentive fan in Regina. Hmmm?

The female conductor walked down the aisle of the car. "Next stop, 30th Street Station," she announced. "Please have all tickets and passes for inspection."

Regina displayed her pass upon request and continued speaking. "I haven't had the chance to listen to the CD you gave me the other night. Things have been a little hectic for me, but I will give you feedback when I do."

I retrieved my pass from my coat to flash at the conductor. "Everything okay?"

The R3 pulled into 30th Street Station as several passengers came aboard searching for the remaining empty seats so they wouldn't have to stand during the train ride.

"I have a few issues I'm dealing with right now, but I'm optimistic things will get better."

I sighed. "I hear you loud and clear."

"Is everything okay with you?"

"Today was just one of those days. I'm glad it's over."

Regina touched my journal. "I could tell."

I smiled in embarrassment. "Sorry."

"What are you apologizing for?"

I shook my head and stared out the window as the R3 departed from 30th Street Station on its way to University City. "I don't know."

Regina turned my head towards her by touching my chin. "Hey, Chris, talk to me."

Her fingers felt so gentle and soft against my goatee, but their strength penetrated deep into my soul. Her face was so lovely and I could have stared into those alluring brown eyes forever.

I shared all of my frustrations with Regina: the acquisition of Aurora by American Sentinel, breaking up with Ronnie, the relationship woes with my family and my latest bout of writer's block. She sat there and listened to every word I said while the R3 made its way from 30th Street Station to University City to its next destination at Lansdowne. Although we had only met two days ago, I felt very comfortable opening up to her. There was something genuine about Regina's concern for my well-being.

She ran her index finger across her throat. "You do have a lot on your mind, Chris. I can understand where you're coming from."

I sighed. "Sometimes it isn't easy."

"No one ever said it would be. Things could be a lot worse. In spite of everything that's happened this week, don't let it interfere with your writing. You've been blessed with a beautiful gift to express your thoughts that touch others in a positive way. Keep writing no matter what obstacles you encounter, okay?"

"Thanks. I appreciate such inspirational words coming from the great poetic Regina Simmons."

Regina slapped my arm. "Boy, get out of here with that foolishness."

"Don't be shy. I heard some good things about you."

She raised her eyebrows with inquisitive expression on her face. "Oh really?"

I nodded. "Both Gene and your girlfriend, Cami, spoke highly of you the other night. However, I wouldn't know since you haven't shared any of your poetry with me. So what's up with that, Flipper?"

Regina laughed. "Okay, let's back this up for a minute. Number one, you don't know me that well to call me Flipper. Number two, I think you are a very good poet, but don't make me have to brush off my skills and put your ego in its place, Kid. It would be quite ugly."

"I was just joking."

"Lighten up. I knew you were and I'm just teasing you. Maybe you need to go out and have some fun tonight."

"Lansdowne, next stop!" the conductor blared as she made her way down the aisle.

Regina gathered her belongings. "It was nice seeing you again."

"You, too, Regina. Thanks again for listening."

Regina stood up and handed me her business card. "No problem, Chris. You're going to be just fine. Listen, if you ever need to talk, please don't hesitate to call."

I retrieved mine from my wallet. "Thanks and don't you be a stranger, either."

She placed my business card in her purse. "Sounds good. I'll be in touch."

"Have a good one," I replied.

She waved goodbye, walked down the aisle and got off the R3 train. I watched her walk up the stairwell and turn towards the train when it pulled away from the station. I patted my journal and smiled because Regina's words and concern really made my day. I pulled out my pen and picked up writing down my thoughts from where I left off.

Chapter Eight
Regina

The bootleg CD of old and new R&B slow jams was lying on my chair inside my cubicle. There was a Post It note attached to the front with the following words:

Regina,

Here's your CD. You can pay me after lunch.

Ted

I hoped some of the songs would rejuvenate my spirits. A serious case of heart palpitations kept me from getting a good night's sleep. I lost count how many times I tried to drift off only to wake up clutching my chest. At times, I thought I was in cardiac arrest. My pajamas were soaked in perspiration when I decided to get out of bed and get ready for work. I knew I should have called out in sick. I couldn't believe Marcia did so by leaving a message for me on my voicemail. She had the nerve to ask me if I could attend her back-to-back meetings in her place at nine thirty and ten thirty. She assured me, "They're going to be brief. All you have to do is take notes, Regina. Trust me." Ha. Never mind the last meeting went forty minutes longer than anticipated, or that I had my own work to do along with covering her rear end. I was planning to see Cami so she could do something with my hair on my lunch hour. Now, I might have to cancel my plans in order to get caught up.

The telephone rang. I should have ignored it, instead I answered it.

"Hello?"

"Ah, hello? Gigi?" the familiar voice of my ex-boyfriend, Keith Andrews, responded.

I sighed. "How are you?" I wasn't in the mood to speak with Keith. He had left a message for me late last night. What kind of imbecile calls somebody at work when they're not there? Damn, talk about desperate. However, I needed to take this chance to set things straight between us.

"I'm well. I was calling to say hi. I was thinking about you, honey. I sent you some flowers the other day at work. I left a message for you last night and – "

"Yes, I know," I interrupted. "The flowers were very thoughtful, Keith, and I thank you. But can I ask you a question?"

"Sure."

"What have you been smoking that would possess you to call me at my job at 10:25 p.m.?"

"I'm sorry for calling you so late, baby. I tried to reach you at home, but your phone number was disconnected and I forgot your cell phone number. You've been on my mind for some time. I just needed to talk with you."

Keith didn't have my old phone number because it was disconnected after I moved out of my apartment in Mt. Airy. I had recently moved into my grandparents' home in Lansdowne. After Pop-Pop died last winter, I inherited the property. Keith suggested, "Sell it so we can make a fast buck." Since when did *we* come into play concerning any decision *I* would make about *my* grandparents' house? Besides, I couldn't sell it because I had too many memories growing up there. I wanted to keep the house in the family for sentimental reasons. Keith told me I was being stupid and my feelings were hurt from his insensitivity. He knew or should have known, how special Nana and Pop-Pop were to me.

"Let's get something straight, Keith. My hours of employment are from 8:30 a.m. to 5 p.m., Monday through Friday. What you did was stupid and crazy. I don't appreciate you using my work number to leave your personal messages for me. Okay?"

"It's cool and it won't happen again. I just had to hear the sound of your voice to know that you're okay."

I rolled my eyes toward the ceiling. "What do you want from me?"

"I miss you, baby. I was wondering if we could get together for dinner and work things out," Keith begged.

I ran my fingers through my hair and shook my head. "I'm sorry, but I don't think that's a good idea."

"Why not?"

"Well, for starters, what would your live-in girlfriend think about us having dinner together?"

"C'mon, Gigi, I've told you before, Monique and I aren't like that. She's an old friend who needed a place to stay because she was having problems with her husband. I told her she could crash at my place until she got herself together. Besides, Monie moved out two days ago."

"And you didn't think it would be a problem with me? Disrespecting your girlfriend by having *Hey Monie* spend a few nights at your apartment?"

"Nothing happened between Monie and me, baby. Trust me."

I sucked my teeth. "So, let me ask you this question? What were her panties doing in your drawer with your socks and underwear when I came over to get the last of my things?"

"What business you got searchin' through my drawers anyway?"

"Don't answer a question with a question. Look, Keith, I'm grateful for the time we spent together, but I'm moving forward with my life. It's nothing personal and I wish you well."

"Well, you know we can still be – "

"Friends?" I interjected.

"Yeah! You know friends still get together and do things once in a while."

"Like hanging out on weekends?"

"Yeah!"

"Kicking it at the club on Friday nights with other professionals?"

"Yeah!"

"Making booty calls in the middle of the night so we can have sex?"

"Yeah – I mean, no! That's not what I meant to say."

"Uh huh. Could you please do me a favor, sweetie?" I teased.

"Yeah?"

"Don't ever call me again!" I hissed, slamming the phone down in anger. That bastard showed his true colors and always knew how to piss me off.

I played the CD and went back to reconciling the monthly bank statement I started yesterday afternoon. The Isley Brothers did their best to try to cheer me up with *Voyage To Atlantis* and so did Deniece Williams singing *Free*, but I wasn't feeling better. My mind needed a reprieve from picking cotton on the Mercury Healthcare Services plantation, so I decided to check my e-mails. There were some new messages waiting for me in my inbox, but there was one that stood out from the rest. It was a rather unexpected surprise: a personal e-mail from Chris.

Hi Regina,

How are you doing? I hope all is well for you and that this e-mail finds you in good spirits. It was nice to see you yesterday aboard the R3 train.

I enjoyed our conversation. Your words were very encouraging and really made me feel better.

As for myself, all is well and I'm not going to complain. Today is a new day, and no matter what the future holds, I will do my best to stay focused on my goals.

Well, Regina, I've got to get back to work. Take care of yourself, stay in touch and keep writing.

:-) Chris

P.S. Last night, I had a burst of creativity and was able to finish the poem I was writing the Monday morning we met. I hope you don't mind me sharing it with you. I would love to hear your feedback. Thanks so much.

Miracle

Luminous, laughing eyes
scintillating, smiling face
exuding exuberance
opening the gateway
into innocence
revealing restless spirits
swirling and swirling,
swirling and swirling
your life, my child
bursting with infinite possibilities;
you are the pride and the reflection
of your parents' love
and the architect of your dreams
to dream big dreams
that exceed the boundaries

of your aspirations
because tomorrow, my child
belongs to you.

I decided to write him back.

Hey Chris,

I'm so glad you are feeling better today. Thank you for sharing Miracle because it is a beautiful poem. You have such a wonderful gift to capture your honesty and integrity inside your words. I'm honored that you shared this piece with me.

I am here today. Work is work and I'm having a so-so day. However, I'm doing the best I can to keep my thoughts positive. That's all any of us can do.

I wanted to ask you a question, Chris. Do you know anyplace where there will be a poetry reading or an open mic this weekend? Right now, I'm feeling a bit creative myself. I enjoyed the Po/Jazz event the other night, but I feel like venting some things off of my chest. It's been a long time coming, but I'm ready to do my thing again. Please let me know.

Duty calls. I'll talk to you soon.
Be blessed!
Regina

I remembered I had brought the compilation CD Chris gave me to work. I retrieved it from my briefcase and inserted it into my CD player. It had a nice sound and I liked the way the music complimented the poetry. There was one track, an a capella track called *Heartbeat* that Chris dedicated to his grandmother, which personally touched me. He recalled memories of her with vivid detail like the beauty of her smile and the taste of her pancakes and German chocolate cakes. I cried because it reminded me of my favorite memories of Nana. While drying my eyes with a Kleenex, I noticed there was a response from Chris waiting in my inbox.

Hi Regina,

It's nice to hear from you, too. I'm sorry to hear you're not having a good day. I hope things do get better for you. Keep your head up and your thoughts positive. Everything will be fine. :-)

Thank you for your comments about Miracle. I'm glad you enjoyed it. My goal was for the piece to be something encouraging for our young, black children. Too often, they're exposed to the negative factors of life. An inspirational, positive poem never hurts and it offsets the negativity. After all, you never know who or what your words will touch.

I do know that there is a poetry reading, Panoramic Poetry, tomorrow night at the October Gallery, which starts around eight. The host called me last week to come through and recite a piece or two. I apologize if this is short notice in asking you this, Regina, but would you like to go with me? I think you would enjoy yourself. Please let me know.

Take care and I'll talk to you later.

:-)

Chris

Cami fastened the black cape around my neck. "So, are you going to go out with Chris or not?"

"I haven't decided," I said. "It is short notice and I really don't know him that well."

I decided to take an early lunch and went to Camille's. Fortunately, the salon wasn't very busy. Therefore, I could get in and out quickly. Besides, if I was late getting back to work, how would Marcia know since she was taking the day off?

The usual cast of characters was in attendance on this hot Thursday afternoon. Lillian, the nosy stylist who got on my last nerves, was curling one of her clients' hair and eavesdropping on our conversation. Khari, the barber/stylist and Lillian's arch-nemesis, was busy fixing his clippers before his next appointment.

"Here you go. The man asked if you wanted to go to a poetry reading. He didn't ask for your hand in marriage. Didn't you tell me the other night how you wished you were back out there reading and singing?"

"Yeah."

"And didn't you ask him about attending poetry readings this weekend?"

"You're right."

Cami hunched her shoulders. "So what's the problem?"

"Well, you know how I feel when it comes to socializing with poets."

Cami's eyes bulged in an exaggerated expression. "You got to be kidding me, hussy! You just trippin' over some bad memories with Leon. That's your problem."

"This has nothing to do with Leon. I'm serious, girl. There was a whole lot of promiscuity going down on the poetry scene back in the day. It was like, *guess-who's-sleeping-with-who-this-week?* And you know I wasn't down with that crap."

Cami elevated the chair. "Hmmm...so, do you get the same vibe from Chris?"

"No, not really. However, you never know."

Cami laughed as she proceeded to run the blow dryer through my hair.

"What's so funny?"

"You."

"And what makes me so funny?"

Cami spoke her piece while massaging oil into my scalp. She thought I was being ridiculous because I was associating Chris with the losers I've dated in the past. Chris was passionate about his writing and the same ambition he had towards his poetry reminded Cami of myself several years ago. Although his invitation was on short notice, she saw this as an opportunity for me to get back out there on the poetry scene. I needed to have some fun and my girl was right. After everything I'd been through this past week, one date with him wouldn't hurt any.

"Excuse me, Cami," Tori, the receptionist, interrupted. "Damon is on the phone for you."

Cami picked up the cordless phone at her station. "Hey baby, what's up? Are you serious? I can't believe you're pulling this shit on me right now! Hold on! Just hold on!"

"Everything okay?" I asked.

"No! Tori, I'm taking this call in my office!"

Uh oh. I never saw Cami this upset in front of her employees and clients. Something was definitely wrong when Cami needed to talk in private with Damon. She always kept a tight lip, but she had an unconscious habit of making innuendos until she was ready to talk. I had sensed her joke about cheating on Monday had some underlining meaning. After this incident, my suspicions were confirmed.

"If you ask me, Regina, I don't think it's a good idea to go out with the brotha. You know dem male poets be trying to hit on women by saying the things they want us to hear," Lillian said.

I knew it wouldn't take long for Lillian to offer her two cents when they weren't needed. She reminded me too much of Darlene because of the way she thought the world should bow down and kiss her conceited ass. Cami mentioned to me that Lillian had a child by a trifling Negro who she was madly in love with and wanted to marry. He didn't reciprocate the same feelings and strung her emotions along to get what he wanted. So I guess you can say she is sort of a male basher because of past experiences.

Khari reached for the screwdriver on his station. "Ain't nobody ask you for your opinion, Lillian. You always stickin' your nose in other folks' business."

"Excuse me, but nobody talkin' to you, Khari. This here is colored folk conversation. When we want some input from the Rainbow Coalition, we'll ask you for some tidbits about your relationship with Becky Sue."

Damn. Everybody in the salon snickered and grimaced at Lillian's comments. I always thought Lillian had a love-hate thing for Khari because he was everything her baby-daddy wasn't: a good, talented and ambitious black man who was a responsible and caring parent to his son. The thing that annoyed Lillian about Khari was his involvement with a white woman. It wasn't anyone's business who Khari dated and girlfriend needed to get over it and get a life.

Khari adjusted the blade on his clippers. "You just jealous because everybody in here got somebody steady in their life except you."

Ouch. That was a low blow to Lillian's ego, but it served her right.

"How many times do I have to tell y'all that I'm on relationship sabbatical until the right man comes along!"

Cami clapped her hands three times after coming from her office. "Hey! Y'all soundin' real ghetto out here! This ain't the projects! Both of you need to chill!"

"Sorry, Boss Lady," Khari sighed.

"Ditto," Lillian mumbled.

Thank you, Lord, for making Cami's phone call short and sweet. I don't think I could have taken another moment of *As the World Turns* at Camille's. At times, I felt sorry for Cami, because she was not only the boss, but also mother and babysitter to those two clowns.

Cami returned to her station. "Tori, I need to cancel and reschedule all my afternoon appointments after I finish Gigi. I have an emergency to attend to."

"No problem."

"Everything okay?" I asked again.

"Yeah, girl, sorry about that outburst."

"It's cool," I said, not pressing the issue any further. This wasn't the right time and place for us to have another heart-to-heart.

Cami brushed my hair and picked up her scissors. "Now, where were we? Oh yeah, I was in the middle of telling you about yourself."

I waved my hands in defeat. "Say no more. I'll go out with Chris."

Cami snipped away at a long, thick strand of my hair. "My girl! I knew you would, hussy. You need to breathe instead of sittin' at home with nothing to do on a Friday night."

"And if the evening turns out to be a disaster, at least I'll have the chance to get back out there on the poetry scene like you said."

She cut another long, thick strand. "There you go."

I stared at Cami butchering away at my hair in the mirror with fervor in her eyes. My right leg began shaking and I felt perspiration developing on my breasts. I had mentioned to her I wanted a change but was uncertain about what hairstyle I wanted. She assured me she had the right one in mind for me. However, this wasn't what I expected. After her conversation with Damon, I wasn't sure if she was in the right frame of mind.

"Ah, Cami?"

"Yeah?" she mumbled.

"Are you sure everything's okay?"

"Didn't you tell me you wanted to try something different?"

"Yeah," I whispered.

"Then relax, would ya? Ole Kissy know what she doin', Ms. Gigi," she replied, winking at my reflection.

I sure as hell hoped so. I didn't want my head to be the scapegoat for her frustrations.

Chapter Nine
Regina

Cami's questions blared from the speakerphone on the nightstand in my bedroom. "So did you give up the booty tonight or not, hussy? What time is Chris gonna wake his ass up in the morning and make your cheese omelet?"

I laughed while hanging my sundress in my closet. "Girl, I think you need to quit watching *Love Jones* for the umpteenth time."

"I know y'all didn't have sex tonight because that's not your style. Otherwise, we wouldn't be having this conversation right now and both of your asses would be knocked out snoring."

I cracked the window open to let in some fresh air. The bedroom felt stuffy and the weather was warm enough so I could turn my ceiling fan on low. "How do you know what's my style? I could have put a hurtin' on Chris so bad, he's lying in a coma as we speak."

"Girl, please! Now you talkin' some beaucoup shit. You know damn well you still a wet-behind-the-ears lil' hussy. You ain't slept with enough niggas yet to get promoted to a five-star slut."

"Hey!" I exclaimed, climbing into my bed. Cami was in rare form at this hour and her jokes only enhanced the good mood I felt from this evening.

"Don't start with me tonight, okay? And don't leave a sistah hanging. I can't believe you're gonna call me after your date with Chris and not tell me anything!"

I ran my fingers through my short bob. "Ha! I should leave your butt hanging after the way you chopped off all my hair yesterday."

"Don't start with me about your haircut. I told you it looks good on you."

"Uh huh. That's what you tell all your clients after you jack their hair up on purpose. I might need to wear a wig until mine grows out again."

"Here you go."

"However, I'm going to let you slide this time."

"Yeah, right."

I wrapped the silk scarf around my head. "Besides, everybody likes my new 'do."

"I told you so!"

"Especially Chris."

"Oh, really?"

"Really!"

I reclined back against the pillow braced between my back and the brass headboard to discuss my date.

Chris and I agreed to meet for dinner at the Philadelphia Fish and Co. before we went to the October Gallery. This was perfect since the reading didn't start until eight o'clock and the restaurant was within walking distance. I was grateful for the chance to unwind. From the moment I said yes to this date, I had been a nervous wreck. I didn't know if it was because of him or because I would be reciting poetry again. Maybe a little bit of both.

We arrived at the restaurant at the same time. I must say he looked great and comfortable in his white linen shirt and khakis. After sipping some Merlot, eating a fabulous meal and sharing stimulating conversation with this down-to-earth brotha, my doubts were erased. Cami was right about Chris being a positive individual who was about something. He was a perfect gentleman: pulling out my seat for me to sit down at dinner; noticing and complimenting my new haircut; and making sure I walked on the inside of the sidewalk away from the street once we left the restaurant. I had to ask myself why this man was still single.

"You look like there's something on your mind, Gigi. Are you okay?" Chris inquired as we walked up 2nd Street.

I tapped my temple with my index finger. "I was deep in thought. I'm sorry."

"What are you apologizing for?"

"I'm a little nervous about reading."

"I know the feeling."

"Yeah, right, Mr. Loverman!" I teased.

He raised his hands in the air. "It's true."

I laughed at his remark because I didn't believe him. Chris projected much confidence when he was on stage and I told him so. He thanked me for my compliment but reminded me that every performer has butterflies before they did their thing, whether it was poetry, acting or singing. He also assured me the vibe at Panoramic Poetry was supportive and the poets and the singers were like family.

We walked through the wooden doors of the October Gallery as the venue's host, Lamar Redcross, stood at the microphone entertaining the audience. The room was mostly full with the crowd surrounding the mic in an amphitheater type arrangement. I was impressed by the beautiful display of paintings and sculptures throughout the gallery. I did recognize a few poets in the audience I saw from the other night at Po/Jazz, including much to my dismay, The Gentleman Poet. I shook my head in disgust as Lamar introduced that foul-breath, trifling Negro to grace us with his erotica nursery rhymes.

I elbowed Chris in his side as he paid for our admission. "I thought you said everybody was like family up in here." At dinner earlier, I told him about my encounter with the self-proclaimed, greatest poet of all time, and we both had a good laugh about his sorry ass.

"Well, Gigi, every once in a while a distant cousin comes crawling out the woodwork at the family reunion to act a fool."

"Hel-lo!"

Lamar made his way over to us. After the two brothas shook hands, Chris introduced me to him. Lamar had that Shemar Moore pretty boy look with a friendly smile, and his sincere, laidback attitude made you feel welcome. Chris pulled him to the side and whispered something, which was out of my earshot. I was curious as to what they were discussing, especially since I heard my name mentioned in the hushed conversation.

"If that's the way you want to roll, Chris, then it works for me," Lamar said. Chris thanked him and returned to me.

"What was that about?" I asked.

"Everything's cool," Chris responded.

As we took our seats in the middle of the last row, I gave him one of my suspicious looks. I knew he was up to something and I wanted to find out.

He nodded. "It's all good. Trust me."

"Hmmm," I murmured.

I sat back in my chair, crossed my arms and tried my best to keep a straight face while listening to The Gentleman Poet recite his latest masterpiece, *She's Hooked on Dick.*

I enjoyed the intimate setting of Panoramic Poetry, which reminded me so much of the early days when I first started reading poetry at Del State. Most of the poets were in their early twenties, and I was impressed by the energy in their voices and the strength of their words. There was a trumpeter and a guitar player who played their respective instruments for each poet or singer with their selection. The doubts I had over my age and the content of my poetry were erased from my mind. Suddenly, I realized we never signed our names on the open mic list.

"Hey, Chris," I whispered. "Did you sign us up to read tonight?"

"They don't have an open mic. You have to sign up in advance."

Damn, I couldn't believe it. I spent half the night trying to memorize some of my favorite poems and now I wasn't going to have the chance to do anything. I let out a sigh of disappointment.

"Don't worry, Gigi, everything's cool. We're getting on tonight."

I raised my eyebrow in concern. "Are you sure?"

"Trust me. You don't have to worry."

"Who said I was worrying?"

"Then why are your hands shaking?"

Chris pointed to my trembling hands resting on my lap. Damn. I clenched my fists tightly.

"Touché," I replied.

Chris smiled and squeezed my wrist. "It's cool, Gigi. You'll be fine."

I blushed. "Thanks."

Lamar made his way to the mic after the next poet finished his performance and entertained the audience with a few jokes before introducing Chris as the next poet. The audience gave him a nice reception.

"What's up, Panoramic Poetry? How's everybody doing tonight?" he spoke into the mic.

The audience gave a half-hearted alright in response to his question.

"Nah, y'all got to show a brotha more love than that! I said, 'How's everybody doing tonight?'"

The audience returned with a loud, energetic *alright* to let him know they were awake. I gave Chris a warm smile in admiration for the way he took command of their attention. He recited his first poem called *Damn*, a hilarious tale about a man meeting a woman on a street corner in Center City only to discover she was really a transvestite. Although I figured out the ending halfway into his performance, I had to give Chris credit for writing such a clever piece. Laughter erupted in the audience when he was finished.

"Now, before I proceed any further," Chris said. "I need to set the record straight. That was not a true story."

There were a few naysayers and hecklers who gave Chris a hard time, but I was impressed by his witty sense of humor.

"I have a surprise for everyone tonight. I'm going to sit down and let someone else come up here and entertain you. I met this sistah the other day and my homeboy told me she's a fantastic poet and singer. Please put your hands together and welcome Ms. Regina Simmons."

I sat in my seat petrified while the audience applauded. I couldn't believe Chris put me on the spot like he did.

Chris adjusted the mic to accommodate for my height. "C'mon, Gigi, don't be shy."

I stood up, grabbed my notebook and gave Chris a slap on his arm and then a hug. I whispered in his ear, "I'm going to kill you, Kid, when I'm finished," before he sat back down in his chair.

"Hello. Please forgive me because I was caught off guard," I said, flashing Chris an evil, playful look while he smiled at me.

"What's up, Regina?" Lamar asked from the back of the audience.

"I'm fine. This is my first time here at Panoramic Poetry. I am impressed by all of the poets and the singers who I've heard tonight."

"It looks like we've got a virgin on the mic tonight," The Gentleman Poet snickered, licking his lips and staring me down from head to toe. There were several oohs in the crowd. If I wasn't mistaken, that fool didn't remember hitting on me at Po/Jazz. That pitiful excuse for a black man was truly a dog with a capital D. I caught a glimpse of Chris's face as he shook his head.

"Let's back this up a minute, son," I returned. "Although this may be my first time here, I damn sure am no virgin on the mic. Okay?"

The audience was cracking up with oohs and dayums to my response. Chris held his head down in laughter while I managed to crack a sly grin. As I shook off the last of my anxieties, I felt my confidence returning.

"Is there anything else you would like to say before I begin?" I asked, raising my eyebrows.

"Nah, it's cool. Do your thing, my sistah," he responded.

"Thank you, my brotha." I turned my attention to the rest of the audience. "I'd like to recite a poem I wrote several years ago, inspired by the Billie Holiday song of the same name. It's been a while since I've done this piece. It's called *Strange Fruit*."

I put my notebook on the ground, closed my eyes and rubbed my hands together. I stood still and opened my mouth to speak into the mic.

Urban trees bear strange fruit
blood on their leaves
blood on their roots
young black bodies rotting in cement cells
and asphalt street corners
strange fruit hanging from societal trees
ostracized, penalized, forgotten.

Perpetual inner city scene
jump ropes dancing to the rhythmic melody
of staccato gunshot concertos
crimson blood trials
finger painting
hopscotch and double dutch spots
cement cracks
where lone iron jacks watch
boys awaken from hoop dreams.

The burned fingers of young men
who traded in
brown sugar highs
for warm glass pipes
the scent of their breath: cloves and cinnamon
now bile and death
still, here lies our fruit ripened and soured
for contemporary crows to pluck
again
for them to emasculate
four scores and one
for poverty to pour
for despair to sow

for desperation to grow
for the worse in them to blossom
here's a strangely familiar, bitter crop
for them to reap
again...

I opened my eyes to a positive response of applause in the art gallery. There were a few astonished looks on various faces in the crowd, including Chris. He stared at me in amazement and displayed an impressive smile when we made eye contact. I winked at him and waited for the noise to subside.

"Thank you so much. I'd like to finish up with a song for you, if you don't mind?"

The audience urged me on with praising comments like "Take your time, Regina," and "You go, girl."

"This is one of my personal favorites by Stevie Wonder. It's called *Overjoyed*."

The musicians began playing their instruments and I sang the lyrics. I couldn't explain the euphoria that overcame me with every note coming from my voice. It felt so wonderful and natural to put my all into expressing myself creatively again. When I was finished singing, I received a standing ovation from the audience. I put the mic back in its stand, picked up my notebook and gave Chris a warm embrace. After returning to my seat, I broke down in tears because no one knew how special this was for me.

Chris wiped a tear from my cheek. "Are you okay?" he asked.

I patted him on his hand. "I'm fine. Thank you for everything."

He smiled at me with both respect and admiration. "No, thank you! You were da bomb, Gigi!"

After the show came to an end, Chris and I stood around and chatted with Lamar and members of the audience. It felt so beautiful to hear some of the comments about my poetry and singing. Even his royal highness, The Gentleman Poet, came over to me and expressed a few kind words before trying to sell me a copy of *Velvet Lullabies*. That imbecile was in a class all by himself.

Chris escorted me to my car and I shared with him my feelings about the night. He was very impressed and told me how speechless he was by my stage presence. He loved *Strange Fruit* because it was very vivid and thought provoking. It was the type of poem which planted a seed in one's mind and made fools think twice about the consequences of their actions before they reaped their unfruitful harvest. He also complimented me on my singing; describing my voice as pure and lovely. This man was giving me goose bumps from head to toe and I couldn't stop blushing.

As we stood next to my parked car, I hugged Chris. "Thanks again for making me feel special."

"No thanks necessary, Gigi. You *are* special and God gave you a special gift, too. Like you told me the other day, don't let anything interfere with your writing and singing."

I unlocked my door. "You have a good night, Chris."

"Gigi, can I ask you a favor?"

I gave him another suspicious glance, uncertain about what he was going to ask me. Lord, please don't let him say something stupid to ruin this moment. I'm really feeling him and there is plenty of potential. "Yes?"

"Can you give me a call after you get settled in so I know you got home safely?"

"And did you call him, Gigi?" Cami asked anxiously.

I laughed out loud. "Damn, listen to you, Nosey Suzy. I don't think that's none of your business, even if you do mind me saying so."

"And if you don't tell me if you did or didn't call Chris, I'm coming over there right now and slap you upside the back of your head, even if you do mind me saying so, hussy," Cami replied as I heard her jingling her car keys.

I couldn't keep my girl in suspense any longer. "Yes, I called Chris, and we briefly chatted before saying goodnight."

"Damn, that's what's up!" Cami yelled. "Go, Gigi, it's your birthday!"

I laughed. "Girl, you're crazy."

"That sounds real good. I'm happy for you."

"Thanks."

"So, when's the next time you're going to see him again?"

"Oh my, what time is it? It's getting real late and I have to go food shopping tomorrow morning."

Cami jingled her car keys again. "Don't start with me."

"And what makes you think there's going to be a second date?"

"You must think I was born yesterday, don't cha?"

I blushed. "Well, we did talk about possibly going to the movies tomorrow evening."

"Hmmm, I thought so. You think you slick, huh?"

"Bye, Cami. I've got to go."

"I'ma let you go, but do me a favor, would ya?"

"What's up?"

"Make sure you buy plenty of eggs tomorrow at the supermarket in case you decide to let Chris spend the night."

Chapter Ten
Chris

The last of the raindrops of the passing storm splattered against my window. I glanced at my alarm clock and saw that the time was 5:48 p.m. I wanted to take a nap before I woke up to meet Regina later. Too excited from our first date, I barely slept last night. She was incredible and I was still at a lost for words to describe her performance.

The telephone rang twelve minutes before the alarm went off. I rolled over and groaned at the sight of my father's phone number displayed on the screen of my Caller ID. Part of me was curious to know what he had to say. However, another part of me wasn't in the mood to deal with his bullshit. So, I decided not to answer and possibly spoil the good mood I was in. I could count the number of times we'd spoken on the phone in the past fourteen years on one hand and still have fingers left over.

Thoughts of Regina drifted back into my mind. I wasn't sure if she was going to call me after our date, but I'm glad she did. I was surprised by her suggestion to go out again tonight. I thought things between us were a little rushed by the way I asked her out, but last night felt natural, so good.

After we said goodnight on the phone, she inspired me to write. I spent a few hours writing in my journal whatever thoughts came into my mind. It didn't matter if it was poetry or not. It didn't matter if the words did or didn't make sense. I gave myself permission to let my thoughts flow on the paper.

Earlier this afternoon, I went over to Gene's apartment with a newfound enthusiasm to get back into his studio after finishing my Saturday morning chores. My boy, baseball cap turned back and cigarettes by his side, was in his producer mode. He sat at his computer during the recording session mixing the tracks. I sipped some water, bobbed my head from side to side, and stood by Michelle, our nickname for the microphone, like a prizefighter ready to go fifteen rounds.

"Man, that was pure butta, Cool C. I want you to go back and double up on some parts in the beginning and towards the end to make it sound better. Aight?"

"Cool," I said.

Gene counted silently and slowly to three before clicking on the mouse to record the track. "Relax and let it flow like butta, baby."

I closed my eyes and listened to the replay. I repeated certain key words and catch phrases in my poem I thought would capture the listener's attention. When it was all said and done, I stepped away from Michelle. Gene gave me an approving two thumbs before he paused the recording.

"That's wassup, Cool C. Man, I ain't heard you sound this excited in a long time. You must've had a second helping of your Wheaties this morning."

I sat down on his sofa and told him he was crazy.

"Nah, seriously! I hear it in your voice. It has an extra lil' umph to give it that special Cool C touch. Just like the way you rocked the mic the other day. What inspired you to write this new piece?"

"I've got something to tell you, Gene. You're not going to believe this one."

Gene reclined in the computer chair and lit a Newport. "Uh oh, this sounds like it's going to be good."

I went into details about my date with Regina and reminisced about everything – from the e-mail conversations we exchanged on Thursday to the small talk we had on the phone the previous night. I expressed how her body language and stage presence was powerful when she recited *Strange Fruit* and how her amazing voice would put Mary J. Blige to shame when she sang *Overjoyed*. I joked about starting a Regina Simmons fan club and not only would I be a lifetime member, but would throw my name in for president.

Gene sat back and blew smoke in the air. "I wish I could have seen Flipper in action. I told you the girl got mad, crazy skills when she lets loose."

I sighed and stared out into space. "Yeah, she was something."

Gene looked at my face and started laughing.

"What?" I asked.

"You feelin' sumthin' for Flipper, ain't cha?"

"Get the fuck out of here!"

"Ya can't fool me, yung bah," Gene said, slipping into his faux West Indian accent whenever he dispensed love advice. "Me an atoritee at luv."

"Oh, so you an authority at love? What do you know about love just because you happily married? Huh? Besides, you graduated from Cheyney University. All you niggas were about spankin' that ass."

"No, you didn't just go there. How you gonna sit up in my crib talking shit, 'what do I know about love?' Man, who do you think schooled your ass about the sistahs? Y'all muthafuckas from Lincoln couldn't tell the difference between sex and love, even if y'all got instructions."

Occasionally, we would rib each other in good humor since our alma maters were rivals.

I admitted to Gene that I was attracted to Regina since we met. My news was no surprise to him, though. He could tell how I felt since the other night when Regina and I were glancing at each other. There was nothing but praise from his lips about her character and thoughts. Some of the female poets back in the day acted worse than the males who were after sex. However, Gigi wasn't like that; she was all business when it came to her craft. He was surprised when she disappeared from the poetry circuit without any explanation. He recalled she dated this one brotha who came around to Buttamilk shows. Supposedly, he was a singer and had some skills, but there was something shady about his demeanor and look. Gene always felt bad vibes about him and wouldn't even give the brotha a feature. Although Regina was bananas about the guy, Gene never said anything to tell her different. I could hear the regret in his voice, but there was no sense in him wallowing in the past. Needless to say, he thought we would make a good couple, and so did I.

The alarm clock went off at six o'clock. With a burst of energy, I jumped out of bed and into the shower. While getting dressed, the telephone rang again. I took another glance at my Caller ID and saw Regina's phone number displayed on the screen.

I picked up the receiver and placed it between my ear and shoulder. "Hello."

"Hey, Kid! What's goin' on?"

Damn, she sounded so sexy. Even her nickname for me sounded sensual.

"Nothing. Just getting ready."

"Oh, really. You sound like you're up to no good over there. I hope you'll be on your best behavior and not try to embarrass me again. Don't make me have to hurt you tonight."

"Excuse me, Ms. Simmons, but I'll have you know that there's nothing up my sleeves except the two arms."

"Oh, so now I'm *Ms. Simmons*. Earlier this week, it was *Regina*. Last night, it was *Gigi*. Would you please make up your mind, Mr. Harrington?"

I sat on my bed and laughed. I loved her sense of humor. It was off the hook. Gigi asked if we could take a rain check on the movies. Instead, she was in the mood to have some fun in Center City. She wanted to have dinner at Lockette's, a new two-level restaurant on 11th Street, and depending on the weeknight, that featured jazz, live music, comedy or karaoke. Her suggestion meant I would have to change my clothes, drive into Philly, and find reasonable and affordable parking. Before I could think of an excuse not to do so, I found my lips agreeing with her. Love certainly made a brotha do things he didn't want to do, but Regina was definitely worth it.

"I'll see you in a lil' bit, Cool C," Regina flirted before hanging up the phone.

I hung up the phone, shook my head and laughed. That girl was too much. I then turned and stared at the blinking red light on the Caller ID box. My curiosity got the best of me and I picked up the phone to check my messages. I should have known better than to listen since he was in his usual drunken stupor whenever he called me.

"J-j-junior! This is dear old Dad! Just callin' the Junior to see how you're doin'. H-h-haven't heard from you in a long time. Guess you're doing okay since we hardly hear from you anymore. It's al-al-alright. When you find the dime and the time, g-g-give dear old Dad a call. Nice talkin' to you, Junior."

Asshole. I slammed the phone down in anger. Dad wasn't an alcoholic, but drinking beer was his therapy to deal with his emotional situations. My grandparents were alcoholics and growing up in that environment had its negative influences on his life. Unfortunately, they trickled down into his marriage with my mother and into our relationship as father and son. Since our falling out, the few phone conversations we'd had, he never had the strength to express his feelings while sober. I remember the conversation we had three months after my college graduation when he called me out of the blue one Sunday afternoon. He cursed me out and made some hurtful remarks. It didn't help matters any since I had been drinking that day, too. We exchanged some nasty comments for a good ninety minutes until I decided to hang up.

I changed my clothes, brushed my teeth and hair, and left to pick up Regina. She didn't live that far from me. Therefore, it took me less than fifteen minutes to get to her home in Lansdowne. She'd mentioned the house belonged to her grandparents and that she moved in not too long after her grandfather had died. It was a nice, small brick home with a lawn and a patio. I parked my car, walked up to the front door and rang the doorbell. The scent of the fresh cut lawn and the flowers in her garden told me that Gigi didn't play when it came to maintaining her home.

Regina opened the door and greeted me with her lovely smile, followed by a tight embrace. "You're late, Kid! What took you so long?"

I glanced at my watch. "I'll have you know I happen to be ten minutes early in spite of the change in tonight's plans, Flipper!"

She punched me in my arm. "Didn't I tell you that you don't know me well enough to call me Flipper?"

"Consider it payback for the Cool C comment."

"Touché. Come on inside. I'm almost ready."

I followed her into the living room and she told me to have a seat on her couch. Regina turned down the volume of the Les Nubians CD, then walked off into the dining room to finish putting on her earrings.

I was impressed with her art collection displayed throughout the room and adorned up the stairway. Wooden African masks and statues enhanced the aesthetic motif she was trying to create. I traced my fingers across the magazines spread across her coffee table: *ESSENCE*, *Black Enterprise*, *Heart & Soul,* and *Newsweek*. I wasn't in her home for less than two minutes and already I was comfortable. If she decided to cancel our dinner plans and order pizza or Chinese take-out, I could have spent the rest of the evening chilling with her indoors.

"Can I get you something to drink, Chris?" she asked.

I picked up the latest issue of *Black Enterprise* sitting on her coffee table. "Nah, I'm cool."

Regina walked back into the living room and turned off the CD player. "Well, if that's the case, I'm ready to rock and roll."

She looked damn gorgeous in her lavender pantsuit! This lady was definitely someone who was all business, just like Gene commented at his apartment.

Regina snapped her fingers. "Hello? Earth to Chris? Yoo hoo!"

I shook my head to come out of my daze. "Sorry. You look stunning, Gigi."

"You're not too bad looking yourself, Kid."

I placed the magazine back on the table, stood up and followed Regina outside to begin our night together.

Karaoke was taking place on the first floor of Lockette's. I could hear the brave *American Idol* wannabes giving their all to sing like their idols. The audience's response was a good barometer of their success. During dinner, Regina would do impersonations of some of the songs we could recognize below. She almost made me choke on my drink when we overheard someone singing Patti LaBelle's *Somebody Loves You Baby*. Regina went into her routine, exaggerating her facial expressions and flapping her arms like a bird to imitate Patti's onstage theatrics. I almost had a heart attack from laughter. Others, like the waiter and a few customers, also had a rough time. Everybody around us clapped when she was finished.

Regina stood up and took a bow. "Thank you very much, ladies and gentlemen. No autographs, please. Encore in five minutes."

"Girl, you're a nut. I'm surprised you did that."

She sat back down and laughed. "Why are you surprised? Didn't I tell you I was a riot?"

"I thought it applied only at work."

"Oh no, whenever the mood strikes," she said, sipping her drink. "Besides, Kid, you needed that one. You look like there's something nagging you."

I rested my hands on the table. "What makes you think there's something on my mind?"

She put her elbows on the table and rested her chin on her clasped hands. "A few times tonight, I noticed your brow was furrowed. You had the same look the other day on the train going home."

I softly bit down on my bottom lip. I didn't want to tell her I was thinking about Dad's message. I don't know why it disturbed me the way it did, and I tried my best not to let it ruin the evening.

I glanced off to the side momentarily and then made eye contact with Regina again. She raised her eyebrows twice and gave me a clever smile.

She sat erect and put her hands on the table. "Anything you'd like to share?"

I let out a sigh of relief. "I'm sorry, Gigi. You caught me thinking."

"About?"

Our waiter, Gerald, came over to our table to clear our remaining dishes. "Can I interest you both in some dessert?"

"I'm fine," she replied.

"I'm okay. Can we have the check?"

"Sure, no problem," Gerald answered, walking away from our table.

We stared at each other and sat in total silence for a few moments before he returned with the check. She nodded and gave me this curious, concerned smile.

"Everything's cool. It won't happen again."

She pointed her finger and winked at me. "It better not, Cool C. I already gave you fair warning: don't make me have to hurt you tonight."

I smiled. "Well, you better be careful because I might enjoy that, Flipper."

"Touché," she replied while bulging her eyes and displaying a sly grin.

After I paid for dinner, we went downstairs to watch the karaoke in the Mahogany Room. Regina wanted to participate and I don't know if it was the liquor I drank or my guilt for letting my thoughts go astray, but I did, too. I wrote both of our names on the sign-up sheet. Fifteen minutes later, they called my name. Regina was caught by surprise and laughed when I came up to the stage. I selected Stevie Wonder's *All I Do* and did my best not to butcher the lyrics in spite of my non-singing vocals. I managed to elicit a few laughs from the audience, including Regina. A few hecklers did their best *Showtime at the Apollo* gestures by waving me offstage. I received a modest round of applause for my karaoke debut, but it was nothing compared to the hug Regina gave me. That was worth my embarrassment.

The emcee called Regina's name and she came on stage. She rubbed her hands together and selected DeBarge's *A Dream* for her performance. The audience fell silent when she sang the first lyric. Her voice captured their full attention and they were caught in her spellbinding web. If I had a pen and paper, I would have signed up a few people for her fan club. After she finished singing, everybody stood up and gave her a standing ovation. She stepped offstage, exchanged handshakes and salutations with a few people, and came back over to me. I gave her a hug and a kiss on her cheek.

She blushed and held my hand. "Thanks, Chris. Are you ready to go?"

"Yeah, let me go to the bathroom."

"It sounds like a – "

Regina paused and let go of my hand. She stood frozen in her tracks and the color in her cheeks rushed away from her face. Her mouth hung open and the words slowly emerged from her lips. "Oh my God."

I didn't notice the brotha standing there in front of us staring at Regina. We were about the same height, but his skin was a shade lighter than mine. His hair was in cornrows and he sported a well-trimmed beard and mustache. I didn't recognize him, but the anger inside my blood boiled when he opened his lips and spoke with his suave voice.

"Hello, Gigi. Long time, no see."

Regina murmured his name, "Leon."

Chapter Eleven

Regina

I couldn't believe Leon was standing there. It had been six years since the last time we'd seen each other. I sighed to gather my composure. The memories and the emotions – the good and the bad – were coming too fast for my mind and my heart to handle. I could barely speak his name, let alone mine or anyone else's. Part of me wanted to run away. Another part of me wanted to slap the taste right out of his mouth. I couldn't move, but I didn't know what to do. I wasn't going to break down, at least not in front of him or Chris. Damn, Chris looked the same way I felt about that bastard's presence; annoyed as hell. Lord, give me the courage to get through this moment because I need you now more than ever.

Leon extended his hand to shake mine. "How've you been, Gigi?"

I crossed my arms, maintained eye contact with him and murmured, "Fine."

He retracted his hand after he got the point. "You look like you've been taking care of yourself, girl."

Chris cleared his throat as Leon shifted his slanted Chinese eyes toward him.

"I'm sorry," I apologized, allowing my anger to get the best of my manners. "Leon, Chris. Chris, Leon."

Leon extended his hand and grunted, "My bad. Wassup?"

Chris shook his hand, sucked his teeth and exchanged a not so amicable "Wassup." The tension in the room was awkward and intense. Leon turned his head towards the bar and adjusted the collar on his silk shirt. I could tell there was something on his mind. I wished he would make his peace and leave us alone.

"I didn't mean to intrude on your evening," Leon said.

Chris nodded. "It's cool, brah. No harm done."

I glanced at Chris with an incredulous look. Stevie Wonder could see things weren't cool. The apologetic look on his face when we made eye contact was enough for me to forgive him for putting his foot in his mouth.

"I was headed upstairs with my girl, Kiya, to eat dinner. She went to the bathroom and I overheard the emcee call your name. I recognized your voice, came over and saw you throw down. Damn, it's been a long time since I've heard you sing."

"Yeah, it has been. Almost six years."

Leon chuckled briefly and grew silent as the sweat began to form on his forehead. I raised my eyebrows and waited on his response.

"Leon! Hey, baby," a female voice broadcasted from outside the lounge.

Leon turned towards her, displayed a one million dollar smile and waved to her. "Hey, baby."

As Kiya walked towards us, I immediately recognized her. She recently came to work at Mercury Healthcare Systems a few weeks ago. I'd seen her from time to time on the elevators and in the cafeteria. You could easily identify this unforgettable, five-foot hoochie walking down the hallways with her medium-sized frame: Yaki # 2 hair weave stitched into her scalp, which was pulled back in a ponytail; a tattoo of a strawberry on the right side of her neck; green colored contact lenses that adorned her eyes; and a protruding belly to indicate she was several months pregnant.

Kiya rubbed her hand on Leon's shoulder. "There you are. I was lookin' for you, baby."

"Kiya, I want to introduce you to an old friend of mine, Regina Simmons. Regina, this is my girlfriend, Kiya Garvin."

An old friend of mine? He had some nerve introducing me that way considering our history. I prayed for the Holy Ghost to give me some extra strength because World War III was about to erupt if I lost my cool and went upside his head.

Kiya stared at me for a hard second before we shook hands. "I know you. I've seen you around at work. It's nice to meet you."

I smiled halfheartedly, seeing right through her transparent smile to know she didn't care for me. However, I wasn't going to lose any sleep tonight over the revelation because the feeling was mutual.

"Likewise. Kiya, I'd like to introduce you to my date, Chris."

"Wassup?" Chris said.

Kiya smiled at Chris and nodded. She then grabbed Leon by the hand, rubbed her belly and whined, "Baby, I'm starvin'. We're gonna be late for dinner and you know how moody I get now that I'm eatin' for two."

I stared at Leon who avoided eye contact with me. He ran his fingers through his cornrows, squeezed Kiya's hand and cleared his throat before speaking.

"Umm, yeah, we've got to go," Leon mumbled. "It was nice seeing you again, Gigi. Nice meeting you, Chris."

Chris and I watched Leon lead Kiya towards the stairs, then we stared at each other for a good minute studying our body languages and waiting for the other to say something.

Finally, Chris rubbed his lips together and asked, "Didn't you say you had to go to the bathroom?"

"Yeah."

He rubbed my forearm. "I'll meet you by the front door in a few minutes?"

"Sure."

I don't know how long I paced back and forth in the bathroom wearing out the soles of my shoes and rambling aloud. I didn't care about the strange looks the other ladies were giving me until they cleared out the bathroom mumbling to themselves or their girlfriends about my behavior. Every profane word and thought crossed my mind when it came to that bum, Leon, and his girlfriend, Smarty Jones.

All the questions and the things I wanted to say came to me after everything had transpired. Why did I allow this incident to ruin my evening with Chris? Why didn't I slap his face when he tried to shake my hand? Why didn't I tell him off like I wanted to for the day when the shiftless Negro told me he didn't want anything to do with me and walked out of my life after I told him I was pregnant? Why did that hoochie emphasize she was pregnant?

I gathered my bearings together as best as I could, giving myself another look in the mirror to make any adjustments to my appearance: straightening my collar; touching up my lips with gloss; and running my fingers through my hair.

I wasn't sure what Chris was thinking about the incident, but I could tell he felt uncomfortable, too. It didn't take a rocket scientist to figure out there was something in the past between Leon and I. Even Kiya sensed it. It also didn't help my cause to flash Chris that look when he opened his mouth. He was doing his best to be supportive for me during this situation. Damn, I screwed up.

I opened my pocketbook to see if I had my trail-pass and a R3 schedule handy. Although he didn't strike me as the type of guy who would leave me high and dry, he's a man and why should he be any exception? It only took a man to let the small head hanging between his legs impair his thinking when his pride was wounded and I wasn't taking any chances. After tonight, what's the worse that could happen to me than being abandoned on a date and having to catch the train home?

The ride home on I-95 in Chris's Ford Explorer wasn't as horrible like I imagined. The twenty minute drive was filled with moments of lighthearted conversation followed by intervals of silence. Long intervals of silence. I'm sure we were both thinking about what had occurred, but didn't bring it up for fear of offending the other. About the third interval, Chris turned on the radio to break up the monotony. I was relieved to hear something, anything to smooth things over. He turned to WRNB and we laughed when we heard Patti LaBelle's *Somebody Loves You Baby.*

Chris tapped me on my shoulder. "Are you ready for your encore?"

I giggled. "Sorry, Kid, I'll have to take a rain-check on that performance."

Chris pulled up to the side of my home and turned off the car. He turned on the interior lights and drummed his hands on the steering wheel while I searched for my keys.

We spoke in unison, saying, "I wanted to tell you – "

We laughed and gave the other permission to speak. Chris won the battle when he conceded, "Ladies first."

"Thank you, Chris, for the lovely evening. As always, I had a great time and enjoyed your company."

Chris nodded, stared deeply into my eyes and remained silent.

"I also want to apologize to you for what transpired between us and Leon and Kiya. Leon was an ex-boyfriend of mine who treated me like an afterthought. It had been a long time since I'd seen him and a lot of painful memories came back to me all at once. He took advantage of my generosity and love for him. I went through a very difficult period in my life towards the end of our relationship. When I needed him the most, he wasn't there for me."

I sighed and grasped for strength in my breath to fight the tears threatening to spill from my eyes. Chris held my hand and rubbed his thumb across my palm.

"You don't have to apologize for anything, Gigi. I got the impression that you two had dated in the past and things weren't smooth. I was proud of the way you handled the situation like a trooper. I don't know what I would have done if the shoe was on the other foot."

I blushed. "Boy, please."

"I'm serious. And if there's anyone who should apologize, it's me."

"What for?"

"Part of me felt jealous of Leon's obvious attraction for you and his apparent shame about everything that went wrong in your relationship. I think he still has some feelings for you. I could see it in his eyes when he stared at you and the way he abruptly left with Kiya. There was definitely something he wanted to say to you."

Chris's last comment made me think because that would definitely explain Leon's behavior tonight. I sucked on my teeth and realized maybe he had a valid point.

I leaned over, giving him a kiss on his right cheek.

"Thanks, Kid, for being so understanding."

"You're welcome."

Chris opened his door and walked around the passenger side to let me out. We hugged and said goodnight, but I noticed a strange look on his face. I wasn't certain how to decipher the glow in his eyes, but I felt like there was something he wanted to say to me. He promised to call once he got home. I nodded but decided to let my observation pass. I watched Chris drive off into the night once he saw me open the front door and walk into my home.

My first impulse was to pick up the telephone and call Cami to tell her everything, but I thought it better not to do so. Knowing girlfriend the way I did, her crazy, ghetto self would have woken up her sons, Duane and James, placed them in the back seat of her Toyota Camry, grabbed Damon's Louisville slugger, swung by my place to pick me up and tracked down Leon and Kiya, so she could break their kneecaps.

I needed this time to sort through my feelings regarding the past. Leon's appearance tonight brought back memories from my life six years ago: my unexpected pregnancy and his response; my diagnosis of Grave's Disease; Nana's struggle with Alzheimer's Disease; and my decision to have an abortion. I walked upstairs to my bedroom, took off my clothes and sat back in my bed. Picking up a picture of Nana, I traced her face with my index finger. I always loved her smile because it was so beautiful and full of life.

Six years ago, I temporarily moved back home and offered my assistance the best I could. My grandparents were my immediate family and there was no other choice in the matter. We did the best we could not to put Nana in a nursing home. The time spent watching her every move and the safety precautions made around the house –

leaving no doors unlocked, removing the knobs on the stoves at night and padlocking all the knives in a separate drawer – were exhausting. Eventually, the fatigue took its toll. Pop-Pop was affected the most, and it was the first time I ever saw him cry since Mama's passing. How heart-wrenching it must have been for him to know the woman he loved since the age of nineteen did not remember who he was, or to witness her physical deterioration day by day when she needed assistance in taking a bath or changing her clothes. There was no way I would be able to handle being pregnant under those circumstances, no matter how hard I wrestled with my decision to keep the baby.

I fell asleep in my bedroom waiting for Chris to call me. The telephone woke me around 12:15 a.m., almost a half hour after he dropped me off. I picked up the phone and let out a sigh of relief when I heard his voice.

"Hey, you," I said. "I thought you almost forgot about me."

"I'm sorry I didn't call you sooner, but that wasn't the case. I could never forget about you, Gigi."

I shook my head and smiled. "Hmmm."

"I had a creative moment when we were talking. I didn't want to talk with you right away until I finished writing this poem."

I didn't know if I should have been flattered by his gesture or ticked off because of his selfishness. I forgave him and understood from the artist's perspective. I was totally speechless and floored listening to him recite his new piece.

Creative waters descend
upon the shores of my third eye
as my body and soul
are rocked steady
by the jubilant sounds of
Stevie Wonder's voice
singing All I Do
when I envision
iridescent irises

of a light brown hue
tattooed into
my memory
generating tranquil thoughts
that breathe life into
intellectual stimulation
in this time, in this place
where you are
admired and desired
for many moons
to come.

I sat in my bed for a good, long moment in a state of surprise, searching for the right words to describe how he made me feel.

"Hello? Are you there?"

I reached over to turn on the speaker phone and smoothed my hair.

"I'm here, Kid. I can't believe you wrote that poem for me. It was so beautiful. I'm very touched by your words."

"You're welcome. I wanted to let you know, in my own poetic way, you weren't an afterthought in my eyes."

I closed my eyes, trying to articulate my thoughts. My right leg was shaking because this man knew how to pull my heart strings.

"Are you okay?" Chris asked.

I wiped away a tear from my eye. "I'm fine, baby. Just thinking."

"About?"

"Some things that have been on my mind lately."

"Well," he said, "I am a good listener, if you want to talk."

I nodded. "Yeah, I'd like that. Do you mind?"

"No, not at all. I'm listening."

"Well, not on the phone."

"Huh?"

I opened my eyes and took off my bra. "Please don't think of me being forward for suggesting this, but could you come over tonight so we can talk?" I couldn't believe I said that. Damn. "Hello, Chris? Are you still there?"

His silence was killing me. Lord, please don't let me screw things up.

"I'm still here," he replied. "I don't know what to say."

"I apologize, sweetie. Please don't get the wrong impression of me."

"It's not like that, Gigi. It's cool."

I exhaled a major sigh of relief. "Thanks. I wanted to share my thoughts with you and I'd like you to be here with me when I do. Besides, I enjoy talking with you face to face."

I cringed when I heard the last sentence come out of my mouth. What kind of mojo did Chris put on me? It was driving me crazy. I can't remember the last time any man made me act this way. I reached for the baby powder on the nightstand and sprinkled some in my hands.

"Are you sure?"

I rolled my eyes at the speaker phone while massaging baby powder onto my breasts. "No, I'm Regina. And if you ask me again, then you can forget about it and stay home."

Chris laughed. "Okay. I'll see you in a few."

"Bye," I said, pressing the off button.

Chapter Twelve

Chris

I should have been asleep in my bed dreaming about Gigi. Instead, I was sitting in my SUV outside of her home at 12:55 a.m. I didn't expect her to ask me to come over tonight. I mulled for a good ten minutes over whether or not I should even do so. It was only our second date and she was already inviting me over. Most women invited a man to their place this late for only one reason, and I have had my share of booty calls. Gigi didn't strike me as that type of sistah, but I really didn't know her that well. Part of me took into careful consideration our encounter with her ex at Lockette's. I liked her, but I wasn't expecting to be the brotha-on-the-speed-dial to lift her wounded pride. I didn't know what she was up to, but I'd soon find out.

After walking up to her house, I was greeted at the front door by Gigi wearing a fuchsia bathrobe, a silk scarf wrapped on her head and holding a composition notebook. She looked too sexy and relaxed in her loungewear.

"Hey, Kid!" she said, giving me a hug.

"Hey, yourself," I replied, inhaling the scent of her body. Damn, she smelled so good. I walked through the front door and into the living room. I was digging the mood Gigi constructed to stimulate her creativity: the wooden lamp and a large Yankee mango scented candle on the end table were the sources of illumination; a small brass incense holder sat on the coffee table and filled the room with lavender; Vivian Green's *What Is Love* was playing on the CD player.

Gigi shut and locked the door. "Thanks for coming over. Please have a seat. Can I get you anything?"

I sat down on the sofa. "Nah, I'm cool." Gigi sat down on the opposite end and placed her notebook on the coffee table. I smiled. "Are you alright?"

She untied her bathrobe to reveal she was wearing a baby blue t-shirt. "I'm fine, Chris. I needed to see your face when I tell you what I have to say."

I stroked my goatee. "Okay?" Her words aroused my curiosity.

Gigi inhaled and sighed. "This is difficult for me to say, but I'm attracted to you."

"Is that all? Girl, I've been known that," I said, waving my hand.

She landed a hard jab into my right arm that hurt more than I let on.

I laughed. "Damn, Gigi, I was just playing."

She cocked her eyebrow and replied, "Look, Kid, you may be cute and cocky, but you ain't all that. I'm being serious."

"I'm sorry," I mumbled sarcastically.

She rolled her eyes and playfully smirked. "We'll see. Anyway, I've enjoyed our dates and I'd like to get to know you. It's been a while since someone has made me feel the way you do, but I've always avoided dating poets."

I laughed. "That's funny you should say that."

"Why?"

I rubbed my arm. "It looks like we have a lot in common."

"Really?"

"Yeah, I'm feeling you, too, Gigi. I'm glad we've had the chance to get to know each other. I've never dated any female poets before because I've seen too many bitter sistahs on open mics airing their dirty laundry about the brothas that did them wrong. It was brutal."

Gigi laughed and slapped my thigh. "That is too funny."

"But there's something special about you, girl, and it doesn't matter about the poetry. I don't want you to think I'm the type of guy that's all about sex. I wasn't trying to seduce you with the poem I wrote tonight. It was something that came from my heart…an expression of the way you drive me crazy. Sometimes, I just can't help myself."

She blushed. "I appreciate and respect you for your sincerity. Believe me, you never struck me as the playa type like your homeboy, Greg."

I shook my head and put my hands in the air. "Nah, girl, that's your peeps. I can't claim ownership of that nigga."

"*Excuse me*," she said, slapping my thigh.

"Wassup?" I replied, widening my eyes.

"Do me a favor?" she asked.

"Yeah."

"Please don't ever say the *N-word* around me or in my house again. It irritates me when our people constantly use that word to identify ourselves like some badge of honor without realizing its historical origin and its derogatory connation."

I nodded. Gigi had a good point and I definitely had to give her respect. "You're absolutely right. I apologize."

She nodded in return. "Apology accepted. As you were saying, he's somebody's homeboy, not ours."

The CD player shuffled discs and *Spanish Guitar* by Toni Braxton came on.

I smiled and murmured aloud.

"What's up?" Gigi asked.

"I like this song. This is one of my favorites."

She rolled her eyes, sucked her teeth and said, "I bet it is."

I shook my head. "Don't hate. It's not like that."

"If you say so."

"No, I like the way she admires the brotha's passion for his guitar. She paints a beautiful picture that makes you feel like you're there with her in this crowded Spanish café. I feel the same way whenever I hear you recite poetry or sing. You are so talented and gifted, Gigi."

She tilted her head, smiled and then reclined back against the arm of the sofa. Her eyes became withdrawn and her lips were pressed together.

I reached for her hand. "Are you okay?"

"I'm thinking about what you said," she replied, squeezing my hand.

"Did I offend you?"

She touched my cheek. "No, you didn't. There's something you need to know about me."

The CD player shuffled discs and a new song came on. An acoustic guitar was playing in the beginning of what sounded like a rock ballad. The beat and the lead singer's voice were familiar, but I couldn't remember the group's name.

Gigi murmured, "Now this is one of my favorites."

I scratched my head. "What's the name of this song?"

"It's *Iris* by the Goo Goo Dolls," Gigi answered, rubbing her temple with her index finger. "This is from the *City of Angels* soundtrack."

I nodded and remembered seeing the movie last week on cable. The song had a nice tempo and I admired her selection. It showed me she wasn't afraid to be open-minded or versatile. I tried to get Gigi to speak, but she put her finger on my lips to silence me. I could see girlfriend can be quite elusive.

"Now that's a powerful song that speaks volumes, unlike your girl, Toni," Gigi said.

"Please!" I replied.

She waved her hand. "It's a testimony of a man's devotion for the woman he loves and the risks he would sacrifice for their relationship."

I laughed. "If I were you, girl, I wouldn't go around telling black folks about that one. That's like those brothas and sistahs you hear about that secretly watch *Friends*. Please don't tell me you watch that corny mess?"

She sucked her teeth and crossed her arms.

I stood up from the sofa. "Damn, Gigi, you watch *Friends*?"

She rolled her eyes towards the ceiling. "No, I don't watch *Friends,*" she snapped. However, the attitude in her voice revealed the truth behind her lie.

I sat back down and put my hand on her shoulder. "It's okay, girl. I won't tell anybody. I'm not going to turn you in to the homies so they can revoke your ghetto pass."

Gigi laughed. "You got issues, Kid," she said, pointing her finger at me.

The song ended and another disc was shuffled into rotation. This time it was Erykah Badu's *Otherside of the Game*. We smiled, gave each other a high-five and started singing the chorus.

Gigi stood up, grabbed my hand and led me to the center of the living room. "I want you to dance with me," she requested.

"Dance with you?" I asked.

Gigi nodded and like a lovesick puppy, I obeyed her instructions by putting my arms around her waist and pulling her body closer.

She rested her head on my chest and whispered, "Dance with me, Chris. Hold me. Don't say another word." The scent of her perfume, the softness of her hips and the music's melody had put all my cognitive senses on lockdown.

She purred like a kitten. "Hmmm."

"What's up?"

"I can tell how much you care about me."

"How so?"

She stepped back a few inches and stared at my erection. "It looks like your friend is very excited."

I sighed and closed my eyes. *Damn,* I thought, *why did my dick have to play me like that?*

She tapped her index finger on my chest and kept staring at my shorts. "I hope you weren't planning on using that tonight, Kid. You know, sometimes people have hidden agendas."

I shook my head. "Not me," I replied. "I meant everything I've told you."

"Okay," she said, maintaining a respectable distance between us.

I kissed her forehead and held her tightly, then sighed and started rubbing the small of her back. "Speaking of hidden agendas," I said. "Wasn't there something you were about to share with me?"

She rubbed my shoulders with her hands. "It's hard for me to explain what's going on with me."

I raised her chin with my fingers. "I'm listening."

After exhaling a deep breath, she nodded and revealed to me the problems she had with her thyroid. I could hear the uncertainty and concern in her voice when she told me about the lump her endocrinologist found that wasn't picked up on the ultrasound. She confessed her hesitation about sharing the information with me since she didn't know how I felt about her.

Erykah Badu's voice faded in the background and D'Angelo began singing the introduction to *Lady*. I pulled her body closer, touched the back of her tapered nape and whispered in her ear, "I'm here for you, Gigi, and I'm not going anywhere."

She smiled and whispered, "Thank you, Chris."

Damn, her lips were so succulent. I did my best to fight my feelings, but I leaned over to kiss her. To my surprise, she didn't pull away. Our tongues were wrestling for penetration and position in each other's mouth. The more she pressed her breasts into my chest, the faster her heart beat grew.

Pulling away from her body, I sighed a hearty "Dayum!"

"You got that right," she added, shaking her hand.

I rubbed my head. "Well, it's getting late. I need to get going."

"You shouldn't be driving home this late," Gigi suggested, grabbing my hand.

I patted my denim shorts for my car keys. "Nah, I'll be alright."

She walked over and turned off the CD player. "Chris, it's okay. You can spend the night." Then, she turned on the hallway light and blew out the candle.

"Are you cool with that? I mean, um, you know – "

"Relax, Kid. Trust me," she said, turning off the lamp.

Taking my hand, she led me upstairs to the second floor. I almost tripped when I climbed the final step of the dimly lit hallway. She turned the knob to the door on the right of the stairway and flicked on the light switch. I had to shut my eyes momentarily to allow them to adjust to the room's light.

"Welcome to the guest quarters of Chez Simmons, Monsieur Harrington," she said while patting my back.

I glanced around the room. A twin bed was placed towards the far right. A wooden computer desk with a PC was near the door. The shelves were cluttered with envelopes, papers and magazines. A gray and white, stuffed animal dolphin was perched at the top. A wooden stand in the far right corner displayed porcelain and lead crystal dolphin figurines on its four shelves. The walls were peach and bare with the exception of a watercolor painting that hung above the desk. It was a beautiful scene of a school of dolphins swimming in the ocean near a lighthouse.

She picked up the stuffed animal and handed it to me. "Say hi to Tyler, Chris."

"Okay," I said, staring at Tyler. The dolphin thing was beginning to spook me.

"Don't be shy, Chris. Give Tyler a hug. He won't bite you."

I glanced at girlfriend like she was crazy. Obliging, I squeezed the fins and suddenly Tyler began to vibrate and make dolphin screeches. Startled, I let go and jumped back from that damn thing.

"What the – ? Girl, have you lost your mind?"

Gigi picked up her toy and laughed at me. "Gotcha!" she exclaimed, stroking Tyler. "That's what you get for messing with me."

I chuckled and waved my hands in defeat. "You got me."

She put Tyler back on the desk. "The bathroom is to your right. I'll be back. Make yourself comfortable."

Gigi walked down the hallway and into her bedroom as I sat on the bed to take off my sneakers. I took off and folded my Allen Iverson jersey and shorts, sitting them on top of the sneakers. She returned shortly, carrying a blanket and a jar of Palmer's cocoa butter.

"Just in case you get the chills," she said, handing me the blanket.

I sat it on the desk's chair. "Can I ask you a question?"

A smirk appeared on her face. "Uh oh."

"Don't start. It's not that bad."

"Okay," she murmured, rolling her eyes.

"What's up with the dolphins?" I asked, touching her silver pendant.

The look on Gigi's face went from playful to pensive. She sucked her teeth for a few seconds, pulled back the covers and told me to lie down. I did as she said, climbing into bed as she sat down on the mattress. She ran her tongue across her lips and untwisted the jar's lid before she finally spoke.

"When I was seven, my parents and I spent the summer at Cape May the week before the Labor Day holiday weekend. They rented a home not too far from the Cape May Lighthouse. I remembered Mama had this fascination with lighthouses."

She dipped her fingers into the jar and rubbed her hands together. Then, she massaged the cocoa butter onto my face and continued her story.

"One evening, Daddy and I were walking on the beach. Mama had a headache and decided to spend the night resting. The stars were beginning to appear in the sky. We were watching the waves come into the shore and that's when I spotted a school of dolphins. It was a family of two adults and a calf. Daddy picked me up in his arms and said, 'Look at the pretty dolphins, Angel. They're one happy family just like us.' That was the last summer I spent with my parents before they died in a car accident four weeks later."

"Regina, I'm sorry," I said, glancing at her solemn face and then at the painting.

She placed the lid back on the jar and sat it on the floor. "It's okay, Chris. I wrote my first poem about that experience and dedicated it to Daddy. Would you like to hear it?"

I nodded. Gigi closed her eyes, rubbed her hands together and bobbed her head. I felt the strength of her words and her soft voice hit me in my heart when they emerged from her lips.

There was a beacon of hope
radiating from your heart
like the slivers of silver moonlight
swimming across the ocean waves
by the lighthouse that resided
near the shores of my imagination
where the dolphins played
and my eyes looked towards Heaven
in my quest for wisdom
and I saw you
an angel in flight
whose gentle wings kissed the clouds
as you ascended to the stars
you who resuscitated my joy
to breathe, to love, and to live
through the power of prayer.

I stared up at the ceiling. "It's beautiful, Gigi. What's it called?"

"Intangible," she replied, rubbing her hand across my chest and picking some lint off my white t-shirt. "Are you okay?"

"I was just thinking."

"About what I said?"

"Yeah, and about my father."

"Is everything okay between you two?"

I sighed. "Not really. We don't exactly have the best relationship in the world."

"Some people don't, but it's okay," Gigi said, tilting my head towards her. "If there's one thing I can tell you, Chris, is that it's never too late to tell someone that you love them. Don't wait until tragedy strikes." She leaned over to give me a goodnight kiss before she picked up the cocoa butter, stood up and turned off the lights.

I said goodnight to Gigi and watched her leave the room, shutting the door behind her.

There was no way in hell I could fall asleep after hearing her story and poem. I didn't have the strength to look at the painting on the wall. It was like staring into Gigi's eyes and seeing my reflection in her pupils. The more I saw my face, the more shame and guilt I felt for all the foolish things Dad and I had said and done over the years. I'm not sure how long I tossed and turned before I sat up. I put my face in my hands when I saw Tyler staring at me with his disapproving, black eyes. I raised my head and said, "I know," when I glanced back at him.

Needing to relieve myself, I stood up, opened the door and walked towards the bathroom. After opening the door and feeling the tile wall for the light switch, I flipped it, turning on the lights. The color scheme of her bathroom was the same as mine, pink and black, and the room smelled like peaches. I noticed the unplugged potpourri dish sitting on the mantle along with her toiletries and was surprised she didn't have any dolphin paraphernalia like a toothbrush holder or a toilet bowl brush.

Before I had the chance to shut the door, I heard Gigi screaming from her bedroom, "No! No! Please God, I'm sorry! I didn't mean to do it." The next sound I heard was something shattering when it fell to the wooden floor.

I ran down the hallway and knocked on the door. "Gigi! Are you okay?"

I heard her climb out of bed, turn the knob and crack the door open. I slowly entered her bedroom and saw her sitting on the edge of the bed crying, "I didn't mean to do it." Her hair was an unruly mess and her t-shirt was drenched in sweat.

"Gigi, are you alright?" I asked, sitting beside her.

"Oh, Chris," Gigi mumbled, wiping away her tears and breathing erratically. "Hold me." She grabbed my body tightly and I could feel her heart pounding like a drum.

"It's okay, baby. I'm here. You're safe," I whispered, stroking my fingers through her hair.

"Please hold me," she sobbed, trembling in fear.

Chapter Thirteen

Regina

Chris rocked me in his arms. "It was a bad dream, Gigi, that's all," he said, wiping the tears from my face.

He tried to assuage my fears by talking to me, but I was too scared to talk, move or think. The nightmare I had made me too hysterical and incoherent to do anything. Chris tried to get me to stand up, but I shook my head and moaned. He rubbed my shoulders and said, "We'll move when you're ready." I held him tighter.

I couldn't recall when I dozed off, but I did remember leaving Chris alone after telling him about the dolphin story with Daddy and reciting *Intangible*. I never shared that experience or the origin of that poem with anyone before, not even with Cami. In the past, I would lie about the dolphin symbolism if anyone ever inquired. I could have done the same to Chris, but for some strange reason, I didn't want to.

I told him everything and could tell something was bothering him. As I spoke, his eyes drifted away from mine and towards the ceiling. When I asked if everything was okay, he briefly mentioned his troubled relationship with his father. I expressed my feelings, said goodnight and left him alone to deal with his issues while I went to my bedroom to deal with mine. Once alone in my room, I pulled out an old photo album from my childhood and sat in my bed reminiscing about Mama and Daddy. I felt jealousy towards Chris, Cami and everybody I knew who ever fought with their parents. It was wrong for me to harbor those feelings and I shouldn't have. They could never understand what it was like to grow up without a mother and father. I wanted to go back to Chris so we could talk about everything, but my pride wouldn't let me. Instead, I wallowed in my own pity party until I cried myself to sleep.

I dreamt Chris and I were dancing together and alone in a grand ballroom. I didn't know exactly where we were, but the impressive appearance of the crystal chandeliers and the black and white tile floor suggested a five-star hotel like the Four Seasons or the Ritz Carlton. There was a terrace that had a clear view of Center City where the stars were sparkling in the night sky with the full moon.

I was wearing an elegant, strapless black gown and a pearl necklace. My hair looked fantastic and there wasn't a strand out of place. Chris, my black knight in shining armor, was dressed to kill from head to toe wearing a tuxedo. We were lost in our own private world, dancing to Anita Baker's *Caught Up In The Rapture*, Teena Marie's *Portuguese Love*, Kenny G's version of *What A Wonderful World* with Louis Armstrong, The Isley Brothers' *Between The Sheets*, Luther Vandross' *Here and Now*, Prince's *Adore*, and Stevie Wonder's *Ribbon In The Sky*. The moment was so magical and perfect as I rested my head against his chest. That's when I heard the faint voice of a little girl saying, "Mommy."

I looked into Chris's eyes. "Did you hear that?" I asked.

"Hear what?" Chris replied.

"A girl's voice," I said.

Chris turned and looked around the empty room. "I don't see anyone."

"Mommy," the voice called from the terrace. I saw her standing out there, a little black girl wearing a yellow t-shirt and a denim skirt. Her hair was in pigtails and her skin complexion was almost the same as mine.

"There she is, Chris," I said, pointing at her.

Chris glanced at the terrace. "Gigi, I don't see anything."

"She's right in front of us!"

She took three steps into the ballroom and said, "Mommy, why did you leave me behind?" Then, she turned around and went back out to the terrace. A thick mist of fog surrounded her and my view of the city.

I ran towards the terrace. "Stop!"

Chris stood still and yelled, "Gigi, come back. There's nobody there."

I went outside and chased after her, but the fog was too thick and I couldn't see anything. I felt like I was running forever until I tripped over something and fell to my face, landing hard to the ground with sand and gravel in my mouth and eyes. When the fog disappeared, I found myself lying on the beach. I stood up, wiped the debris from my body and looked around. The air smelled like salt water, the sea gulls were flying and chirping above in the sky, and the sun was setting. Although it had been years since I'd been here, I knew I was in Cape May.

"Oh, Lord, please tell me what's going on?" I asked.

"How could you, Angel?" a voice called from behind me. I turned around and saw Daddy and Mama standing there. They looked just like they did the last summer we spent together. Daddy looked so handsome, energetic and relaxed in his cut-off blue jean shorts and white t-shirt. Mama was wearing her favorite black bathing suit with the purple floral imprint and the straw hat she bought that week.

"How could you throw away our grandchild's life, Regina?" Mama asked, extending her arms.

"Oh, Mama, I didn't mean to," I said, extending my arms toward her. "It was a mistake. I'm sorry."

While reaching out to my parents, Mama stepped back from me and I fell again. Suddenly my legs felt as though they were being pulled into the ground. Looking around, I realized I was sinking in a pit of quicksand.

I squirmed and pleaded, "Mama! Daddy! Please help me."

"You should have died, Angel, not us," Daddy said as he stepped back and they turned to walk away from me. By now, my entire body was almost submersed in the murky pool.

"No! No! Please, God, I'm sorry! I didn't mean to do it!" I screamed until I woke up after hearing Chris knocking and calling my name outside in the hallway.

I slowly rose to my feet with Chris's help. He placed his arm across my back and escorted me to the rocking chair in the right corner. My sheets were scattered across my mattress along with my scarf and the photo album. I sat down while Chris kneeled down and picked up the broken lamp, Nana's picture and the telephone I knocked off the nightstand in my sleep.

I raked my fingers through my hair. "Leave that mess alone. I'll take care of it."

"It's no problem. I got it," he said, placing Nana's picture on the nightstand.

I clenched my teeth. "I said, *I'll take care of it!*"

Whoa. I put my hands to my lips and covered my mouth. I couldn't believe I raised my voice and spoke to him that way. By the surprised look on his face, neither could he. He stood up, sat down on the edge of the bed, and rested his hands on his thighs.

I lowered my head. "I'm sorry. I didn't mean to say that."

"Don't worry about it. You're still shaken up from the nightmare you had. Do you want to talk about it?"

I shook my head. Chris walked across the bedroom towards me, raised my chin to look me in the eye and smiled. Not able to look him in his eyes, I turned my head away from his face. He nodded and sat back down on the bed. We then sat in silence for a few minutes glancing around my bedroom.

I coughed. "Chris, could you please do me a favor?" I asked.

"Sure."

"I'd like to be alone right now. It's nothing personal, but I need some privacy to sort through some thoughts." I watched as Chris rose and walked towards the window, where he stood for a few moments before walking out of the bedroom.

I didn't move from the bed until Chris was dressed and ready to leave. Damn, I didn't want him to go, but I wasn't in the mood for talking. Why couldn't I find the power to ask him to stay with me?

Against my own will, I got up from the bed, escorted him downstairs to the living room, turned on the lights and unlocked the front door. Chris walked outside and then stood at the top of the steps staring at me.

He rubbed his hands together. "Um, I'll call you to let you know I made it home safe."

I nodded and whispered, "I'll be listening."

While holding my hand, he leaned over to give me a kiss on my cheek and searched my eyes for me to tell him not to leave. I looked into his eyes and opened my mouth, but I couldn't find the words to do so. I simply closed my mouth and stared at the brick step.

Letting go of my hand, Chris said, "Goodbye, Gigi."

"Goodbye," I replied, while waving my hand and watching him walk towards his SUV.

I closed the door once Chris drove away. After lighting the candles, I turned out the lights and sat down on my living room sofa. I couldn't believe I let him walk away like that, but I didn't have any choice. The nightmare spooked me more than I realized, and I wasn't ready to share everything about my past with him, especially the abortion. Besides, with all the problems I've been having with my thyroid, maybe now wasn't the right time for me to pursue a relationship with Chris. At least, until I had some concrete answers about my prognosis.

After sitting in silence for ten minutes, the telephone rang. I didn't move, but instead, I let the answering machine do its thing while I sat there and listened to Chris's voice.

"Hi, Gigi. It's me, Chris. Um…I…um, I don't know what I'm trying to say, but… um…damn. I'm sorry. I wanted to let you know that I do care for you and that I'm here for you. I'll do my best to be patient and be understanding. Take care and I'll…um…talk to you later."

I rested my head against the arm. "I hope so, Chris. I really do hope you will understand and forgive me someday for what I have to do."

Chapter Fourteen
Chris

I saw Gigi waiting at the platform from my window seat when the R3 train arrived at the Lansdowne station. This was the first time I had seen her this week since I left her place last weekend. She didn't return my call from the other night as I had hoped she would. Whatever she dreamt that night must have been real deep. I remembered how spooked she was, but if she was up to it, we could talk before we arrived in Center City.

Gigi climbed aboard the train, took off her sunglasses and walked down the aisle trying to decide where she wanted to sit. It must have been Dress Down Friday at her job because she was wearing an overall, denim short piece and a purple shirt. I removed my gym bag from the empty seat next to me and waved to get her attention. Looking surprised to see me, she paused in her tracks. Biting down on her bottom lip, Gigi waved to me and sat down in an empty seat that was three rows ahead of mine. The passenger standing behind her – a heavyset, white female in her mid forties with excessive makeup plastered across her face – sat beside me. The funk from her cheap perfume made me want to vomit. No, Gigi didn't play me like that. I balled my fists to keep cool and not let it bother me, but it did.

The next twenty minutes riding aboard the train felt like an hour by the time it arrived at Suburban Station. I kept debating to myself whether or not I should get up and sit next to Gigi. Instead, I stared at the back of her head, wondering what was up with her. She never once turned around to look at me. Maybe it had something to do with her ultrasound appointment on Monday and she wasn't ready to share the results with me. Okay, I could understand if she weren't an open and straightforward person.

Gigi stood up and waited for the departing passengers to clear the aisle. Before exiting the train, she turned towards me and we stared at each other for a brief moment. The smile on her face lacked the warmth it had on our dates. She waved goodbye and departed. I picked up my gym bag, excused myself from Tammy Faye's big sister and rushed to follow her.

I threw my gym bag over my shoulder, stepped up my pace and called out her name, but she kept walking slowly and meticulously. Not knowing if she could hear my voice over the noise in the station, I said her name again. She paused at the bottom of the stairway leading up to the street level and turned around to face me. Her arms were crossed over her breasts.

"Hey, you, what's up?" I asked while sitting my gym bag on the red tiled platform.

She rubbed her forearms. "I'm fine, Chris. How are you?"

"I'm cool," I said, rubbing my hands together. "Um, is everything okay?"

A computer-generated voice announced over the loudspeakers that the 8:15 a.m. R2 train was about to arrive shortly on Track # 3. Gigi's eyes drifted back and forth between the ground and mine as she slid the top of her sneaker between the grooves of the tile.

"I'm alright. Thanks for asking."

"Well…um…please forgive me for saying this, but you don't act like you're alright. I haven't seen you since Sunday, and I was concerned about you. I know you told me you were suppose to have an ultrasound done on Monday for your thyroid. How did things go?"

The R2 pulled in and several passengers got off and walked upstairs. Gigi turned her head towards the silver vehicle and held the brass staircase rail with her right hand. "Things went well."

I touched her chin with my fingers and turned her head towards me. "You know you can always talk to me about anything."

She hunched her shoulders. "Thanks. Um, Chris, aren't you going to be late for work? I don't want you to miss your train."

I stroked my goatee and shook my head. I couldn't believe she was acting this way. Her awkward body language was enough to convince me I wasn't going to get any straight answers from her by pressing the issue. I sighed, picked up my gym bag and hung the black strap over my shoulder. "Yeah, you're right. I'm sorry to bother you."

"No problem. Um, I'll give you a call later this afternoon," Gigi said, walking upstairs and heading off to work.

I stood there on that platform and watched the R2 take off to its next destination. I felt like a first-class fool wearing my heart on my sleeve for someone I thought was attracted to me. Only God knew what was going on with Gigi because I certainly didn't. I kept convincing myself I wasn't at fault, even though I felt like I was for some strange reason. Maybe this was a sign that things wouldn't have worked out between us in the long run. The more I tried to rationalize the matter, the more confused I became and there was no use stressing myself out.

I sat at my desk pretending to work, but everything that transpired between me and Gigi was still fresh on my mind. I kept telling myself to let it go, but I couldn't. Okay, so we only went to dinner twice and shared one kiss. But damn if that kiss wasn't all that. I must have spent the next half hour writing, deleting, rewriting, deleting and finally rewriting an e-mail to Gigi before sending it to her. The way I was tripping over this girl was driving me crazy and I needed to get my head right.

The people at American Sentinel were making their presence known throughout Aurora with some major shakeups and they were taking no prisoners. Almost three quarters of the employees in the Electronic Data Processing Department, including the vice president, received pink slips on Tuesday morning. George Gibson, the vice president of the Audit Department, was called to an emergency meeting in Human Resources along with the vice presidents of Accounting and Payroll. Yeah, things were getting real ugly around here. My telephone rang and I picked up the receiver.

"Audit, Chris speaking."

"Hi, Chris. It's me, Paulette."

I turned my head and looked over my left shoulder towards Paulette's cubicle. Sure enough, she was sitting there, calling me on her telephone, speaking in a hushed tone. Of all my co-workers in this damn department, Paulette Deavers was my least favorite. Girlfriend was a natural born ass kisser and an undercover racist. I could tell how much she despised blacks by the way she spoke down to tellers at bank audits. She hardly ever had two words to say to me except for hello and goodbye. This was going to be one interesting conversation.

"Yes?" I asked.

"Do you know why George was called into HR?"

I stared at Paulette, who was now glancing at her PC. "No."

"Hmmm...must be something shady going down. What do you think?"

I leaned back in my chair. "I don't know."

"Hmmm. Well, if you hear anything, please let me know."

I nodded. "Okay."

"Thanks," she said, hanging up the phone as if our conversation never took place. She didn't even look in my direction.

I hung up the phone, turned around, slapped my hand against my desk and cracked up laughing. I didn't care if Paulette turned my way or not because I had seen it all this morning. First, Gigi, and now this fool since her ass was on the line just like mine. I didn't think Ms. Thing even used a word like *shady* in her vocabulary. My telephone rang again and I picked up the receiver.

"Audit, Chris speaking."

"Hi, son. How are you doing?"

"Hey, Mom. What's up, pretty lady?"

"Nothing, just checking up on you. I haven't heard from you in a while and just wanted to make sure you're still alive and well."

"Thanks, Mom. I'm still alive, but I'm not sure about being well."

"I've known that for years."

I laughed. "That was cute, Mom, real cute."

"Are you alright?"

I lowered my voice so my co-workers couldn't hear me. "I'm just going through it at work and with someone I met recently who was bugging out on me today."

"Well, if I were you, I wouldn't worry about it. You can only worry about the things you can control. All the things you can't, just put it in God's hands and let Him take care of the rest. Besides, you worry too much, son, and you need to relax."

I touched my chest. "*I* worry too much? I wonder from whom I inherited that trait from."

"Not from me you didn't! At least, not from my side of the family."

"Speaking of family, I forgot to tell you I'm going to Dad's retirement dinner tonight."

"So, you finally decided to go? What made you change your mind?"

I sighed. "I had a brief conversation last weekend with the sistah I met about our relationship with our parents. I felt a little guilty about some of the things that have gone down between Dad and me. I called Sam last Sunday and told him I'd be there."

"I'm proud of you. I'm glad you took the first step to make amends with him before it was too late."

"Yeah, she also told me something along those lines."

"Who's that?"

"The girl I met. Her name is Regina, but everybody calls her Gigi."

"Hmmm. Well, I'll say a special prayer for you and Gigi that things will get better."

"Thanks, Mom, I appreciate it."

"That's what mothers are for, son. But let me ask you one question, Chris?"

"Shoot."

"Please don't tell me you two work together. You know you have a bad habit of dating your co-workers and all the trouble it's brought you in the past."

I laughed. "You didn't have to go there, Mom. Since you did, and correct me if I'm wrong, but didn't you meet Dad at your first job?"

"Yes, I did."

"And correct me if I'm wrong again, Mom, but weren't you the first person to marry him?"

"You're right and I was also the first person to divorce him."

The front door of the Audit Department opened and I could hear George walking into our office, returning from his impromptu meeting. He announced to everyone that there was a mandatory joint staff meeting at eleven o'clock in Conference Room 5A with the accounting and payroll departments. Afterwards, he went into his office and slammed the door loudly. The time displayed on my PC read 10:48 a.m.

"Um, Mom, I'm going to have to call you back. We're about to have a meeting shortly and I've got to get ready."

"Okay. Give me a call anytime if you need to talk."

"Thanks. I'll talk to you later. Love you," I said, hanging up the phone. I grabbed a legal pad and pen and made my way to the meeting with the rest of my department. George's office door remained shut and he hadn't emerged yet. Whatever was discussed at the meeting with the VPs was about to trickle down to us peons in each department.

I returned to the Audit Department along with some of my co-workers after the meeting came to an end at 11:20 a.m. Everybody was in a somber mood, including Mary, who sat down at her desk, took a look around the office and sighed heavily. I walked past George's office and saw the door to his office was opened and the lights were turned off. His personal belongings – pictures of his family – were still intact and dispersed across his desk. Part of me wanted to gather them in one pile and shatter every glass frame into a million pieces with a sledgehammer after the shit that just went down. I plopped down at my former cubicle and opened the manila envelope I was given at the meeting. I perused through its contents once again: a letter of termination from the HR Department of Aurora, a severance check for four week's pay and a letter of recommendation for employment signed by each department head.

A representative from American Sentinel National Bank was present along with the VPs of Accounting, Payroll, and Human Resources. He was a white male in his mid to late forties with graying, black hair and a receding hairline. He was dressed in a dark, navy blue suit and a metallic silver tie that didn't complement the outfit he wore. Three stacks of manila envelopes were by his side and piled adjacent to one another, an envelope for every employee in the three departments. George was MIA from the scene of the crime, but two security guards stood on opposite sides of the room – two swollen, tall and buffed brothas with stone cold faces who looked like they could have done some time at Graterford. Neither one blinked or flinched during the entire meeting. Then again, nobody else did for that matter.

The representative politely introduced himself and thanked everyone for coming together on short notice. I could smell the stench of shit on that cutthroat bastard's breath the moment he said those words. Hitler began his presentation by reminding everybody of American Sentinel's acquisition of Aurora. He rambled for almost a good five minutes about how the acquisition would mean progression for not only the bank's customers but to the entire organization as a whole. Then, he wasted no time cutting to the chase and informed us that all staff, senior level, and managerial positions in the three respective departments were eliminated, effective today. Each employee who had been employed with Aurora longer than a year would receive a weekly severance package equivalent to his or her years of employment. The VPs would be retained as independent consultants to help make the necessary transition successful from Aurora to American Sentinel. Hitler asked us to turn in our IDs and any departmental keys by 12:30 p.m. to their respective department head and leave the premises. Then, he thanked us for our time and abruptly left the meeting followed by the Tiny Lester twins watching his back.

I shook my head and had to laugh about today's events. This was definitely a day to remember. While reaching for the phone to call Mom to let her know what happened, I noticed the red message light blinking. I checked to see if I was still able to access my voicemail now that I was officially terminated. To my surprise, I could, and there were two messages waiting for me from Sam. His voice was excited and out of breath. He told me to call him immediately. I called his cell phone and he answered after the first ring.

"Hello, Mom?" Sam asked.

"No, Sam, it's me."

"Damn, Chris, where you been? I've been trying to get a hold of you for the past half hour. C'mon, damnit, what the hell is up? Move it, move it," Sam replied, screaming at traffic while he was driving.

"Whoa, slow down, lil' brother. I'm here. What's up?"

"It's Dad, Chris."

"Yeah, I know, Sam. Tonight is his retirement party and you don't have to worry about me not showing up. I told you on Sunday that I'll be there. Okay?"

"Yo, Chris, shut up! Would you just shut the fuck up and listen?"

I glanced at the receiver, surprised by the tone of his voice. "Sorry, my bad. Wassup?"

"It's Dad, Chris. Mom called and told me Dad had a heart attack this morning."

I sat down in my chair in shock by what Sam had just said.

"Hello, Chris? Are you there?" Sam asked.

I scratched my head. "I...I'm here. When did it happen? Where is he? How is he?"

"I don't know all the details yet, but it happened while he was at work. He was taken to Presbyterian and the last I heard from Mom, she said he was in critical but stable condition."

"Shit! Okay, where are you?"

"I'm on the Schuylkill and should be there in ten minutes."

"What room is he in?"

"I don't know. I think they took him to the emergency room. I'll call Mom and find out. Then, I'll call you back."

"Don't bother. I was fired today."

"Damn, Chris, I'm sorry to hear it."

"It's cool. I'll meet you there after I get my things together."

"Okay, I'll see you soon," Sam said, hanging up the phone.

I hung up the receiver and covered my nose and mouth with my hands. I couldn't believe Dad had a heart attack. Damn, how fucked up was that, especially on his last day at work.

I sat there for a good five minutes before emerging from my trance after Paulette came back and started gathering her personal belongings. I got myself together and threw the few possessions I had on my desk into my gym bag. I handed Mary my employee ID and office key, wished her the best of luck and left Aurora to go to Presbyterian Hospital.

Chapter Fifteen
Regina

Cami placed the e-mail printout on the table, slid it towards me and shook her head. "You're dead wrong for what you did to Chris this morning, hussy. It was foul and you know it."

I picked up the printout, folded it in half and placed it beside my iced tea. "Tell me something I don't know," I said, staring outside the window of the Marathon Grill and watching the traffic drive down Chestnut Street.

Cami hunched her shoulders. "I don't get you, Gigi. You invited the brotha over to your home at one o'clock in the morning. You told him how much you were attracted to him. You let him almost spend the night, but only asked him to leave because you got scared over a nightmare you had. Now, you're blowing him off without a good reason. Would you please explain to me what your problem is?"

I put my index finger to my lips. "And would you please lower your voice? I don't need everybody within earshot to know all my business."

"Sorry," she whispered.

I rested my forearms across the table. "I didn't intentionally blow Chris off without a good reason. Right now, I need to get the results back from my ultrasound. I can't go any further with him until I know what's going on with me."

We sat straight up when our waitress, Jamie, brought our orders to the table. I placed the e-mail back inside my purse. She asked us if there was anything else we needed. We both said, "No, thank you," and Jamie attended to the customers sitting two tables to our right.

Cami unwrapped the silverware inside her napkin and started cleaning the utensils. "And did you tell him that?"

I lowered my head. "No, I didn't."

"Hmmm," Cami said, shaking her head. She glanced at the fork with a disgusted smirk and snapped her fingers to get Jamie's attention. The petite and gaunt brunette returned to us and Cami asked if she could replace the fork with one that didn't have spots. Jamie politely complied with her request and went towards the kitchen.

After inspecting my utensils for cleanliness, I placed them on the table after finding no spots and laid my napkin across my lap. Cami crossed her arms, leaned back and stared at me with that *know-it-all* look written across her face.

I hunched my shoulders and whispered, "Okay, I was wrong. How many times do you want me to say it?"

She ran her fingers through her braids. "We both know you were wrong, hussy. The thing I don't understand is…"

Jamie returned to our table with a clean fork. "I'm sorry about that, Miss. Is there anything else you need?"

"No, sweetie," Cami replied. Jamie nodded and walked back towards the kitchen to pick up another order.

Picking up my utensils, I started cutting my chicken salad. "What is it that you don't understand?"

Cami massaged her temples with her hands and lowered her voice, saying, "The thing I don't understand is the whole time Chris was over your house you two didn't get your freak on?"

I dropped my utensils on the plate. "You're sick."

"Damn, Gigi, I taught you better than that."

"Look, hoochie mama, it wasn't that type of party."

She waved her hand and chuckled. "Don't tell me the thought never crossed your mind the entire time he was there?" She raised her eyebrows waiting for a response.

I blushed. "Well, maybe once when we were dancing."

"Mm hmmm."

"And maybe again when he leaned over and kissed me."

"Are there any other intimate details from your evening you didn't tell me about?"

I sighed. "No, but I did rub cocoa butter on his face before he went to bed."

She reached over and grabbed my hand. "Aw, Gigi, you rubbed cocoa butter on your man's face because he was ashy. You so sweet."

Laughing, I slapped Cami's hand away from mine, almost causing her to knock over her water, but she caught the glass. Upon hearing the maitre d's voice, I looked across to the table beside us. I pressed my lips together when I saw Kiya, Leon's girlfriend, walking towards us with one of her hoochie girlfriends from Mercury Healthcare. Immediately upon noticing me, Kiya began rolling her eyes and I gave her a fake *it's-good-to-see-you-too* smile. She asked the maitre d if they could have another table closer to the bathroom. The maitre d obliged and led them to the opposite side of the restaurant. While walking, Kiya turned her head towards us, rolled her eyes again and scratched the bridge of her nose with her middle finger. I shook my head and laughed at her immaturity.

Cami gave me a bewildered look. "What the fuck was that all about?"

"That's her," I replied.

"Who?"

I sucked my teeth. "Leon's girlfriend."

Cami leaned across the table. "The pregnant chick with the tacky weave and the nappy roots?"

I nodded, mentioning to Cami about my encounter with Leon and Kiya after Chris and I had dinner.

She slammed her hands on the table. "Girl, why didn't you say somethin'?" A few customers turned their heads in our direction.

"Will you settle down before you make a scene?"

"Oh, hell no! We gonna handle this matter to-day!" Cami snapped, tapping her index finger on the table.

"Handle what?"

She pointed towards Kiya. "You just keep your eyes on *My Little Pony* and tell me when she gets up and goes to the bathroom. I'll follow her and you wait two minutes after I get up to follow me. We'll let her handle her business and when she steps out of the stall," she paused, punching her palm. "That's when we'll beat her ass down!"

"Are you out of your mind?" I asked, lowering my voice. "You're talking about attacking a pregnant woman in a public restaurant."

She bulged her eyes. "And?"

"And suppose her girlfriend catches wind of your plan?"

Cami put her hands on her hips and rolled her neck. "Girl, please. I got toothpicks in my kitchen that are thicker than that skinny bitch."

"Excuse you!"

Cami rolled her eyes. "My bad."

I shook my head. "Let it go. I love you with my heart and soul, but I'm not going to jail for you over something stupid and childish."

"C'mon, hussy, don't be a punk. I'm telling you we can…"

"No!" I interrupted.

Cami picked up her utensils and started cutting her salmon fillet. "Damn, I can't believe you're gonna let her play you," she said, taking a bite out of her meal.

I took a sip of my iced tea. "I'm not paying that fool any mind."

"You're better than me."

"Actually, I feel sorry for her."

"How so?" Cami asked, taking another bite.

"Because Leon's not in love with her."

"And how do you know he ain't in love with her?" she spoke, chewing on her food.

"That's what he told me when we talked on the phone Wednesday."

She coughed and almost choked. "Hold up! Rewind this for a minute." She cleared her throat. "Did you just say you talked to Leon on Wednesday?"

"Yes, I did," I replied, taking a bite of my salad.

"My, my, my," Cami muttered, sipping her water. "Aren't you full of surprises this afternoon? So, what did you two talk about?"

I sipped my iced tea, sat my glass on the table and filled Cami in on the details of my conversation with Leon as we finished our lunch.

Two days ago, I was sitting in my cubicle reviewing journal entries and playing with the dolphin mobile swing on my desk. I was counting down the minutes until five o'clock and I had a lot on my mind. I kept thinking about Chris because I felt bad about asking him to leave the way I did. I wanted to give him a call or e-mail him, but I didn't. I was too damn stubborn to communicate with him.

Then, there was the result of the second ultrasound I had done on Monday, which revealed there was something that the first one didn't pick up. I watched the lab technician identify a small mass in my right thyroid as he made notes on his computer. During the procedure, I couldn't speak, but afterwards when it was finished, I asked him what he found. He made an evasive comment about not being properly qualified to diagnose his findings, but assured me the results would be sent to Dr. Fitzpatrick by the time we met on Friday. That crap really pissed me off. However, there was nothing else I could do but wait.

The telephone rang and I answered it, hoping it would be either Chris or Dr. Fitzpatrick.

"Hello?" There was a brief silence on the other end, but I could hear the person breathing. "Chris?"

"Hi, Gigi. It's me, Leon. "

I sucked my teeth. "Hi, how are you?"

"Cool. And yourself?"

"Copasetic."

He laughed. "Yeah, you always were when it came to handling a crisis. I mean, things around you could be fallin' apart, but you always came through like Jordan in the NBA Playoffs to score the winning shot. A champ, that's what you are, girl."

I rolled my eyes. "Thank you for the compliment."

"No problem, babe."

"Excuse me, but I am not your *babe*! Don't get it twisted. Okay?"

"You're right. No disrespect meant."

I ran my fingers through my hair. "Apology accepted. So, this is definitely a surprise. Is there something I can help you with, Leon?"

"Um, I wanted to tell you, Gigi, it was good seein' you last Saturday night at Lockette's."

"You already did before you had dinner with Kiya."

"Yeah, you're right. I did. Sorry."

"Yes, you are, but it's okay."

"That was a good one. You got me, or as you always like to say, 'Touché.'"

I smiled. "Uh huh...and speaking of Kiya, congratulations on your expecting bundle of joy."

Leon sighed. "Oh, yeah. Gee, thanks."

Oh, yeah. Gee, thanks. Hmmm. "You don't sound very excited."

"Don't get me wrong, Gigi, I am excited about the baby and all. But...um...me and Kiya are having some problems. I mean...um...that's expected when it comes to children."

"Well, all that matters is that you're both in love and you'll do what's right for the baby."

"Yeah, I guess so. Just because you're having a baby with someone, though, doesn't necessarily mean you're in love with them."

Whoa. I didn't see that comment coming. "If you don't mind me saying so, Leon, it's getting late and I have a train to catch.

Could we get back to my original question? Is there something I can help you with?"

Leon told me that seeing and hearing me sing again brought back some good memories when we were dating. During his reminiscence, there were also some bad memories that came back to him. Things that shouldn't have been said or done. I understood and told him I didn't harbor any ill feelings. He also realized he had some unresolved issues that needed closure and asked me if we could get together for lunch or meet somewhere to talk face to face. I expressed it wasn't a good idea, but I'd think about it. He gave me his phone number and I told him I wasn't making any promises, so he wouldn't be disappointed if he didn't hear from me. He understood and we said goodbye.

"Mm hmmm," Cami mumbled. "For a moment there, I thought you would take the jackass up on his offer."

I stared out the window. "Well, I didn't promise that I would, but I didn't promise that I wouldn't, either."

She put her elbows on the table and rested her forehead on the palms of her hands. "I don't believe you. What is your problem?"

I crossed my arms and leaned back in my chair. "Maybe Leon isn't the only one with unresolved issues about our past relationship."

Cami shook her head and sighed. "You know, I am so sick of seeing good, black women like yourself turning down positive, black men in favor of raggedy, good-for-nothing brothas that treated them wrong. Can't you see that cheating bastard is trying to run a game on you?"

I raised my eyebrows. "Excuse me, but my grandparents didn't raise a fool. Trust me, I know what I'm doing."

She put her hands on the table. "If you say so, but it doesn't sound like you're making any sense at all."

"Oh, so you're an expert on relationships, huh?"

"I never said I was an expert, but I do have some experience seeing as though I'm married."

"So, let me ask you a question, Mrs. Monroe? Do you always walk around in public without your wedding ring?" I asked, staring at her bare left hand.

Cami slid her hands underneath the table, licked her lips and searched for a response. "I lost it the other night doing the kids' laundry."

I chuckled. "Uh huh."

"You can think what you want. That's my story and I'm stickin' to it," Cami said, looking across the restaurant to avoid eye contact with me.

I nodded. "Okay. I'll let you slide for now, but we'll pick up this conversation later." Checking the time on my cell phone, I realized I had thirty minutes to get to my appointment with Dr. Fitzpatrick.

She glanced at her wristwatch. "Yeah, I've got a touch up to do when I get back to the salon."

I saw Jamie walking between her customers' tables and waved to get her attention. As she approached, I asked her if we could have the check for our lunch. Jamie nodded and went towards the front of the restaurant.

I was planning to meet up with the girls later this evening at a poetry venue April kept hounding me about the entire week. She heard from one of her relatives about this place right off of South Street that was going to start featuring poetry and singing. Ever since April read for the first time at Po/Jazz, the poetry bug had bitten her. I couldn't blame her since I felt the same way after my first reading. Cami said she would meet us there but first had to take care of something important after closing the salon.

Cami pointed across the restaurant. "Gigi, look!" I turned my head and saw Kiya walking towards the bathroom. She smiled, rubbed her hands and said, "Let's do this."

I gritted my teeth. "I said, *let it go!*"

She pouted and leaned back against her chair. "Damn, hussy, I'm just playing."

Shaking my head, I said a silent prayer for Cami, asking the Lord to please forgive her for the things she says out of her mouth.

Carol opened the door to the receptionist area of Dr. Fitzpatrick's office. "Hi, Regina. How are you feeling today?"

I stood up and grabbed my purse. "I'm fine, Carol. And yourself?"

She held the door open for me. "Fine, thank you. Dr. Fitzpatrick would like to meet with you in his office. Right now, he's treating another patient, but he'll be with you shortly."

We walked down the narrow corridor past the examination room where I could overhear him behind the door. Carol opened his office door, told me to have a seat and asked if there was anything she could get me. I said, "No, thanks," and she closed the door, leaving me alone in his office.

After sitting down in the comfortable black leather chair and resting my purse on the floor, I noticed a manila folder lying on his desk with my name on the tab. While reaching over to run my index finger across the spine, I kept telling myself to be patient and stop being nosy, but that was easier said than done. I leaned back, crossed my arms and tapped my foot. Growing impatient, I kept checking the time every two minutes. I let out a sigh of relief and stood up when Dr. Fitzpatrick finally opened the door.

"Good afternoon, Regina. How are you?" he asked, shaking my hand.

"Just fine," I replied, sitting back down in the chair. He closed the door, sat down in the chair behind his desk and picked up my file. "Well, here we are again," I said while sitting up straight and crossing my legs.

He opened the folder. "Yes, we are. I have the results from your ultrasound and I do have a few questions I'd like to ask you."

I put my hands on my leg and rubbed my knee. "Sure."

"Have you been experiencing any difficulties breathing and/or swallowing for the past two weeks?"

"No."

"Do you recall as a child being exposed to an x-ray machine around your neck at the dentist or in the hospital?"

I shook my head, uncrossed my legs and leaned forward. "No, not that I remember."

"Does your family have a history of thyroid disease on your mother's side?"

"Um, not that I am aware of. My mom passed away when I was seven."

"I see."

"Please forgive me for interrupting, but am I alright?"

He nodded and apologized if he scared me. I accepted his apology, crossed my legs and again rested my hands on my knee. He explained that the ultrasound revealed there was a tumor in my right thyroid. He wanted to perform a thyroid biopsy this afternoon by sticking a fine-needle through my skin, inserting it into the gland and removing a small sample of tissue. The procedure would take no more than ten minutes to perform, but before he could do so, I would need to read and sign a consent form to understand the risks. The purpose for the biopsy would be to determine if the tumor was benign or malignant.

"Are you trying to say I might have cancer?" I asked, running my hand across my throat.

"It is a possibility. If so, it's hereditary or occurred through exposure to radiation at an early age. Based upon what you know and told me, I think the chances are slim, but we'll see."

I uncrossed my legs. "If I do decide to do this today, how long before you will know?"

"The results should be back within three days. I'll give you some privacy so you can read the consent form. Would fifteen minutes be okay?" he asked, handing me the papers.

I nodded and took the papers. He then shut the door and left me alone in his office to make my decision. I stared at the forms, thinking about everything that was said. The thought of being diagnosed with cancer frightened me big time. I didn't know Mama's medical history at all, but I couldn't recall Nana having any problems with her thyroid. I put them down on his desk and exhaled a deep sigh, then placed my forearms on my thighs and rested my head on top of my fists.

"Lord," I whispered. "Please help me get through the next phase of this ordeal."

Chapter Sixteen

Chris

By the time I arrived at the hospital, Dad was being transported from the emergency room to the intensive care unit for evaluation. Sam and Evelyn, my stepmother, were sitting in the waiting room consoling one another. Neither one noticed I was standing outside by the partially opened door and listening to their conversation. Sam had unbuttoned his shirt collar and rolled up the blue sleeves to his forearms. Tiny beads of sweat were developing around his hairline and his brown eyes were affixed to the ugly, burgundy carpet. Evelyn tapped the heels of her black pumps against the floor. She rested the coffee cup she kept sipping from on the table by her side.

"Everything's going to be alright, baby. We've got to stay strong for your daddy," Evelyn said, picking lint from her pink blouse.

Sam shook his head. "What if he doesn't make it, Mom?"

"Your daddy is a fighter and a survivor. Trust me, he's going to pull through."

I felt weird observing them like an outsider, but I always felt this way whenever I spent time with Dad, Evelyn and Sam. My stepmother went out of her way to make me feel uncomfortable when I came over to visit on the weekends. She treated me like shit by reprimanding me for petty things to let me know I wasn't appreciated in her home. I'd be a billionaire today if I had a dollar for all the times I was told to turn down the volume on the TV when I was playing video games on my Atari 2600 or watching Saturday morning cartoons or pro wrestling because my stepmother couldn't hear herself think. Or, if Sam picked a fight with me and couldn't have his way, I was the one who received the blame for starting trouble. Evelyn would never punish him because he was young and didn't know any better. To make matters worse, Dad never came to my defense and would take her side in any argument she and I had.

I knocked on the door and took two steps into the room. "Ahem, hello." Both Sam and Evelyn looked toward my direction.

"Hey, Chris," Sam replied. "What took you so long to get here, man?"

Evelyn displayed a disgusted grimace on her face and pressed her lips together as she glared at me. I sat down in the empty seat on the left and placed my gym bag on the floor.

"I got here as fast as I could. How is he?"

"They took Dad into intensive care not too long ago," Sam sighed. "They were having trouble unblocking his arteries. We're waiting to see what's going to happen next."

"Oh, boy. Uh, how are you doing, Evelyn?" I asked, turning my head towards my stepmother.

She brushed a strand of her shoulder-length, brunette hair with golden highlights from across her face. "Dandy. I was wondering if and when you were finally going to show up, Christopher."

I balled my fists. Evelyn knew I hated whenever she or Dad would call me by my full name or Junior. "Well, what counts is that I'm here."

She took another sip to finish the rest of her coffee. "Sam was trying to find you to let you know what had happened."

I tapped my fingers against the arms of the chair. "Yes, I know. At least, *he* was considerate enough to do so."

"Damnit! Why do y'all have to start this shit?" Sam stood up.

Evelyn rose from the couch and put her right arm around Sam. "I'm sorry, baby. I didn't mean to upset you."

He gently removed her arm and pulled some change from his pocket. "I'll be back, Mom. I'm going to get a soda."

Sam left the waiting room and Evelyn sat back down at the far end of the couch. She reached for her purse on the floor, sat it on the couch and pulled out a pack of Newports and a lighter. I stood and picked up an issue of *Sports Illustrated* to pretend I was reading. She pulled a cigarette from the paper carton, put it in her mouth and lit it.

Evelyn glanced around the room and gritted her teeth. "Shit, you can't find an ashtray whenever you need one." I bit my tongue for my family's sake, not reminding her that we were in a non-smoking facility. As she used the empty coffee cup to accommodate her needs, I shook my head and flipped through the magazine. I wished Sam would come back soon to alleviate the tension between us.

"So, Chris," Evelyn said, blowing cigarette smoke in the air. "How's your mother doing?"

I rested my elbows on the forearms of the chair. "Mom's doing okay. I told her what happened to Dad and she'll keep him in prayer."

She nodded. "Hmmm, that's nice."

I knew Evelyn well enough to know she didn't care for Mom and was making conversation. It was cold blooded the way she manipulated her way into Dad's life and the two had an affair. At the time, they both worked for the same accounting firm and pretty much hooked up the way I did with Ronnie. Dad did Mom wrong, and she didn't deserve to be treated like shit, especially from the man who promised to love her for better or worse.

"Excuse me, Mrs. Harrington," a male voice with a heavy accent called from the entrance. Evelyn and I turned our heads towards the door and saw an Asian physician standing there holding a clipboard. He was dressed in a green surgeon's outfit and stood about Sam's height, five feet seven.

"How is my husband, Dr. Chen? Is he going to be okay?" she asked, standing up.

"Your husband is being prepped for surgery," Dr. Chen replied.

"Oh my God," Evelyn said, crossing her arms. She sat back down and tried her best not to cry, but was unsuccessful in holding back her tears.

"What's up with Dad?" Sam asked, walking back into the waiting room. Dr. Chen shared the news of their unsuccessful attempt to unblock Dad's arteries. They needed to perform a coronary artery bypass to redirect the flow of blood into his heart. With this news, my half brother lost it, too, and held his mother for emotional support before Dr. Chen left to prepare for surgery. I wanted to cry, but couldn't and I didn't know why. Maybe because I didn't feel close to Dad like Sam did.

I rose from my seat and walked outside the room to call Mom on my cell phone and give her the latest update. She left work at two o'clock and arrived in less than a half hour to join us. It was good to see her again and she looked beautiful in her green dress. Her natural brown hair was shorter than Evelyn's but had a touch of gray at the temples. Although my parents' separation and divorce were nasty and bitter, she never held any grudges against Dad. If anything, Mom did her best to make sure I loved and respected him in spite of the way he did her wrong or treated me like shit. She understood my frustrations with Dad and Evelyn and gave me much support, with the exception of my decision not to have anything to do with him after he didn't attend my graduation from Lincoln.

There was an awkward tension in the waiting room between Mom and Evelyn due to their history. However, they were somewhat cordial with each other when Mom first arrived. Mom did her best to put aside her feelings for Evelyn, but my stepmother kept to herself, directly spoke to Sam or indirectly murmured aloud when she wanted to say something to my mother or me. Mom allowed her phony ass to slide for now, given the circumstances.

We managed to occupy ourselves by watching soap operas and talk shows or talking about the good memories we had about Dad. It was weird for me to see us acting like a family after all the bad things we said or did to each other over the years. It was almost 4:45 p.m. by the time Dr. Chen returned to the waiting room, wearing a surgical cap with his mask dangling around his neck from its string. Evelyn was the first to stand, followed by Sam, Mom and me.

"How is he, Dr. Chen?" Evelyn asked, squeezing Sam's hand tightly.

"Yeah, how's my Dad doin'?" Sam inquired.

Dr. Chen smiled. "Mr. Harrington is going to be just fine. He's recovering and they're preparing a room for him as we speak."

Everybody let out a collective sigh of relief. Evelyn clasped her hands in prayer and thanked the Lord for saving Dad. I put my arm around Sam and gave him a tight hug. Mom smiled and nodded in agreement with everybody's sentiments.

"Can we see him?" Sam asked.

"Yes, can we see him?" Evelyn echoed.

Dr. Chen removed his surgical cap. "He's unconscious, but you can see him for a few minutes. Follow me."

We walked through the automatic metallic doors to the recovery room and saw Dad lying on a bed beside a portable EKG machine. Two nurses were monitoring his post-surgical progress. He looked so helpless and vulnerable wearing a white gown and electrodes with adhesive pads attached to his arms and legs. I could see bandages wrapped around his chest through the slightly transparent gown. His skin complexion was olive and his hair, eyebrows and mustache were completely gray.

Mom rubbed her chin and then massaged my shoulder. I glanced at her and then touched her back. Dad had grown so much older since the last time either of us had seen him. Sam and Evelyn held hands and stood there motionless, observing his chest rise and fall slowly with every breath.

"I hate to cut your visit short," Dr. Chen said, breaking the silence. "But we need to let Mr. Harrington get his rest."

Mom and I slowly followed Dr. Chen while Evelyn and Sam didn't move. Mom turned around and tapped Evelyn on her shoulder. She looked at Mom, nodded and motioned for Sam to follow. After returning to the waiting room, Evelyn and Sam sat back down on the sofa. Mom told me she was heading home and asked me if I was going to stay or if I wanted a ride. I decided to leave with her and asked Sam to call me with Dad's room number so I could swing by and visit tomorrow. Mom and I said our goodbyes to Sam and Evelyn, then headed to her car.

The Friday afternoon traffic on the Schuylkill Expressway wasn't too congested for the rush hour. Mom had the windows up and the air conditioner on to avoid the smell of driving through the oil refineries and waste disposals surrounding Southwest Philly. That part of the city could smell funky, especially in the summertime heat. She did most of the talking during the ride, as the image of Dad lying there in the recovery room was fresh on my mind.

"Are you okay, Chris?" Mom asked, pulling into the left lane and driving towards the exit for the Platt Bridge.

I rested my head against the car seat. "I was thinking about how much older Dad looked today."

Mom sighed. "I know. It's been almost twelve years since the last time I saw him."

"Yeah, it's been a while for me, too."

"Well, I told you how foolish it was for you to do what you did."

"I reached out to him and he hurt my feelings. Can you blame me?"

"Regardless of his actions, he's still your father and two wrongs don't make a right. He was wrong for not coming and you were wrong for trying to cut him out of your life. You two are so much alike."

"No, we are not!" I replied.

"Oh, yes, you are." Mom pointed her finger at me. "That's why you and Sam don't get along, just like your father doesn't get along with his siblings. Also, you wind up getting involved with those insecure women who need a relationship to validate their existence, just like your father did with your stepmother."

I shook my head. "You never met the last girl I was interested in."

"I didn't meet her, but the few I've met were enough for me. Especially the one you were dating at the bank. What was her name?"

I sucked my teeth. "Veronica."

Mom nodded her head. "Uh huh, what happened to her?"

"No comment. So, what do you want me to do, Mom?" I asked, hunching my shoulders.

"You have to let go of the anger you have towards your father. Know it's not easy for me to say this, and believe me, I speak from experience, but you'll never be able to feel what love is all about until you let go of whatever ill-feelings you have."

"And what, pray tell, is love all about, Mom?" I inquired sarcastically.

"Smart ass," Mom slapped my arm. "Love always begins within you. If you can't love yourself for who you are, then how can you expect to find happiness in life?"

I scratched my head and continued listening.

"And I'm not talking about your relationship with women either. It applies also to your writing, your career and your family. Unlike your father, you have enough sense to realize you won't be able to find contentment through a job, a relationship, or how much money you have accumulated in a savings bank. Too many people place so much emphasis on external factors instead of looking within themselves. If they did, they'd discover how truly blessed they really are."

I let her words sink into my thoughts, not thinking Mom would come at me this hard. Still, she did have a valid point.

"Well, here we are," Mom announced while putting the car in park when she arrived at my apartment complex in Lansdowne.

I unbuckled my seat belt. "Thanks, Mom, for the lift home and the support today."

She patted my shoulder. "That's what mothers are for, son. What do you have planned for tonight?"

I shook my head. "Nothing. It's been a long day and I need some rest."

As I stepped out of the car, she told me not to beat myself up too much about what she said and reminded me I was still her child. Then, she winked at me and smiled. I couldn't help myself from laughing. Mom asked me to give her a call if I needed anything or just wanted to talk. I promised to do so, shut the door and watched her drive off down Lansdowne Ave.

I loosened my tie and unbuttoned my shirt collar after turning on the air conditioner in my living room. After getting a Heineken from the refrigerator, I collapsed on the sofa, thinking that today was one of those days I'll never forget. First, Gigi blew me off on the train; next, I lost my job at Aurora; and then Dad had a heart attack and bypass surgery. Damn, I would have stayed in bed this morning if I knew all this would happen.

I thought about my future. I wasn't too worried because I did have some money put aside for rainy days. Plus, the severance check from Aurora was a blessing in disguise. I reached over, picked up my gym bag, and sat it on the sofa. After opening the zipper, I looked through the bag at its normal contents: gym clothes, sneakers, underwear, deodorant, towel, brush, socks, etc., including my journal and a few pictures I had at work. However, the manila folder with the check was missing. I searched the other compartments and found nothing. I dumped everything out of the bag and onto the floor, searching frantically through the pile. No manila folder. Shit, where the hell was it?

"Calm down, Chris!" I yelled. "Stay cool!"

I stood up, went to my bedroom and saw the red light on my Caller ID box blinking. Picking up the phone, I listened to the four messages.

"Hey, Chris, this is Sam. If you're home, man, please pick up. I tried callin' you at work, but you didn't answer. Mom called me and said that Dad had a heart attack this morning on his last day at work. Please call me soon."

"Cool C in the place to be! What's goin' on, man? This is Gene. I'm just hittin' you up to say wassup and to make sure everything is everything. Everything is cool on my end and I wanted to let you know I'm co-hosting a gig tonight at the 2nd Street Soul Café called Spitfire. There's going to be some poetry and singing. If you ain't too busy tonight, I definitely want you to come through and bless the mic with a lil' sumthin' sumthin'. Aight? Get back to me. Peace."

"Hi, Chris, it's…um…me, Ronnie. I heard what happened this morning in your department. Mary called me because she found your severance package and gave it to me before she left the bank. Give me a call when you get the chance so I can make arrangements to get it to you. It's…um…been a while since we've last spoken and I'd like to make sure that you're doing well. Bye."

I exhaled a sigh of relief while listening to Ronnie's voice.

"Hey, Chris, it's Sam. I wanted to let you know that Dad's hospital room is three thirteen. He's still resting, but Mom and I are going to stay with him until visiting hours are over. Thanks again for being here today. Um, I'll talk to you later."

I grinned after hearing Sam's message. I thought about what Mom said and nodded. It looked like I had some issues I needed to address with family and a few relationships. I called Ronnie but the answering machine clicked on. I left a message telling her thanks and asking her to call me when she had the chance.

Exhausted, I took off my clothes and jumped into the shower. By the time I finished, she still hadn't returned my call. I reclined on my bed to rest for a few minutes, glancing out the blinds of my bedroom window. Dusk was setting in across the sky as the color changed from baby blue to hazy purple. I don't know what time I drifted off to sleep, but I do remember the phone ringing and waking me up at 8:22 p.m.

"Hello?"

"Hi, Chris, it's me," Ronnie said.

"Hey, how are you doing?" I asked.

"I'm fine. I should be asking you that question."

I stood up and closed the blinds. "I'm alright. Thanks again for what you and Mary did."

"It's no problem. So…um…what's new?"

"Well…um…it's been a crazy day."

"Uh huh. So, when can I give you your folder?" Ronnie asked.

"I was thinking if there was some place we could meet tonight where I can pick it up from you. That is, if you don't have any plans."

"Well, my cousin, Denise, is planning to go out later tonight and she asked me to baby sit her daughter, Brandi. She's on her way shortly, so tonight may not be good for me."

I nodded. "Well, it would only take a few minutes. I can swing by, come to the front door, and you can hand me the folder."

"Yes, I could do that," Ronnie sighed. "I was hoping…um…we could sit down and talk, if it wasn't too much to ask? It would only take a few minutes."

I shook my head, knowing this wasn't going to be easy. The last thing I wanted to do was say the wrong thing to make her tear apart my severance package.

"Hello, Chris? Are you there?" she asked.

I ran my hand across my bed sheet. "I'm here. Look, Ronnie, I –"

"I know what you're thinking, Chris, and I'm not trying to seduce you," Ronnie interrupted. "Besides, by the time you arrive, Brandi will be here, and you know I'm not the type to do something disrespectful with a child in my place."

I rolled my eyes towards the ceiling. Who did girlfriend think she was trying to fool? Although she might not try anything while Brandi was there, I wouldn't put it past her. Then again, how did I know she was telling me the truth about the babysitting part?

"Hello, Chris?"

I remained silent and so did Ronnie. She held all the cards and there was no way out of playing her game. "Okay, I'll see you in a few."

"Thanks," she replied, hanging up the phone.

I slammed down the phone and hit the palm of my left hand with my fist. Fuck, how could I have been so stupid to leave the package behind? Ronnie was probably parading around her place like a head cheerleader. Left with no other choice, I put on my clothes and headed over there to face the music because this was going to be a long night.

Chapter Seventeen

Regina

The sidewalks on South Street were packed with friends, college students, and twenty-something and thirty-something straight and gay couples of different races hanging out on a Friday night. Police officers patrolled the streets to keep traffic moving and ensure nobody stepped out of line. I saw Dar and April standing in front of the Blockbuster at the intersection of South and 2nd Streets. The closer I approached them, the better I could see the frown on Dar's face as she mumbled something under her breath.

"Hey, Gigi," April said. "You look great. I like that blue scarf."

"Thanks," I replied, adjusting my purse. "Nice sundress." April looked stunning in her yellow sundress with her braids pulled back in a ponytail.

"Damn, why you wearin' that thing around your neck, hot as it is tonight?" Dar asked, puffing away at her cigarette.

"It's good to see you, too," I said, checking her over from head to toe. She had a lot of nerve to even attempt to criticize anything I wore since I could see the outline of her girdle underneath her blouse. We exchanged a standoffish glare, daring the other to make a smart remark.

"Okay, ladies, let's not start anything," April interjected, stepping between us. "Cami's not here to help me referee. Until she meets up with us, how about you two chillin'."

I tapped my foot, waiting for Dar to open her mouth. If she was going to go there, I had no problem also telling her about those blue jeans that barely fit her big ass.

She blew smoke in the air and said, "Whatever!"

I waved my hand. "I don't know about this, April. I've had a bad day. Maybe I should have stayed home."

Dar's face lit up with excitement. April held her notebook to her chest, shook her head, wrapped her right arm around mine and pleaded with me to support her tonight. Dar spat another ignorant remark as she put out her cigarette on the pavement. We rolled our eyes at her. April pouted her lips, pleading with me not to change my mind.

"You got me, April." I shrugged.

She gave me a tight hug and yelled, "Thank you!" A twinge of pain shot across my collarbone.

"You're welcome," I replied while stepping back and rubbing my neck.

April pressed her lips together. "Uh, are you okay, Gigi?"

"I'll be fine," I coughed, stepping from the pavement and onto the cobblestone street. I turned towards my friends and said, "Let's go."

Both April and Dar stared at me and then at each other. Dar hunched her shoulders and crossed the street. April followed reluctantly but still had that concerned look on her face. She kept staring at me, trying to determine if I was telling her the truth.

I paused and crossed my arms. "Will you please stop that? I'm okay. I think I'm coming down with something." I coughed again, hoping she believed me. Unlike Cami, April didn't know me well enough to know I was lying.

She squeezed my forearm. "I'm sorry, girl. Just lookin' out for you."

I smiled, gave her a hug and whispered, "Apology accepted." Closing my eyes, I asked the Lord to forgive me for deceiving my friend.

Pain would shoot across my collarbone if I made any sudden movements that jerked my neck, like April's hug did. The biopsy also left a swollen bruise on my neck that I concealed with the scarf. An ordinary band-aid would have roused some questions, and outside of Cami, I wasn't ready to share the news with anyone until I received the results.

"Look, if y'all gonna get a hotel room, then it's fine with me," Dar interjected. "Otherwise, we gonna be late for the show."

April and I glared at her as she walked towards the 2nd Street Soul Café.

"C'mon, let's go," I said as I glanced at my cell phone and saw that it was almost 8:35 p.m. I prayed Cami was on her way to keep her sister-in-law in check before she said or did the wrong thing.

After we paid our admission and April signed her name on the open mic listing, we walked into the restaurant and sat down at an empty table three rows from the stage and near the front door. Although the size of the room was small compared to Brave New World, I liked the 2nd Street Soul Café the moment I stepped through the door. It was intimate and classy, the way any commercial property should be in that part of the city. The owners made sure everything was satisfactory from the white tablecloths and red candles on each table to the paintings by African American artists that decorated the green wall, which obstructed our view of 2nd Street.

A female poet, with caramel skin and honey-colored locks, and who I saw last week at the October Gallery, stood on the stage reciting a powerful poem. Dressed in orange Afrocentric garb, she had the predominantly female audience hooked into her flow. I couldn't remember her name, but I did recall her poem's title, *My Idea of Heaven*, a beautiful tribute to our deceased heroes like Malcolm X, Medger Evers, Billie Holiday, Nina Simone and Miles Davis.

"She's real good," April sighed, with a gleam of excitement in her eyes and her smile.

"She's alright." Dar puffed away at another cigarette, unimpressed. "Oh shit!"

"What's up?" April turned towards her.

Her face radiated like a light bulb.

"He's here! The poet I met last week," Dar pointed across the room.

April and I looked across the room and there he was, The Gentleman Poet, sitting in the front row talking to Gene. Whatever that second-rate, Rick Fox wannabe had to say was apparently getting on Gene's nerves. Agitation was displayed across my friend's face as he stared at the floor and rubbed his bald head while Greg rambled and placed a chapbook and CD on the table. Gene nodded and slid the contents towards him. His Royal Highness, with a devious smirk on his face, sat back in his chair.

"I gotta get myself together." Dar stated as she adjusted her ponytail.

I shook my head at her. If she had an ounce of common sense, she wouldn't waste her thoughts and time on that clown.

"Ooh, isn't that Chris's friend, Gene?" April asked.

I nodded. "Yeah."

"I was hoping he'd be here tonight. I haven't seen him since I left the bank."

I slid my hands underneath the table and clenched my fists. Although April's comment was innocent, I needed to check myself. Listening to her mention Chris's name and detecting the excitement in her voice made me feel jealous.

The poet wrapped up her piece and the audience serenaded her with cheers and applause. Before leaving the stage to sit back down at her table, she thanked everyone. Gene placed the chapbook and CD underneath his armpit, went to the stage and picked up the microphone.

"Give her some love, y'all. One mo' time for Sistah Aziza," Gene said while everybody clapped. "That's wassup! Next up on the mic, this brotha is the author of the book, *Velvet Lullabies*." Gene held up the chapbook and CD. "And he's coming out with a new CD called *Sensuality and Me*. Put your hands together for The Gentleman Poet."

As the audience clapped, Pretty Ricky strutted towards the stage like he was the king of the world. Gene handed him his contents and the microphone, walked off towards the front door and leaned against the wall to light a cigarette.

"Excuse me, girls. I'll be right back." I stood up and went to the front.

Gene blew smoke in the air and shook his head as Greg got himself together. I could tell he was pissed off big time. He didn't even notice me approaching him.

"Hey, stranger." I smiled.

Gene closed his eyes and smiled. "Yo, Flipper! Wassup!" He opened his arms as he hugged me.

I patted him on his back. "I'm fine. Are you alright?"

"Some folks are a fuckin' trip," Gene replied, escorting me to the other side of the wall. "I'm cool, Flipper. That muthafucka walks in here like he owns the joint and expects somebody to bring him on stage right away. He spoke to Nate, the person who's supposed to be here running things, earlier today about coming through tonight. I told him to sign the open mic list like everybody else, but he don't believe in signing his name on anybody's list."

I crossed my arms. "Are you serious?"

Gene rolled his eyes and sighed.

"Where's Nate?" I asked. "If this is his venue, then shouldn't he be here?"

"Exactly!" Gene shrugged. "He called to let me know he was runnin' behind schedule. He told me to get things started and I did. Greg kept hounding me about his turn. Finally, I gave in just to shut him the fuck up."

I rubbed his arm. "I'm sorry to hear that."

"Nah, it's cool." Gene took another puff of his cigarette. "Everything's gonna be alright. So, wassup with you? Ya know I gotta get you up there to do sumthin'."

I waved my hands. "Not tonight."

"What?" Gene shrugged. "C'mon, Flipper, we go back like fried fish dinners from the West Philly cornerstore on Saturday nights."

"You know that was corny as hell," I laughed.

"True dat, but I can't have one of my Buttacups just sittin' in the audience and not represent. Besides, Cool C told me what you did last week at Panoramic Poetry."

I clasped my hands together and stared at the ground. Chills went through my body just thinking about how bad I treated Chris this morning. Like April, I was also hoping he would show up tonight so we could talk about what happened. Assuming he still wanted to speak with me.

"So, how 'bout it, Flipper? Can we get you on stage tonight or not?" He outstretched his arms and waited for my response.

I admired Gene's power of persuasion. He could sell heat in the desert to an Iraqi. I wasn't sure if my voice would be strong enough to sing, but I might be able to get away with a poem. "One poem." I held up my index finger and gave him another hug.

Gene nodded. "Aight"

"Yo, Gene," a voice called from behind us. "Man, I'm sorry to leave you hangin', but I'm here."

We turned around toward the front door and saw a brown skin brotha wearing glasses, a Philadelphia Eagles baseball cap, a dark blue shirt, tan khakis and brown Timberlands. He stood a few inches shorter than Gene.

Gene sighed. "Man, Nate, where you been all this time?"

"My bad." Nate extended his fist to give Gene a pound. My friend reluctantly did so. "I had to pick up my boy who I want you to check out. He's right behind me."

Nate's friend walked through the door and took two steps back when he saw me. Of all the people I was expecting to run into tonight, Leon was the last person I wanted to see.

"Leon, this is the guy I was tellin' you about," Nate said, pointing towards Gene.

Leon turned in Gene's direction. "I remember you from Buttamilk at the North Star Bar." He extended his hand towards Gene.

"Word? You look kinda familiar." Gene shook his hand and squinted his eyes at Leon trying to remember him.

"Oh, yeah," Leon nodded. "That's where I met the lovely lady standing beside you for the first time."

So now I'm a *lovely lady* instead of *an old friend* when your baby's mama is away. I bit my lip and rubbed my shoe into the floor. Gene shifted his eyes towards me, back to Leon and to me again. He nodded and a disapproving scowl appeared on his face.

Gene blew smoke in the air. "Yeah, I remember you now."

"So, how's it goin', Gigi?" Leon asked, ignoring the tone in Gene's voice.

"Fine," I shrugged.

Nate looked at our faces. "Ahem, did I…um…miss something?"

"I'm sorry, Nate." I extended my hand towards him. "My name is Regina. We all happen to be old friends."

"Yeah," Gene chimed in. "Flipper is one of my old school poets and singers who's gonna be doin' sumthin' later on."

Nate nodded. "Oh, that's cool. Nice to meet ya."

"Hmmm." Leon stroked his chin and nodded. The way he kept gazing at me made my skin crawl.

"Excuse me, fellas," I straightened my blouse. "I should be getting back to my friends."

"Do you mind if I have a word with you in private, Gigi?" Leon asked.

I mulled his request over for a few seconds and looked at Gene, who was examining my face for a response. I nodded my head to let him know it was okay.

"Look here, Nate." Gene handed him the open mic list. "Why don't you take over hosting for me while I step outside to finish the rest of my cigarette?" Nate disappeared back into the restaurant and Gene walked out into the night. He paced back and forth, but made sure we weren't completely out of his eyesight.

I crossed my arms, leaned my shoulder against the wall and stared at Leon. He rubbed his hands and pressed his lips to gather his thoughts.

"It's good seein' you again," Leon said.

I rolled my eyes. "Thanks."

"Look, Gigi," Leon ran his hand through his cornrows. "We...um...probably didn't expect to see each other tonight – "

"You've got that right," I interjected.

"And like I told you the other day, I really would like for us to sit down and talk. However," he glanced out the window towards Gene. "This ain't the right time and place. I don't want to start no trouble between me and your peoples."

He had a good point, especially if Cami walked through the door right now.

"So, I'm going to make up some bullshit excuse for Nate and bounce."

In the past, Leon didn't give a damn about anyone's feelings and would have stood his ground regardless if he were wrong. Looks like time, maturity and a baby on the way could change a person. I nodded.

Leon smiled. "Thanks, Gigi." He squeezed my hand and held it for a few moments before pulling Nate to the side and whispering something in his ear. Goosebumps were dancing across my forearms and I couldn't move or speak. I had forgotten how warm and strong his hands felt. The memories of the two of us holding hands and taking long walks, sharing our dreams about singing and poetry in the beginning of our relationship haunted me. I remembered once telling him whenever he held my hand, I always felt safe and secure. Why the hell was this happening to me?

After a few moments, Leon gave Nate a pound and a hug. Before he walked out the door, he looked at me and said, "Call me."

"Leon," I said.

"Yeah?"

Reaching into my purse, I pulled out my business card and a pen. I should have been shot for what I was thinking as I scribbled my home phone number on the back. I walked towards Leon and handed it to him. He stared at the card and then gave me an amicable grin before leaving the restaurant.

Tracing my fingernails along the doorway, I murmured aloud, "Why me, Lord?" I saw Gene watching Leon walk down 2nd Street.

He dropped his cigarette on the ground, put it out with his foot and shook his head.

Gathering my thoughts about what had transpired, I went back to my table. Dar was in her own world, grinning from ear to ear and listening to The Gentleman Poet recite his signature piece, *Sixty Nine Degrees of Separation*. April had an exasperated look like the majority of the audience.

"For the way that brotha bragged about himself, I thought he would have sounded better," April said, rolling her eyes.

"He's a piece of work, girl," I sighed. "That's why I had to leave the room."

"Shhh. Y'all need to quit hatin'," Dar said.

"Whatever," April and I replied in unison.

I checked the time on my cell phone. It was almost nine o'clock. Where the hell was Cami? She told me she was going to have a meeting with the employees after they closed for the night, but she should have been here by now. She made it a rule that there were no appointments after five o'clock on Fridays, unless it was something special like Easter Sunday, so everybody else could be out of the door no later than eight o'clock. I dialed Camille's and no one answered. I dialed her cell phone and still no answer. I left a message for her to call me when she could.

"Did you get in touch with her?" April asked.

I shook my head.

"Y'all worry too much. She said she'll be here."

Cami was usually punctual about time and would have contacted us if something was wrong. April shrugged and I turned my chair around just in time for Greg to finish his performance. The audience gave him an exasperated, half-hearted applause for his efforts, except for Dar who stood on her feet to give him her own personal standing ovation. He looked towards our table and flashed a sinister smile.

Almost a half hour had passed and six poets came and went before Gene called April's name on the open mic. Dar and I put our hands together and gave her an extra special applause while everybody clapped. She thanked everyone, opened her notebook and read her first poem, *Deep Waters*. In nervousness, April rushed through the poem in the beginning, but caught herself somewhere in the middle and slowed down. I enjoyed her use of imagery when she compared her lover's features to the beauty of the sea. Nice job. While she searched her notebook to find the next poem she wanted to read, Greg glanced towards us and made his move, sitting down across from me. Dar locked her eyes on the object of her desires as he kept staring at me. Just sitting across from him made bile rise in my throat.

"Well, it's good to see you again," Greg said.

"Thanks," Dar replied, grinning.

"Huh?" Greg glanced at her.

"You remember from Po/Jazz?" Dar inquired.

He nodded. "Oh, yeah! Good to see you, too."

Dar rambled about how much she enjoyed reading his chapbook, clueless to the fact the bastard wasn't the least bit interested in her. Still, Greg sat back and allowed her to stroke his ego with compliments. Never once did he take his eyes off of me while I did my best to concentrate on April's performance.

The Hispanic waitress came over to our table and brought me the Merlot I ordered five minutes earlier.

"*Gracias,*" I said.

"*De nada,*" she replied.

"*¿Hablas español? ¿No?*" Greg teased a strand of his curly, long hair.

"Can I help you with something?" I inquired, hunching my shoulders.

He leaned over and touched my arm. "*Tu poesía respire a la vida en mi alma. Tu voz es tan atractiva y hace que mi corazón salta un golpe.*"

No that fool didn't try to hit on me using Spanish! Who did Pretty Ricky think he was by telling me my poetry breathed life into his soul and that my voice sounded so sexy it made his heart skip a beat? Well, at least he took my advice from our first encounter and had a breath mint. I stared at his hand and then gave him a nasty look to let him know never to touch me again. He got the point, waved his hands and said, "*Lo siento.*"

The dejected look on Dar's face when Greg touched me immediately transformed into a grin after he backed off from my chilly reception. She massaged his shoulder and he flashed a transparent, fake smile to lift her spirits. Was she that dense not to realize he was playing her?

"I think it's about time you left." I crossed my arms. "I'm trying to watch my friend."

Dar gave me a look as if I had lost my mind, but I didn't care.

Pretty Ricky glanced dismissively at April. "Your friend needs to work on her writing and delivery."

"Excuse me, but I don't think you have any room to talk about anybody's writing."

"Gigi," Dar whispered.

"I'm not sayin' your girl doesn't have any talent." Greg waved his hands in the air. "But you can tell she's got a long way to go."

I laughed. "Oh, so you're an expert on the spoken word movement."

"My record speaks for itself." He reached into his black bag and gave Dar and me two flyers.

I shook my head and laughed at the headline: GET YO FREAK ON, ONE MO TIME!!! FREAKEASY EROTIC SLAM, ROUND TWO!!! CUMMING AT CHA!!! The latest erotic slam was going down one week from this Wednesday with a cash prize of two hundred dollars. Now I had seen everything tonight and then some.

"You have got to be kidding." I placed the flyer on the table. "Son, let me tell you something. You're not as good as you think. Okay?

"Oh, so you think you're better than me?"

"I never professed to be better than you. However, it's jackasses like you who give poets a bad name." I pointed my finger at him. "You have absolutely no originality or versatility. All you ever talk about is sex."

Dar gritted her teeth. "Gigi!"

"Regardless of whatever you have to say, anyone with half a brain can see that's your entire M.O. from your poetry to your wardrobe."

Greg wiped imaginary dust from his Tommy Hilfiger jeans and chuckled. "Let me remind you that we live in an age where sex sells the majority of all consumer products. Human beings are carnal by nature. And anyone with half a brain realizes that. I'm just out gettin' mine. All I'm sayin' is what every horny female in this audience wants to be told by either their boyfriends or husbands when they come lookin' for some love and affection."

"Oh, really?" I laughed, putting my hand to my heart.

"If they can't find it at home, then they certainly come out lookin' for it in the streets or the clubs. They know the rules of the game and come out playin' ball. Sometimes I might not be the top draft pick, but plenty of females will choose me for some one-on-one."

"That's right, baby." Dar patted him on his back.

After listening to this jackass and his signifying pigeon open their mouths, I stood corrected.

"Why do you think people get into the entertainment business?" he asked. "They wanna get laid and get paid. All the actors, the rappers, the musicians and the singers want the same. I'm just bringin' it to the poetry world. If you're going to talk the talk and walk the walk, then you better look the part." Greg stood up from his chair. "After all, clothes do make the man."

I rested my elbows against the table and chuckled.

"And in spite of what you think about me, it's not all about sex. I'm also in it for a few dead presidents: Washington, Lincoln, Hamilton, Jackson and Franklin."

"You probably didn't know that Ben Franklin was the first President of the United States?" I raised my eyebrows.

"Nice try. George Washington was the first."

I clapped lightly. "I'm impressed."

"Everybody knows Ben Franklin was the second. Later." Greg strolled towards the front door.

"I guess he told you," Dar snorted, oblivious her boo left without her name and phone number.

I laughed and wiped the tears from my eyes.

"What's so funny?" Dar asked. She sucked her teeth and sighed, "You crazy."

"Okay, Dar, if you say so," I exhaled between giggles.

The audience applauded as April finished her last poem and returned to our table. Damn, I missed most of her performance thanks to Pretty Ricky. Gene spoke into the mic asking everybody to give April another round of applause.

"How did I do?" April asked.

I apologized to April and explained briefly what had transpired while Dar sucked her teeth. However, I did give her positive compliments on *Deep Waters*. She smiled and thanked me.

"Okay, everybody," Gene spoke into the mic, "I've got a special treat for y'all tonight. I didn't know this sistah was in the audience, but she and I go back some ways." Gene looked towards me.

Oh, God, I knew what was coming next. I shook my head because Gene was about to pour it on real thick with one of his long winded introductions. He always did for anyone he liked.

"When I hosted a poetry venue called Buttamilk a few years ago," he paused while several people in the audience clapped due to the name recognition. "This sistah was one of our original Buttacups along with Jill Scott and Stephanie Renee. She was also one of our frontrunners for the title of Ms. Buttaworth, because the girl got a set of lungs on her."

April squeezed my forearm and I blushed. Dar frowned, but I wasn't paying her any mind.

"I almost had to get on my hands and knees to beg her to do sumthin' tonight. She did say she would bless us with one poem." Gene held up his index finger. "Everybody, show some love for my girl, Regina Simmons."

The audience applauded as I made my way to the stage, where Gene held my arm to assist me up the wooden stairs. Giving him a hug, I whispered thanks and adjusted the microphone to accommodate my height.

"Hello," I said. "Is everybody feeling good tonight?"

The audience responded with some alrights and fine.

"Hi, Regina! How you doin'?" Greg shouted, standing beside Nate next to the wall. Several faces in the crowd, including Gene's and April's, were annoyed by his arrogance.

I smiled. "I'm fine."

Pretty Ricky bent over and whispered something in Nate's ear. I said a quick prayer, asking the Lord to forgive me for what I was about to do. I knew vengeance was His, but some people needed to be put in their place.

"Before I begin," I continued. "I want all the ladies in the audience to give themselves a round of applause. Don't be shy, girls, because we look good tonight."

The females in the audiences clapped and cheered.

"Give it up for the ladies," Greg yelled, clapping his hands.

"And fellas, give yourselves a round of applause because y'all got it goin' on, too."

The males in the audience barked, including Greg. *Good*, I thought, *I gotcha right where I want you.*

"Some of y'all," I stared right at The Gentleman Poet and smiled. "Look damn good up in here."

Greg and a few males barked again while several ladies booed.

I combed my fingers through my hair. "And for those men who fall into that category, y'all need to quit frontin'."

Laughter erupted across the audience along with a few oohs.

"I'm not hatin', but regardless of where you go," I said, holding up my index finger. "You always see that one brotha who's always wearing the latest gear from A to Z. And he knows he's three months behind in his rent."

Laughter erupted again as a few people fell out their chairs. Gene and April were clutching their sides in serious pain while Dar sat back, crossed her arms and looked at the floor. A few heads turned toward The Gentleman Poet, whose pathetic smile was replaced with a pathetic sneer.

"The water company shut off his plumbing and PECO has sent him his final notice. But the mentality of this fool is I got it goin' on because he thinks clothes make the man." I turned towards Pretty Ricky, who looked like he was about to cry.

"Well, everyone, I'm here to let you know, by the title of my poem, that *Clothes Don't Make the Man*."

I heard a few uh ohs in the audience before I closed my eyes. Gene yelled, "Don't hurt 'em, Flipper." I rubbed my hands, smiled and recited my poem.

For the love of money
you spend beyond your means
even though you are broke as a joke
and can't afford to pay attention
straight from the Phat Farm
livin' the lifestyles of the rich and the famous
at the Men's Warehouse, City Blue, and Lord & Taylor's,
ridin' aboard the American Express,
searchin' for new merchandise to Discover,
lookin' fly in your DKNY, Sean John
and Roc-A-Wear sweatsuits,
double breasted Stacey Adams pinstripe,
Ralph Lauren Polo shirt, Tommy Hilfiger jeans,
Timberland boots, Florsheim wingtips
and $150 brand new Nike Air Jordan sneakers
and you can't spell either Armani
or Versace to save your ass
because image is everything to you,
money is only good to spend on new clothes
to add to your extravagant wardrobe
so forget about saving for rainy days
and investing for the future
because that crap is played out

like Sergio Valenti, Cazelles,
L.L. Cool J Kangols,
Two-tone Lee jeans, Troop leather jackets,
and Chuck Taylor Converse sneakers
because it's all about the Benjamins, baby,
and you got to get yours
drivin' down South Street on the weekends
in your mama's brand new, four-door Lexus
with your conniving gold-digger by your side,
frontin' on your car phone like "you da man"
tryin' to impress your fragile ego.

The audience erupted in both cheers and applause. A few people, including Gene and April, rose to their feet. Pretty Ricky gritted his teeth and glared at me with nothing but contempt. I blew him a kiss to let him know the feeling was mutual, then took a bow, thanked the audience and went back to my table while shaking a few hands.

Gene made his way to the stage and adjusted the mic. "Dayum! Tell the truth, Flipper. Tell the truth." He smiled broadly. "One more time for Regina Simmons."

"That was da bomb, Gigi!" April gave me a high five.

"Thanks, girl," I laughed.

"You ain't right," Dar snapped. She rolled her eyes, stood up and walked outside.

Good, I thought, *your boo's going to need your help picking up the pieces to his shattered ego.* Maybe you can get his phone number for some one-on-one playing time.

"Forget her, Gigi." April waved her hand.

I shook my head. "Believe me, I'm trying."

"Look here, everybody," Gene said. "That's going to do it for our open mic portion. We're gonna be taking a five minute intermission and then, we'll be bringing up our feature poet for the night."

"Yo, Gene," Greg yelled from the side. He stared at me as he spoke. "Can we open the mic back up after the feature?"

There was a mixture of laughter and exasperated sighs throughout the audience. I couldn't believe that bastard had the nerve to say that. Damn, talk about being sensitive as hell.

April slapped the table. "No, he didn't!" We both looked at each other and started giggling.

Gene laughed, waved his hands and stepped off the stage to mingle with a few folks. Pretty Ricky was in hot pursuit.

"Oh my God," I said.

"Damn, Gigi, you hurt the brotha's feelings," April replied.

"He's a big boy," I coughed. "He'll be alright."

"Or he'll be something else," April added.

"Hel-lo."

"What time is it?"

I glanced at my cell phone. "Almost nine-fifty. Where the hell is Cami?"

"Good question." April nodded. "We better get Dar so we can find out what's going on?"

I nodded. Cami's behavior tonight was unusual. It was not like her to miss out unless there was an emergency. After paying for our drinks, we headed for the front door. Gene walked towards the front with Greg pestering him about getting back on stage. April and I paused while they walked toward us.

"Hell no!" Gene raised his voice to Pretty Ricky. "Let it go!"

"Well," Greg sneered as he glanced my way. "Look who's leaving so soon."

Gene turned towards us and hugged me. "Yo, Flipper, you were on point tonight!"

"Thanks, Gene." I patted him on the back.

"And yo, April," Gene extended his hand. "You were good, too. I was definitely feeling your pieces."

"Thanks," April blushed.

"Ahem." Greg cleared his throat while his eyes remained locked on mine, anger oozing from every pore.

"Can I help you with something?" I asked.

Gene stepped in between us, but I waved him off, stepping closer to Greg while maintaining eye contact with him. He bit his lip and I could see water forming in his eyes.

"Yo, everybody," Nate announced from the front door. "This sistah smashed some dude's car window with her fist and she's about to go at it with this couple."

April ran outside with a few people to find out what the hoopla was all about. It was probably something stupid and blown out of proportion since black folks loved to exaggerate. However, I still had to deal with Pretty Ricky and his bruised feelings. He stared at me and then at Gene, who stood by my side ready to defend me. As he backed off and walked towards the bathroom, I let out a sigh of relief.

"Whew," Gene exhaled. "Man, that could have been ugly."

I smiled and shook my head. After tonight, I didn't need any more drama.

"Gigi!" April called from the front door. "Come quick! Dar's flipping out and about to fight Cami!"

"What?" I yelled, running outside along with Gene. Sure enough, Dar was screaming at Cami and some dark-skinned brotha with salt and pepper hair and a gray beard. Her right hand, bloody, swollen and lacerated, was all in the guy's face and Cami's. I didn't know who he was, but by the way he was screaming at Dar, apparently he was ticked off. Cami stood there screaming back and forth between the two parties with shards of glass in her braids and cuts on her face. What the hell was going on tonight?

"Who the fuck do you think you are breaking my car window?" he yelled, pointing at the shattered passenger window of his Lexus parked against the curb.

"Who the fuck do you think you are kissing my sister-in-law?" Dar asked, screaming back at him.

"What?" April and I yelled in unison. We looked at each other and then at Cami, totally surprised by what Dar just said.

"Look, Dar," Cami yelled. "Your monkey ass needs to get a grip and calm the fuck down!"

"Don't tell me to calm the fuck down, bitch," Dar screamed. "What the fuck do you think you're doin' cheatin' on my brotha with this raggedy muthafucka?"

"You better watch who you callin' a raggedy muthafucka," he said, pointing at Dar.

"Shut the fuck up, Derrick!" Cami yelled. "And you shut the fuck up, too, Dar!"

This entire fiasco was unbelievable. Cami was cheating on Damon? I felt like I was watching a bad episode of *Cheaters* meets *Jerry Springer* and everything was about to explode. A small crowd of patrons from the restaurant and pedestrians were gathering around us.

"Don't tell me to shut the fuck up! I'll beat both of y'all's asses down right here!"

Uh oh. Given Dar's present state of mind, I'm sure she could.

Derrick stepped right into Dar's face. "You ain't gonna beat shit down!"

Dar's eyes bulged out. "Come on wit' it!"

Cami stepped between Dar and Derrick. "Will you both please shut the fuck up?"

"Fuck you!" Dar punched Cami in the face, causing her to fall to the sidewalk. Several people moaned a collective "Whoa!" One ignoramus yelled, "Dayum! Did you see that big bitch knock that skank bitch on her ass?"

Immediately, April and I rushed over and grabbed Dar's arms while Derrick rushed to Cami's side. We pulled her back as best as we could, but she was too strong. My neck started to ache from the struggle as I lost my grip. Dar tossed us aside and lunged after Derrick, swinging her fists like a lunatic. Gene and two brothas grabbed her and pulled her towards the restaurant.

"Let me go!" Dar screamed and kicked. April and I tended to Cami, who was slowly rising to her hands and knees.

Derrick bent over and asked, "Baby, are you alright?"

Cami coughed and spat blood. "Go, Derrick. Just go."

Derrick grabbed her hand. "You might need to see a doctor. What if you – "

"Get the fuck out of here!" Cami screamed.

"You heard her, Derrick." I rolled my eyes. "Leave!"

He nodded and rose to his feet. "If that's the way you want it, I'm out!" He exchanged a few obscenities and death threats with Dar, who was still being restrained, before he drove off.

"Let me go, y'all! I'ma beat the living shit out of you, Cami! I'ma tell Damon everything I saw tonight! Your ass is fuckin' grass, you hear me?" Dar hissed and wrestled with Gene and the fellas as they took her back inside the restaurant.

Cami rose to her feet and yelled, "Shut up, bitch!"

"Are you alright?" I asked, wiping blood from her cheek with a tissue. Her face looked like Angela Bassett's in *What's Love Got to Do with It.* "Derrick may be right about seeing a doctor."

"I'm cool. Just get me out of here, Gigi."

"Who the hell was that?" I asked.

"Yeah," April added. "And what the hell has been going on with you?"

"Look, I need to get away from here so I can think." Cami shook her head. "I'll explain everything. I promise. Okay?"

I saw sincerity in her eyes and knew she was finally telling me the truth. I nodded. "Okay."

April agreed to stay with Dar until she cooled down, if that was possible. I promised I would contact her later on after Cami and I spoke. We left as the police arrived at the restaurant. She didn't want to stick around, so we discreetly made our way to my car. During the walk to the parking lot, I tried to get Cami to open up, but she wouldn't. *Okay,* I thought, *your stubborn ass may not be in the mood to talk now, but you can't keep silent forever.*

Chapter Eighteen
Regina

Cami was still cleaning herself up in my bathroom by the time I changed clothes and went back downstairs. After pouring us two glasses of Pinot Grigio, I sat back and listened to Kindred's *Far Away* on the CD player. I couldn't believe my girl was cheating on Damon. I prayed that wasn't the case, but I needed to hear her side of the story before I made any judgments. During the entire ride to my home, she didn't say a word. Her cell phone rang repeatedly, but she never answered it. I wished she'd put the damn thing on mute so I didn't have to listen to that annoying theme from the movie *Halloween*. I felt like Michael Myers was going to attack me at any moment.

I heard her flick the light switch off and shut the bathroom door before she joined me in the living room. She sat down on the sofa and rubbed her chin. Her bottom lip was swollen from Dar's sucker punch.

"Do me a favor, would ya, Gigi? Remind me to knock the living shit out of Dar the next time I see her."

"Here you go," I said, handing her an ice pack.

Cami rested it against her chin. "Woo! Damn, that's cold."

"What did you expect?" I slid her drink towards her. "Well, here's a lil sumthin' to ease the pain, sweetie."

Cami glanced at the glass. She tapped her fingers against the coffee table and licked her lips before she reluctantly declined my offer.

"Hmmm," I said. Cami was never the type to let good liquor go to waste. I remembered on Senior Cut Day at her cousin, Cheryl's house, she polished off two cases of Bartle & James wine coolers by herself after the rest of us got sick.

"Damn, what happened to you, hussy?" she asked, pointing at the band aid on my neck.

I shook my head. "Oh no, we're not about to change the subject." I crossed my legs and took a sip of my drink. "I'll fill you in on the details about my day after you tell me what's going on with you."

Leaning against the arm of the sofa, Cami started to speak until her cell phone rang again. She reached into her purse, checked the number and answered it.

"Hey, Ma. I'm alright. I'm at Gigi's. How are the boys? Oh shit." Cami ran her fingers through her braids. "Sorry, Ma. Look, if Damon calls again, tell him you haven't spoken to me. Just tell him that, would ya?"

Uh oh. Guess Dar opened her big mouth and spilled the beans.

"I'm not asking you to lie, Ma." Cami gritted her teeth, rolled her eyes and lowered her voice. "I know who I'm talking to and I'm sorry. I can't deal with him right now. I'll explain everything to you tomorrow, okay? I gotta go, Ma. Love you." She slammed her phone shut and screamed, "Fuck!"

I ran my fingers through my hair. "You okay?"

"I'm sorry." She leaned her head against the back of the sofa and stared at the ceiling as tears ran down her cheeks.

"It's going to be okay," I said, grabbing her hand.

Cami wiped her eyes. "I…um…don't know where to begin."

"Take your time."

She pulled a rubber band from her purse and wrapped it around her braids. "You know Damon and me have been together since we were teenagers. Like any couple, we've had our share of good times and bad problems. Well, Gigi, we've been having nothing but bad problems ever since the salon opened. I told you how the shit really hit the fan when he got laid off from work six months ago."

I nodded, knowing how Damon struggled temping here and there, but never finding anything permanent. She stuck by Damon's side no matter what and always supported him in his decisions. My girl was in love with her man. But I also knew how his attitude grew more resentful due to his insecurities of Cami being the main provider. I thought about all the magazine articles I'd read about husbands who couldn't deal with their wives making more money.

"The arguments got real vicious. Although I was tempted to really let him have it, I never disrespected him as a man and a father for the boys' sake. You know how much they adore their Daddy. When he saw he couldn't belittle me and shatter my pride, do you know what that asshole had the audacity to do?"

I hunched my shoulders.

"He decided 'we ain't gonna have sex anymore'," Cami said, mocking Damon's deep voice. "'Now, whatcha gotta say about that?'" She tapped her index finger on the coffee table.

I laughed. "No, he didn't!"

"Oh, hell yes, he did," Cami hissed, rolling her eyes. "He also had the nerve to start sleeping on the living room sofa."

"So, how long did that last?"

"About two weeks. Then, he came crawling back into our bedroom. I guess he got tired of sleeping alone and masturbating."

I cringed. "Ill!"

"And like a lovesick, horny fool, I gave him some. However, things were never the same between us romantically after that. We grew apart and became perfect strangers living under the same roof, just raising our sons. Sex was nothing but our therapy for every argument we've had since then. Hell, the man would start a fight with me over stupid shit like me soaking my panties in the bathroom sink."

I shook my head. "That's not love."

"You got that right," Cami said. "I fell out of love with Damon because I felt like a piece of meat. I've lost count how many orgasms I've faked these past few months."

"Was he cheating on you?" I asked, hoping her answer would explain his behavior and why she might be messing around.

"No, he wasn't." Cami sighed heavily. "I had a private investigator watch him for almost a month, but he found nothing."

I poured more Pinot Grigio into my glass. "So, where does Derrick come into play?"

Before she could answer, Cami's cell phone interrupted our conversation. She checked the number and turned off the ringer. It didn't take a rocket scientist to figure out who was on the other line. One minute later, my telephone rang and Damon's voice on my answering machine confirmed my suspicions.

"Cami! Cami! Pick up the muthafuckin' phone! I know you're over there! What the fuck is Dar talkin' bout she seen you kissin' some other dude tonight? Yo, Gigi, tell that ho to pick up or else I'ma come over there and break your fuckin' windows!"

My heart jumped several beats when I heard him say that. As ghetto as Cami was, Damon was two steps ahead of her. I wouldn't put it pass him to follow through with his threat.

Cami sprang from the sofa, picked up the phone and screamed, "Shut the fuck up, Damon! You ain't gonna break shit, so quit huffin' and puffin'! And who the fuck you think you are callin' me a ho? I dare your muthafuckin' ass to come over to Gigi's and say that shit to my face!"

I couldn't believe Cami stood there cursing him out and talking trash. What the hell was she thinking? I went to get my cell phone to call the police, but she shooed me to calm down and have a seat. How the hell did she expect me to calm down with her deranged husband hell-bent on breaking my windows?

"Fuck!" Cami yelled after hanging up and sitting back down on the sofa. "Why me? Why me?" She buried her head in her hands.

I stared at her in complete disbelief and asked, "Have you lost your damn mind?"

"My marriage is so fucked up," Cami said, staring across the living room.

I snapped my fingers twice to get her attention. "Hel-lo?"

"Huh?" Cami raised her eyebrows. "Chill, hussy. Damon ain't comin' here tonight, so you ain't got shit to worry about."

"Yeah, right!"

"He can't get over here 'cause our car is in the shop. He doesn't know what SEPTA route to take to get from Wynnefield to Lansdowne. And if he did," Cami glanced at her watch. "Ain't too many buses runnin' this late."

"Okay, Sherlock," I said, crossing my arms. "Hasn't Damon been to my house before? Yes, he has. Doesn't he have friends who drive cars? Yes, he does. Don't you have my address written down in your phone book? Yes, you do."

Cami sighed. "Yeah, Damon's been to your house before, but he has a poor sense of direction drivin' outside of Philly. Yeah, most of his friends do have cars, but they ain't never been to the suburbs. They have trouble finding *my* home. Besides, do you think a bunch of North Philly muthafuckas are gonna be ridin' around an unfamiliar neighborhood in Delaware County at night? That's an invitation for the police to give 'em a beatdown."

I ran my fingers through my hair and rolled my eyes towards the ceiling.

"Look," she said, leaning forward and rubbing my shoulder, "I know Damon and he wouldn't do anything to hurt you to get to me.

I sipped my wine. "How could you be so stupid to have Derrick drop you off at the restaurant knowing Dar would be there tonight? And who the hell is he anyway?"

Cami sighed and told me Derrick was one of Khari's clients who worked downtown in Center City as a personal financial planner. She said he always looked sexy and fine coming into the salon in his double-breasted suits and polished shoes. Derrick was also a playa who always hit on any pretty lady that caught his eye. Although he knew Cami was married, it didn't stop him from making an occasional pass at her.

About four months ago, Derrick came into Camille's when Khari wasn't there and offered my girl fifty dollars to cut his hair and hook his beard up since he had an emergency meeting that afternoon.

Cami's first instinct was to tell him no, but she thought if he was foolish to pay that much money for a twenty dollar haircut and beard trim, she'd be a bigger fool to turn down a thirty dollar tip. At first, she felt disgusted by the comments he made about how soft and gentle her hands felt. Although she was repulsed by the way he smiled and glanced at her breasts, there was something about him that turned her on. Maybe it was his arrogance, age or the scent of Cool Water cologne along his neck that made him appealing in her eyes, but apparently, Derrick struck a nerve with her.

He was streetwise, business savvy and resourceful enough to handle his own against any challenge in the boardroom or in the hood. That would explain why he acted like a park ape when Dar shattered the window of his Lexus. He thanked her for hooking him up and handed her his business card, offering a free financial evaluation over lunch. Cami declined the invitation, telling him that she and her husband had sound financial planning. Derrick was only amused by her comment and told her to think things through in case she changed her mind. Two weeks later, after her latest fight with Damon, they met for lunch at the Marriot on 12th & Market Streets.

"I don't believe you," I said, shaking my head. "You're my girl and all, but didn't you realize he was playing you?"

"Stop!" Cami exclaimed sarcastically. "Of course I knew what he was all about, but I had my own agenda, too."

I crossed my arms in anticipation for her response.

"I was tired of being Damon's piece of ass. I needed some love and affection, and my husband certainly wasn't providing that for yours truly. So after we finished lunch, I suggested we get ourselves a hotel room. He was surprised, but didn't hesitate to cancel his appointments that afternoon."

My jaw dropped listening to Cami talk about their lovemaking session. She held nothing back, going into every intimate and nasty detail about the way her body quivered when he planted butterfly kisses on her breasts, shoulders and legs; the dampness and the funk of their sweat when flesh rubbed and pressed against flesh.

She floored me when she told me the strength of his arms wrapped around her torso when he held her tight with the sheets entangled around their legs. They didn't expect to rock each other's world, but they couldn't let go of the passion they created that day. Since then, they snuck around having sex at hotels after work or in her home on her days off from the salon.

"Aren't you going to say anything, hussy?" Cami asked, staring at me.

"This is too much for me," I murmured. "I need another drink."

"Well, you can have mine," she replied, sliding her glass towards me.

I chuckled and asked sarcastically, "Don't tell me you're pregnant?" Cami crossed her arms and lowered her head. Her awkward silence revealed the answer to my question. "I don't believe it. You can't be – "

"I am," she interrupted.

"Girl, quit playing."

"I'm not joking, Gigi. I'm pregnant with Derrick's baby. Two days ago, I took an E.P.T. and found out I'm gonna be a mommy." Her face had the same sincere expression as when we'd stood outside the 2nd Street Soul Café.

"How do you know it's his?"

"A few weeks ago, we were gettin' it on in my bedroom and the condom tore."

I swallowed Cami's drink in one gulp.

"I told him tonight after work at the salon," Cami continued. "We talked about our options and our future. Afterwards, he dropped me off on South Street to avoid running into anybody. I walked down 2nd Street, but I didn't expect him to circle the block and pull up in front of the restaurant by the time I got there. Derrick wanted to talk some more, so I got back in his Lexus. He had a change of heart and asked me to think about my decision and reconsider the alternatives. He leaned over and gave me a kiss on my cheek, but I couldn't resist tasting those lips again." She fanned herself with her hand. "I knew I shouldn't, but I didn't see Dar come outside the restaurant. I didn't realize she saw us until she tapped on the window and shattered the glass with her fist."

I shook my head. "Do you know Damon will explode when he finds out you're pregnant?"

Cami gazed at the coffee table. "Believe me, what he doesn't know won't hurt him."

My head started buzzing from all the wine I had drank. Cami's words echoed in my mind like riddles. *We talked about our options and our future. He had a change of heart and asked me to think about my decision and reconsider the alternatives. What he doesn't know won't hurt him.* Damn, she was going to have an abortion. I opened my mouth to say something, but she cut me off.

"Look, Gigi, I'm sorry I brought this up. I was apprehensive to share this with you not knowing how you would react."

I shook my head. It was all too much to digest: the affair with Derrick, the unexpected pregnancy and now this.

Cami looked at me while trying to gather her thoughts, then closed her eyes. "I'm not trying to have three children with two different fathers."

"You know something, Cami," I said, rubbing my thighs. "You're a damn fool."

She sat back with her eyes widened. "Say what?"

"I can't believe you would be so stupid to let your life fall apart like this."

"Okay, hussy, you done put away one too many drinks tonight. In case you forgot, this is my decision, not yours. So, why the fuck are you gettin' so upset?"

"Yeah, I know this is your decision, but that's only the tip of the iceberg. Here I am thinking Damon did you wrong, but it was you who did him wrong."

"Hold up, Gigi, don't – "

"No, I'm not finished," I interrupted. "The way you carried on with Derrick is no different than some chickenhead having sex behind her man's back. And now, you got yourself pregnant by this fool and decide to have an abortion so there's one less skeleton in your closet."

"Don't be draggin' your hang-ups into my situation and tryin' to run my life!" Cami snapped.

"Excuse you?" I asked, raising my eyebrow.

"You heard me! You got a lot of fuckin' nerve to criticize me for doing the same thing you did six years ago!" Cami pointed her finger. "If you remember, I was the one who tried to talk you out of it, but you went ahead and did so! You made your bed, hussy, and laid in it!"

"You're right. I'm not going to deny what I did. But at the time, I was single and Leon turned his back on me. I wasn't ready to deal with a newborn along with taking care of my grandmother and my health matters. You, on the other hand," I said, pointing my finger back at her. "Happen to be married with children and running a business. At your age, you should have known better."

"Get the fuck out of my face with that bullshit!" Cami laughed, waving her hand. "Don't even start with me about age and marital status. In case you forgot, we happen to be the same age. And you got a lot of room to talk since your single ass can't make up your mind when it comes to men. You had an opportunity to get with someone good for you, like Chris, but instead, you blew that chance 'cause you ain't ever let go of your feelings for Leon."

"You don't know what the hell you're talking about!"

"Look me in the eye, Gigi, and tell me I'm wrong!"

My telephone rang in the middle of our argument. We stared at each other, at the phone and then again at each other. The answering machine came on and an *I-told-you-so* smirk appeared on Cami's face when she recognized the caller's voice.

"Hey, Gigi. It's me, Leon. I'm sorry we didn't have the chance to talk like I'd hoped, but it was good seein' you tonight. You always took good care of yourself, so I shouldn't be surprised. I'm really hoping we can get together 'cause I think we both have a lot of things to clear up. Take care and I'll see you soon. Peace."

"Well," Cami said, sucking her teeth. "It looks like I ain't the only chickenhead up here in this henhouse." She clucked to add insult to injury.

If I weren't so pissed, I would have been cracking up at her joke. "Fuck you," I murmured.

Her eyes widened. "Damn, hussy, that was the *F-word.*" She opened her mouth and placed her hands on her cheeks sarcastically.

"You got a lot of nerve callin' somebody a hussy since you enjoy spreading your legs these days and gettin' pregnant by every Tom, Dick or Harry that comes strolling into your salon!" I snapped.

Cami's chest rose and fell. Rage was steaming from her flushed cheeks. I knew what I said was wrong and foul, but I was too angry and drunk to think straight.

"You know somethin', Gigi," Cami said, clasping her hands. "I don't feel any sympathy for you either, since there's a strong chance you might not be able to get pregnant 'cause of your fucked up thyroid!"

I rose to my feet, put my hands on my hips and pressed my lips together. Cami stood up, hunched her shoulders and raised her eyebrows. I couldn't recall us ever having a fight this bad. Sure, we've had some intense arguments, but we always knew where to draw the line. Tonight, we crossed it without consideration or respect for our personal dilemmas. Right about now, I wasn't sure if things would ever be the same between us. Without another word, I unlocked the front door and waited for her to leave, not caring where she would go or how she would get there. She grabbed her belongings, went about her business and didn't look back as I slammed the door shut.

Chapter Nineteen
Chris

"Well, hello there," Ronnie greeted me as she opened the front door. "It's good to see you." She leaned against the doorway in a peach bathrobe, her hair pulled back in a ponytail, smiling and licking her lips.

I shook my head in disgust just imagining what thoughts were going through her sick mind.

"What the hell is that look for?" Ronnie asked, crossing her arms.

"I don't – "

"Didn't I tell you I wasn't trying to seduce you?" she asked, interrupting me.

"Yeah, that's what you said," I replied, not believing her.

"So, what's the problem?"

I scanned her living room from over her shoulder. "Where's your cousin's daughter, Brandi?"

"She's on her way like I told you. She'll be here any moment."

I released another sigh, rolling my eyes towards the ceiling.

"It ain't that type of party between us, Chris. You can't spend just five minutes of your time talking with me?"

I rubbed my forehead and stared at the ground. Given her track record, I still didn't completely trust her. She invited me inside her apartment and I sat down on the sofa, which was close to the front door. Ronnie sat towards the opposite end, smiling away like a simple-minded fool. I wished she'd cut that shit out. The air conditioner felt like it was on full blast in the immaculate and spotless room. She always kept a clean and tidy place and was damn near obsessed with order and putting things back in their proper place. My severance package was lying on the center of her coffee table between a glass vase with fresh cut flowers, a plate of French bread pizza and a glass of soda.

"Here you go, Chris," Ronnie said, leaning over to pick up the envelope.

I nodded and opened it, examining the contents. "I really appreciate what you did."

"No problem. That's what friends are for. Can I get you something to drink?" she asked, putting her hands inside the pockets of her robe.

I shook my head. The last thing in the world I wanted her to think was that we were friends. "Look, Ronnie, let's get one thing straight – "

The telephone on the end table beside her rang, interrupting me. "Hello? Hey, Niecey. Where you at, girl? You shoulda been here by now. Oh no, she didn't. Is she okay? I'm sorry to hear that. Mm hmmm. Mm hmmm. Well, I hope Brandi feels better. Call me if you need anything." She hung up the phone. "Now, what were you saying?"

"Everything okay?"

"Brandi threw up in my cousin's car as they were pulling out the driveway. Niecey decided to cancel her date and stay home with her."

"Oh, I see," I replied, rising from the sofa. That was my cue to go. "Well, it's getting late and I gotta bounce."

"We haven't had the chance to talk yet," Ronnie said, standing up.

I hunched my shoulders. "What do we have to talk about?"

"How are you feeling, Chris? I mean, you got laid off. Are you going to be okay?"

"I'll be fine. Like I told you earlier, it's been a crazy day and I'm tired."

Ronnie reached out and squeezed my hand. "Something's wrong. I can tell."

"I'm cool," I said, waving my hands in the air. "All I want to do is go home and put this day behind me."

"You know you can always talk to me," she pleaded.

I crossed my arms. "C'mon, Ronnie, quit playin' games, okay?"

"What are you talking about?"

"You know damn well Brandi wasn't comin' over here. You probably had one of your girlfriends call you five minutes after I rang the buzzer."

"Unbelievable!" she hissed. "Do you think I would make up some shit like that?"

"Yeah, I do!"

"If that's what you think, then go!" Ronnie snapped, pointing at the door.

"See ya," I said, opening the door.

"Wait, Chris." She pulled my arm and slammed the door shut. "Okay, you were right. Brandi isn't coming over. Well, not until tomorrow night."

"Mm hmmm," I murmured. I knew her lying ass was up to no good.

"I knew you wouldn't have come over if I was alone and I wanted to see you."

"What for?"

She walked towards me, touched my forearm and confessed, "I missed you, baby. I've been thinking about you lately."

I lowered my arms to my side. "What about your friend, Allen? What would he have to say about me being here?"

"Don't tell me you believed that lie."

"No, I didn't," I replied.

"Oh," she murmured, sucking her teeth. "You know I was only messin' with you to make you jealous."

I let out an exasperated sigh. "I'm sorry, Ronnie, but it's over between us."

"Why? Haven't you missed me?"

I shook my head and crossed my arms again. "How do you know I haven't been seein' someone else since we broke up?" Damn, I should have known better than to say what I did, but it was too late. Whether or not I'd ever see Gigi again didn't matter. Ronnie needed to know what time it was and that we were history.

"Well, have you?" she inquired, raising her eyebrow.

I closed my eyes and whispered, "Yeah, I have."

"I bet it's that April bitch from the bank," she hissed. "I knew you were always attracted to her."

I laughed. I knew I shouldn't have done so, but I couldn't keep a straight face.

"What the hell is so funny?"

"I'm sorry, it's not April."

"Well then, who is she?"

"It doesn't matter, and that's none of your business."

"Y'all can't be that serious. We've only been apart for a few weeks now."

"You don't know how serious we are," I bluffed.

"Then why did you come here tonight?"

"To pick up my severance package, that's why," I responded, waving it.

Taking two steps back, Ronnie leaned against the door and untied her bathrobe, letting it fall to the brown carpet. "You can't tell me, Chris," she said, pulling off her "I LOVE NY" t-shirt and throwing it across the living room. "You haven't missed me." She licked her lips, inched her body closer to mine and squeezed her full, erect breasts, wearing nothing but a purple thong.

I closed my eyes and shook my head. Girlfriend was going for broke tonight, but homey damn sure wasn't playing this shit. I walked over, picked up Ronnie's t-shirt, tossed it to her and said, "Put your clothes back on, Adina Howard, before you catch cold standing around in your panties."

She giggled, dropping her t-shirt to the floor. "You crazy, boy."

"I'm crazy?" I asked, laughing and touching my chest with my index finger. "I'm serious, girl. Enough is enough."

"And I'm serious, too, Chris," she pleaded. She wrapped her arms around my torso and pressed her breasts into my chest. "You know you've missed my body as much as I miss yours."

I put my hands on her stomach and eased her away. "Stop it, please," I begged.

She rubbed my forearms. "C'mon, how about once more for old times sake?"

"No," I answered sternly, jerking my arms away. I did my best not to shove her, but she was testing my patience. The severance package fell from underneath my armpit and I bent over to reach for it. Seizing the opportunity, she leaned over to put her arms around my body and kiss me. Caught off balance, our bodies fell to the floor with hers ending up on top of mine and our lips locked in some serious, passionate, sloppy kiss. Ronnie's lips didn't feel or taste like Gigi's, and her pathetic ass only made me want to vomit. Between gulps of air, I asked her to stop, but that only made her come on stronger. Finally, she pulled back and knelt over my body like a lioness stalking its prey.

"You…can't…tell me…how…much…you…missed me," she panted, staring at me with the ferocious gleam in her eyes and wicked smile she always displayed whenever she felt sexually aroused. I knew that expression all too well.

"It's…it's…not right," I murmured, trying to catch my breath. "I'm seeing…someone."

"That's bullshit and you know it," she snapped, unloosening her ponytail to let her shoulder-length hair free.

I bit my lip and turned to the side. *Fuck! Why me?* I thought as I smacked the floor with the palm of my hand.

She sat beside me and stroked my thigh. "Chris," she whispered, turning my head towards her, "I want you so bad, baby. And I know you want me, too." Her fingers began massaging my crotch. I pulled her hand away, but it was too late. "Let me feel you inside of me."

Sitting against the wall, I hung my head between my knees, beating myself up for coming over. I said nothing for a few moments until I rose to my feet, picked up my severance package and replied, "I'm sorry, Ronnie, but I can't."

"She doesn't have to know," she whispered, holding my hand.

I shook my head.

As Ronnie rose to her feet and touched my cheek, I pulled her hand away from my face. She pouted, picked up her t-shirt and robe, and put them back on. Her chest rose and her eyes were dampening.

"Fine! Just do us both a favor and get the fuck out!" she exclaimed, storming off into her bedroom.

I sighed and said nothing as I left Ronnie's place for the last time.

By the time I got to South Philly, it was almost ten thirty. I decided to head down to Spitfire so I could chat with Gene and get a drink or two. I would have been at the restaurant fifteen minutes earlier, but finding an empty parking space at this hour on the weekend was damn near impossible. Fortunately, I lucked out at 4th and Lombard and didn't have to walk too far. I knew the poetry show would be winding down by now and I might be able to catch Gene, assuming he hadn't already left. Since he was hosting tonight, there was a pretty good chance he hadn't, because there was no way he'd be able to do his usual stick and move when he was ready to leave.

I crossed 2nd Street and noticed Gene standing outside the restaurant talking with some brotha about tonight's show. Neither one had noticed me standing a few yards away, so I kept my distance and decided to listen. From the look and the sound of the conversation, things didn't go as well as they planned.

"Man, I'm tellin' you, Gene, your girl and her friends almost fucked things up for me tonight," the guy said.

Gene took a puff of his cigarette. "Don't hand me that bullshit, Nate. Flipper had nothin' to do with the way things were run tonight. They were fucked up from the beginning."

Shit, if I hadn't left my check at work, I could have been here to see Gigi.

"How you gonna talk shit about the way I handled things?" Nate asked.

Gene waved his hands. "Man, I don't even want to talk about it."

"Well, we need to talk about next month's show since we gonna be havin' a poetry slam. I need you to work with my man Greg in making sure things will be tight this time around."

Gene blew smoke in the air, half listening to what Nate had to say. Just from the way he rambled about his ideas and the cockiness in his voice, I could tell this guy was a lot of talk but not much action. After stomaching all of Nate's shit that he could, Gene put his cigarette out on the ground and told him to do whatever he wanted to do with whomever and wherever because he was out. He walked towards me while Nate kept calling his name until he just gave up.

"What's up, brah?" I asked, getting Gene's attention.

"Yo, Cool C, what's goin' on?" Gene shook my hand firmly.

"Everything okay?"

"Nah, but ain't no use in complain'," Gene replied, glancing towards the restaurant. "Where you been?"

"Long story. If you got a dime, then I got the time."

"Yeah, that'll work for me. Besides," he said, rubbing his bald head. "You look like you've got somethin' on your mind."

I nodded as we made our way back to my Ford Explorer to give Gene a ride home.

Parked in front of Gene's apartment building in South Philly, we sat talking for the past half hour. The windows were half cracked so my friend could finish his cigarette and blow smoke outside into the cool night air. I shared with him everything that occurred today while he sat back and listened.

"Damn, Cool C, I'm sorry to hear about your dad. Is he going to be alright?"

"Yeah, he should be alright." I stared outside the windshield, uncertain about his recovery. "I was planning to see him sometime tomorrow, if he is up to it."

Gene slapped his thigh. "Yeah, definitely go visit him to make sure everything's okay. Don't even trip on losing your job 'cause somethin' better is comin' along."

"You got that shit right. I'm not even stressing about the job or that fool Ronnie."

Gene laughed. "Man, that chick was too coo-coo for Cocoa Puffs. Some sistahs are off the deep end when they can't let go."

"Speaking of sistahs off the deep end, what really trips me out is the way Gigi behaved this morning," I replied, hunching my shoulders. "What the hell was up with the way she played me?"

Gene took another puff and blew smoke out the window. He closed his eyes and grew real silent.

"What's up?" I asked.

"Cool C, you my boy and all – "

"Yeah," I interjected.

"Well, she was here tonight with her girlfriends."

"Yeah, I know. I overheard you and Nate talking about her tonight."

"The dude she was dating a few years back was also here."

"Leon," I murmured.

He nodded and told me how Leon arrived with Nate later that evening while he and Gigi were talking inside the foyer. Upon arriving, Leon asked to speak with Gigi in private. They left them alone, but Gene stepped outside to keep an eye on her in case things got out of hand. Although he wasn't eavesdropping, he did see Gigi give Leon her phone number at the end of their conversation.

I leaned back against my seat and gazed out the windshield. I now knew the answer to my question. Leon. "Hmmm," I mumbled nonchalantly.

"You okay, man?" he asked.

"I don't know what to say."

"I'm sorry I told you, but you my boy and – "

"It's cool," I interrupted. "I ain't mad, so don't go there. I've seen too many fools bump their heads today and don't you start trippin', too."

Gene laughed and I couldn't help doing the same.

"So, whatcha gonna do 'bout the next Spitfire show?" I asked, changing the subject.

"Man, I don't care what they do 'cause I know they'll be fallin' apart before the next show."

"What makes you say that?"

"I've been knowin' Nate before I was down with Buttamilk and that brotha is all 'bout himself," he responded, blowing cigarette smoke out the window. "He ain't got any love for poetry like we do. I'd invited him to a few of our gigs, but he would never show. The only reason he started Spitfire was because he got caught up in that Def Poetry hype after watching a poetry show a few months ago. Apparently, dollar signs must have popped up in his eyes. A few weeks ago, he gave me a call and asked me to help him out, but I should have known better."

"So, why did you do it?"

"Originally, I said no, but he promised to pay me for hosting and give me a cut from the door if I spread the word. Everything else would be taken care of 'cause he had a featured poet for the first show and the location of the venue. So, I did my thing, but come to find out, Nate was lazy, a procrastinator and notorious for doin' things at the last minute. A lot of the stuff he was responsible for fell in my lap. After weeks of advertising, the owners didn't confirm the event was going down at the restaurant until the day before."

I laughed and stared at my friend like he had lost his mind.

"Oh, it gets better," he said. "There was supposed to be a band tonight, but he under budgeted for them…so no band. On top of that, the featured spot was promised to two other poets and I had to deal with hurt feelings and bruised egos. And don't get me started 'bout Nate showing up late to his own venue or your boy, The Gentleman Poet."

I held the steering wheel and shook my head. "Damn, that's fucked up."

"You ain't lyin'. It's bullshit like tonight's show that makes me want to step off the scene permanently."

"C'mon, Gene," I said, slapping his thigh. "You don't really mean that."

"Nah, but you don't know how upset I get seein' cats start these poetry venues across Philly for the wrong reasons. When I started Buttamilk with my partners, Kenny and Marv, we did it for one reason only and that was one love. Everybody involved, from the poets, the singers, the comedians and the three of us, had one love for the art and the expression of creativity.

"The first show began as a gathering over somebody's apartment in West Philly, with a few friends reciting poetry or sharing a song. Nobody knew that those weekly pow-wow sessions would evolve into a weekly venue at the North Star Bar. Everyone came out because they had the passion for the art and showed each other nothing but respect. While I understand the art of poetry has evolved and changed since then, some folks on the scene today be trippin' too much over their egos, money, sex or slammin'. Ain't too many venues around anymore that have that magic."

I stroked my goatee, feeling everything he said. "Let me ask you a question," I said, tapping my fingers on the dashboard. "Have you ever thought about startin' Buttamilk again?"

He chuckled, flicked his cigarette out the window and said, "Nah. Buttamilk will always have a special place in my heart, but it wouldn't be the same. Me, Kenny and Marv have moved on and we are doin' our own separate things now. Besides, with Kymm being pregnant, I'm still adjustin' to the fact I'm gonna be a father. After the baby comes, I know my time will be limited."

"Understood."

"But if I did do another venue again, I would definitely incorporate some of the concepts we did. However, it would need a new name. Something catchy, yet simple," he replied, yawning and covering his mouth. "Yo, but I'ma stop runnin' my mouth and get on inside. You need to get some rest."

"Yeah, you're right," I said, giving him some dap.

We said our goodbyes and I watched Gene walk across the street and inside the building.

Pulling away from the curve, I thought about everything we talked about tonight. So many thoughts were scrambling throughout my mind, but the conversation we had regarding poetry ignited something inside of me, similar to the ones I shared with Gigi. I exhaled a deep sigh just thinking about her. Yeah, I was disappointed by what I heard tonight, but I had to move on. Easier said than done, but like Ronnie said earlier, we couldn't have been that serious, especially since Leon was still a part of her life. Better to find out now than to get deeply involved with someone whose heart and feelings were elsewhere.

I turned the radio to WDAS and let Patti LaBelle's *New Day* give me some comfort and a little inspiration on my ride home.

Chapter Twenty
Chris

"Watch it, asshole!" I cursed at the speeding Honda Accord that cut in front of me. God only knew why some idiots felt the need to drive like they were competing in the NASCAR, especially when it was pouring rain heavy and hard. Saturday came and went, and I spent most of the day in bed resting from all the running around I did the day before. Sam left two messages for me the day before to update me on Dad's prognosis and to find out when I was coming by to see him. Feeling somewhat guilty for not returning his phone calls, I needed to see my father before the end of the weekend like I promised.

As I was pulling off the South Street exit from the Schuylkill, the steady downpour turned to a light drizzle. I rode down Spruce Street and through the University of Penn's campus. Cracking the car window, I inhaled the freshness of the air. While driving, I saw a father and son walking down the block underneath a large blue and white umbrella. The boy must have been about twelve, and although I didn't know them from Adam, curiosity was flooding my mind with so many questions about them. Where were they going today? How did they get along? Why couldn't I have had a better relationship with Dad when I was twelve? I shook my head as I pulled into the hospital's garage and parked my SUV.

"Yo, Chris," Sam said as I stepped off the elevator. "Man, I'm glad you made it."

"Yeah," I murmured. It looked like my brother was heading home. "Um, how's Dad doin'?"

"He's good," he replied, setting his backpack on the ground. "He dozed off not too long ago. I was on my way out to get somethin' to eat. Mom came by earlier this morning before she went to church. She'll be back later on."

I nodded. "Cool." I was relieved Evelyn wasn't there so I didn't have to put up with her bullshit.

"Uncle Leroy came by yesterday to check up on Dad."

"Oh, yeah?" I cracked a smile. Uncle Leroy was my father's youngest brother and the craziest person in our family. He had a good heart when it came to family, especially taking care of his children. However, my uncle was irresponsible as hell when it came to money. Dad resented him for his carelessness and often bailed him out whenever he needed to make rent or car payments.

"You okay, bro?" Sam asked, pushing the down elevator button. "You don't look so hot."

I stroked my goatee. "I'm alright. Just got a lot of things on my mind."

Sam nodded, put his hand on my shoulder and said, "Look, Chris, I know you and Dad have had your share of problems and all, but – "

"Hold up," I interrupted, waving my hand. "You don't know jack about my problems with Dad. Okay? So don't even go there."

"Fuck it, man. Why can't you just let it go?"

"Hey, I can't turn off my feelings like a light switch."

"Do you think you're the only one who's had issues with him? Huh?"

I shook my head and listened to my brother remind me that our father had done his share of belittling everybody, from us to our aunts and uncles. Although I agreed with what Sam was saying, it still didn't give Dad any right to treat me or Mom like shit. That's what hurt more than anything else. Sam couldn't relate to that since it wasn't him or his mother on the receiving end of his putdowns.

A pudgy white nurse walking by asked us to lower our voices and stop cursing out of respect for the patients. Sam apologized while I glanced at her before she went about her business.

I clasped my hands. “Yeah, you’re right, but no matter what, it’s hard for me to let go.”

My brother nodded. “I hear what you’re sayin’, bro, but he’s our father. He almost died.”

“Yeah, I know,” I murmured.

“Um, are you gonna be alright? If you want, I can stay with you.”

The down arrow illuminated and the metallic elevator rang as the door opened.

“Go on. I’ll be fine.”

He slung his backpack over his shoulder. “You sure?”

I nodded and promised not to stay too long so I wouldn’t disturb Dad’s rest.

Sam stepped aboard and pressed the button for the lobby level. “I’ll call you later. Okay?”

“Bye,” I said before the elevator door closed. Leaning against the wall, I stared at my distorted reflection in the elevator door. I inhaled a deep breath before making my way down the hall.

I opened the door and slowly made my way towards Dad’s bedside. The humming of the air conditioner, the pulsating beeps of the EKG and my father’s barely audible snore were the only sounds percolating in his hospital room. Even in his sleep, he had the same vulnerable appearance as when I saw him in the recovery room the other day. Running my fingers along the cool metal bedside, I turned on the portable lamp and studied the wrinkles in his forehead and the grayness in his facial hair. It seemed like Dad had aged a few years in the past two days.

He turned his head towards me and slightly opened his eyes. “Sam,” he mumbled in his semi-conscious state.

“It’s me, Dad,” I responded, grasping the metal rail. “Chris.”

Dad blinked his eyes and stared at me. He licked his chapped lips, saying, “Junior?”

I nodded.

He tilted his head and squinted his eyes as he stared at me without saying a word. He opened his mouth as if he was about to say something.

"Are you okay?" I asked.

"You, you put on some weight, huh?"

Of all the nasty comments we exchanged over the years, I didn't know if I should be offended by what he just said. Still, it was quite amusing and it made me chuckle.

I smiled, shook my head, and said, "Yeah, I did."

"Have you been working out?"

"A little bit."

He nodded his head and sighed. "Well, you look like you've been taking good care of yourself."

I raised my eyebrows and stared at him in disbelief. This couldn't be my father lying here and giving me two compliments in a row.

I reached out, touching his forearm. "Thanks. Um, how are you feeling?"

"Not so bad. Things could have been a lot worse considering. How's work?"

"Work is work," I replied, shrugging my shoulders.

"Sam told me you lost your job."

I rolled my eyes, wishing my brother were there so I could punch his ass out. "Yeah, it was one of those things that happened."

"Don't be ashamed about losing your job," Dad cajoled. "Happens to the best of us. After all, it wasn't your fault, was it?"

I shook my head. It appeared I had spoken too soon about not recognizing my father.

"No, my entire department got laid off."

"Oh, I see," he murmured, convinced that I was lying to him. I didn't care if he believed me or not, but he was in the wrong for what he said. Although I felt like telling him off, I didn't do so, and I wasn't sure why. Maybe I didn't want to upset his heart. Or maybe it wasn't worth the effort anymore. Still, there was something I needed to know.

"Can I ask you a question, Dad?"

"Sure."

"What makes you think I was responsible for losing my job?"

"I didn't say you were responsible for losing your job, son. I know you have a habit of starting things with so much enthusiasm, but then giving up when things get tough."

"Like what?"

"Well, how about the time you took violin lessons in the third grade and you wound up breaking the damn thing midway through the program?"

"Are you serious?" I asked, staring at him in disbelief. How the hell could he recall and relate something I did in my childhood to my adult life? Talk about comparing apples to oranges. Yeah, I got bored with playing the violin, but I didn't break it on purpose. I laid it on my bed and accidentally sat on it when I came back from the bathroom. He wasn't there when it happened and even when I told him, he still didn't believe me.

"Well, you asked, didn't you?"

"Don't go there, Dad. Okay?"

He stared at the ceiling, then tilted his head and asked, "So, how's the poetry going?"

"Sam told you about that, too?"

He nodded.

"Oh," I mumbled, staring at the floor.

"Well," Dad sighed, staring at the ceiling. "I hope you weren't planning to become a full-time poet now that you're out of work."

"What's that suppose to mean?" I inquired, tapping my fingers on the rail.

"I mean, you aren't one of those angry, militant poets preaching that revolutionary and kill whitey shit."

I laughed, shaking my head at his ignorant remark.

"What's so damn funny? I'm being serious, Junior. Just because you lost your job doesn't give you an excuse to blame the white man for your misfortunes. Any asshole can call themselves a poet standing on a street corner and talking shit all day long."

I raised my eyebrows. "Hold up, Dad, did you just call me an asshole?"

"No, I'm not calling you an asshole, Junior – "

"Well, it certainly sounds like you are," I interrupted.

"See, you're missing my entire point."

"I'm still tryin' to figure out what the fuck is your point!"

"Hey!" Dad snapped. "Watch your mouth, damnit! Remember I'm still your father."

I shrugged my shoulders. "And?"

"And I'm entitled to some respect."

"For what?" I snapped. "You haven't said or done anything for me in over fourteen years."

"Of course not, since you wanted to be an emancipated minor," Dad replied. "You didn't want my help to pay for your college tuition because you want to prove you can make it in this world alone. You forgot who it was that paid for you to attend a preparatory course so you could get a decent score on your SATs and get accepted to college. So why the hell should I bother doing jack shit for you?"

"I never declared myself an emancipated minor, Dad! That's some sarcastic bullshit you made up! And I didn't ask you for your help because you love nothing more than to rub shit in somebody's face by constantly reminding them of all their failures and setbacks!"

"That's bullshit," he dismissed.

"No, it's the truth," I added. "You also don't have a problem dangling a carrot over somebody's head to let them know what you've done for them financially. There's more to life than money, you know."

"Yeah, well tell that to your Uncle Leroy," Dad said, changing the subject. "Consider yourself lucky you didn't have to grow up and look after a bunch of sorry ass motherfuckers like your aunts and uncles. I'm surprised that bastard didn't come in here yesterday to find out if his name was in my will."

I sighed in disgust. "I don't believe you. Uncle Leroy came by to see you. He's your brother and he cares about you."

"Leroy's selfish, black ass doesn't give a damn about anybody except himself."

"Is that what you think, Dad? Do you really think Leroy came by here to see how much money you left him in your will?"

"I wouldn't put it past him."

I shook my head. "Let me ask you another question, Dad. Considering all that's happened between us, what am I doing here?"

"I don't know. You tell me, Junior. Isn't it ironic that you've barely said a word to me in almost fourteen years and all of a sudden, you come around when I had a heart attack and you've lost your job?"

I slapped the rail. "You know something, Dad, – " I snapped, pointing my finger.

"What?"

I gritted my teeth and glared at my father with so much anger. I wanted to not only tell him off, but to beat the living shit out of him for all the ignorant and hurtful things he ever said about me, Mom, Sam and our family.

"If you've got somethin' to say, just speak your mind," he said.

Taking two steps backwards and clenching my fists, I remembered what Mom said to me the other day: *Love always begins within you. If you can't love yourself for who you are, then how can you expect to find happiness in life?* Until this moment, I never realized how profound her words really were and took a long hard look at myself. Yeah, she was on point with her analysis about Dad and I being alike when it came to our relatives and the women in our lives. My relationship with Sam was no different than his with my uncles. And Ronnie was no different than Evelyn with her insecurities and deceptive acts.

Waving my hands, I whispered, "Forget it. It's nothing."

"Hmmm," he sighed, closing his eyes.

I cleared my throat to gain his attention. "Um, I've got to get going, Dad." It was pointless for me to reason with him anyway. He was too damn stubborn and ignorant to change, and there was no point in getting myself worked up over nothing.

He sucked his teeth, stared at the ceiling again and said, "Well, it was good seein' you, Junior."

"You, too," I murmured while turning off the portable lamp. As I opened the door, I heard him mumbling something about me underneath his breath. I shook my head and left him alone.

Almost a half hour had past before I decided to leave Presbyterian. I sat in the parking garage thinking about everything that transpired during my visit. I called Mom and gave her an update of Dad's condition and also informed her of my conversation. She wasn't surprised by the things he said, but glad I was listening to what she told me. So was I. No way did I want to spend the rest of my life being bitter and wasting my time searching for happiness in all the wrong places.

The rain had stopped and sunlight was peaking through the gray skies. I rode down Chestnut Street, past Drexel University and the 30th Street Station Post Office before making my way back to the Schuylkill in complete silence. The only noise that disrupted the quietness was the ringing of my cell phone.

I put the headset on and said, "Hello."

"What's up, Cool C?" Gene asked.

"Hey! Whatcha up to, brah?"

"Nothin'. Thought I'd call you to see how you were doin'."

"Appreciate it. I'm okay."

"How's your Dad?"

"It's funny you should ask because I just left the hospital. He's fine."

"That's real good to hear. Anyway, I won't keep you long, but wanted to also thank you for the talk we had the other day."

"What for?" I asked, raising my eyebrows.

"Well, after you went home, I started to think about what you said, and there's something I want to run by you when you have a moment."

"Awww, shit! Sounds interesting."

Gene laughed. "Oh yeah, it's gonna be real interesting. But I'm definitely gonna need your help, man."

I looked at the clock on the dashboard. "I was on my way home, Gene, but I got time to stop by your place."

"Nah, you don't have to go out of your way."

"Trust me, brah," I said, shaking my head and smiling. "It's no trouble and I can be there shortly."

"Cool. I'll see you in a few," Gene said, hanging up the phone.

As I made my way off the Grays Ferry Exit and down Washington Avenue, I wondered what Gene had up his sleeve. I'd surely find out in the next five minutes.

Chapter Twenty-One
Regina

A message from Dr. Fitzpatrick was on my voice mail when I came back from another of Marcia's impromptu staff meetings that afternoon. I called his office the day before to receive the results of my biopsy, but hadn't heard anything until now. Clasping my hands in prayer, I listened to him apologize for not returning my phone call. He had been out of the office and the results hadn't come yet. He assured me if they didn't hear anything by noon tomorrow, he'd follow up with a phone call to the lab.

I shook my head and turned on my radio. There was no use worrying about something that was beyond my control. I constantly reminded myself about what my horoscope forecasted in the Daily News: *Today's events will bring you rejuvenation and joy. You will gain the insight you need to move forward with your life.* My telephone rang and I answered it after the second ring.

"Hello?"

"Girl, where the hell have you been?" April asked.

Crossing my legs, I wished I hadn't picked up my phone. April had left me several messages at home and work wondering what happened between Cami and I. Apparently, Cami wasn't telling her anything based on the context from April's messages. I wasn't in the mood to talk with her either and I did my best to avoid her until now.

"Don't act like you're not there, Gigi, because I can hear you breathing. Okay?"

I sighed. "I'm here."

"Why haven't you returned any of my calls?"

"I'm sorry," I apologized, running my fingers through my hair. "I've been busy."

"Don't lie to me. I need to talk to you about – "

"Look, April," I interjected, "I'm sorry for lying to you, but I don't feel like talking about Cami."

"Well, neither did I, since you two fools were ignoring my phone calls, but she called me this morning."

"That's nice," I replied dryly.

"She told me about her affair with Derrick and the pregnancy. She also told me about the falling out you two had."

"Hmmm," I murmured. I couldn't believe Cami brought April into the middle of this. Resting my elbows on my desk, I closed my eyes and said, "Um, this isn't a good time for me and – "

"Gigi, don't," she pleaded. "Hear me out. Please?"

"Look, April, I know you mean well, but what's done is done. Okay? Cami's an adult. She made her bed and slept in it. She went there with me and said some real hurtful shit to my face!"

"I know, Gigi, and I told her she was wrong."

"You did what?"

"I told Cami she was wrong for making that nasty comment. You and I both know she doesn't think before she opens her mouth."

"And did she tell you what I said?"

"Yes she did, and I don't agree with the way you handled the situation. However, that's no excuse for her to say something that horrible."

Reaching for a Kleenex, I wiped a tear from my eye.

"Cami also realizes what she said was cold blooded," she continued. "She was bawling like a baby while we were talking."

"So, now she's remorseful after shooting off her big mouth and I'm supposed to forgive her?"

"No, you shouldn't. You have every right not to speak to her again, but you may have said a few things that hurt her feelings, too."

Although I met April through Cami many years ago and subsequently we became friends, I didn't expect her to take my side. I also didn't want to admit that she had a good point. I wasn't very supportive to Cami.

"Hello?" April inquired.

"I'm here. Can I ask you a question?"

"Sure."

"Why did you call me?"

She paused for a few moments before replying. "Cami wants to talk with you."

I could tell there was something April was hiding by the hesitancy in her voice. "She could have called me herself."

"Yeah, but would you've answered if you knew it was her?"

"Touché."

She laughed, but I didn't see anything funny about talking with Cami again. After all, what else did she have to say? April didn't know, but asked me to think about it. She agreed I had every right to feel the way I did and wasn't sure if she would ever forgive Cami. Speaking to and forgiving Cami was not a priority on my to-do list.

Shaking my head after hanging up the phone, I chuckled when I heard the chorus of Toni Braxton's *Spanish Guitar* fading into the background. That was the third time this week I heard that song and every time I did, my thoughts drifted back to Chris. How could I have been so stupid and stubborn to push him away? Reaching into my purse, I unfolded and re-read the printout of the e-mail he sent me last week.

Gigi,

I apologize for upsetting you or making you feel uncomfortable this morning. I know things must be difficult for you right now, and I should have been patient and understanding like I told you the other night.

You're a very special and beautiful person, Gigi, and you're someone who is truly blessed. And it's not only with your poetry and singing, but it's everything about you. Even as I'm writing this message, it's difficult for me to explain and if we were talking face to face, I'm not sure if I could, but I'd try my best. What I do know is that I enjoy your company and getting to know you. I also enjoy sharing my thoughts with you and vice versa. As I said before, I do care about you and I'm faithful that everything will work out for you. Please know that you will be in my thoughts and prayers.

Take care,
Chris

Ever since our last encounter, I felt guilty for the way I behaved. I kept searching for him aboard the R3, hoping to run into him. I lost count of how many times I picked up the phone to give him a call at work and at home, but didn't follow through. It was time for me to admit my shame and to patch things up between us. Maybe things weren't that bad and it wasn't too late to apologize since Chris seemed like the understanding type. I picked up the phone and decided to call him.

"Audit Department, this is Kelly," an unfamiliar voice answered. I must have dialed the wrong number.

"Hi, I'm trying to get in touch with Chris Harrington."

"I'm sorry, but Mr. Harrington no longer works here," she responded dryly.

"Oh. Um, thank you very much," I said, hanging up the phone.

With the bank merger, I knew Chris was concerned about being laid off from work, but I didn't think it would happen to him. I hoped he was okay.

"Ahem," a female voice called from behind, popping chewing gum.

I turned around and saw Kiya leaning against the entrance to my cubicle. Sucking my teeth, I twirled my pendant's silver chain with my index finger. What the hell did she want? This was the first time I'd seen her since our paths crossed last week at the Marathon Grill. She stared at me and popped her chewing gum.

"Can I help you with something?" I inquired, crossing my leg. I didn't know who she thought she was standing there in those unflattering overstretch pants and run over flat shoes.

"Uh, yeah," she replied, popping her gum again. "I wanna speak with you, if it ain't too much trouble?"

Crossing my arms, I sighed. It was only 2:35 p.m. and I wanted a second opinion from that crackpot astrologer. If anything else, this day had its share of surprises. I invited Kiya to have a seat. She fidgeted her unattractive, pregnant ass into the empty chair by my desk.

Lowering her voice, she said, "Um, this ain't gonna take too long, so I'll get straight to the point."

"Okay."

"I wanted to…um…apologize to you," she said, holding her head down in shame.

"What for?" I asked, raising my eyebrows. First Cami, now her.

"When we first met at Lockette's," she said, popping her gum. "I knew you and Leon had dated just by the way y'all were looking at each other. Naturally, I got jealous, as any woman would if she saw her man's ex."

I nodded. "Mm hmmm."

She popped her gum and stared at the ceiling. "Before we met and all, sometimes I'd see you in the cafeteria gettin' coffee or lunch and – "

"Excuse me," I interjected as she popped her gum in mid-sentence. "But could you please not pop your gum while you're talking?"

She waved her hand. "So, like I was sayin', I was also jealous of you because you work up here in the Accounting Department and I know you got some college degrees, so you makin' some big bucks. I was hatin' on you badly, Regina, when I shouldn't have."

I nodded. "We all have our moments."

"Up until a few days ago," she continued, clearing her throat. "I…um…didn't know all the history between you and Leon. Um, he told me what happened 'bout you gettin' pregnant. I always knew there was somethin' he was hidin' from me when I told him about us havin' a baby. For a week or two, he was silent but kinda distant. When he came back around, he seemed so excited about the baby, a bit too excited at times for Leon. You know what I mean?"

My right leg began shaking as I stared at her.

"Now I understand why. He felt guilty and all about not being there for you. He told me himself. It really hit home for him when he saw you again."

I sighed, remembering Leon's behavior that night. He wasn't the only one whose feelings resurfaced.

"Also, he told me he's not in love with me 'cause – " she paused, her eyes moistening. "Um, he's not sure if he's still in love with you."

I reached for a Kleenex and handed it to her.

"Thanks."

"He said that?"

She nodded. "Yeah."

"How do you feel about that?"

She shrugged her shoulders and said, "It don't matter anyways, 'cause things ain't been right between us for a long time, even before the baby came into the picture. I ain't want to admit it to myself. I was hopin' that maybe it would be different since we gonna be parents, but it's the same ole shit with him, ya know?" Putting her hand over her lips, she apologized for cursing.

I waved my hand and Kiya giggled. Much to my surprise, I cracked a smile. Resting my hands on the desk, I said, "I don't know what to say, – "

"You ain't gotta say nuthin'," she interrupted. "Shit, it don't matter to me how you feel about him. He told me he'd do right by our child, so there ain't no need for me to file any child support papers."

Raising my eyebrows, I chuckled. I didn't believe Leon had the audacity to say that crap. I prayed she wasn't that gullible.

"And I know what you thinkin' 'cause I ain't nobody's fool. I got a cousin who went through the same bullshit a few years back, so I know what I got to do to provide for my baby's future." Kiya smiled, massaging her swollen belly. "Although Leon did me wrong and all, I'm blessed he gave me this child so I can teach my baby what true love is all about."

I pressed my lips, clasped my hands and stared at her. I couldn't find anything to say after hearing the excitement in Kiya's voice about her child. I noticed her face appeared darker than the rest of her body, but there was a healthy glow in her deep-set eyes and cheeks. Glancing in the mirror on my desk, I wondered if I would have had that same look if I had kept my child.

"Um, are you okay?" she asked.

I nodded. "I'm fine. Um, you're not the only one who needs to apologize for her behavior."

"Huh?" Kiya asked, raising her eyebrows.

"I admit that...um...I felt a little bitter, too, about your pregnancy. It was painful for me to know you're going to have a baby by him."

Kiya sucked her teeth and nodded.

Before I could speak, the telephone rang. I excused myself to answer it.

"Hello?"

"Hi, Regina. It's Dr. Fitzpatrick."

"Hi! How are you?" His phone call caught me by total surprise since I didn't expect to hear from him until tomorrow, unless the results came back from the lab.

"Just fine. I hope I'm not calling at a bad time."

"Um, no," I said, glancing at Kiya and pressing my lips. "Can I put you on hold?"

"Sure."

Placing the receiver on my desk, I apologized to Kiya for cutting our conversation short, but told her this was an important call. She nodded and I stood up to assist her. Before she left my cubicle, we stared at each other for a few seconds, exchanged half-smiles and said goodbye cordially.

Sitting in my chair, I picked up the receiver and apologized to Dr. Fitzpatrick for placing him on hold. He understood and told me the results had arrived twenty minutes earlier. My right leg began shaking again. I closed my eyes and prepared myself for the worst. He told me the abnormality inside my right thyroid wasn't a tumor at all. It was the result of a goiter that began developing, but for some unknown reason, paused midway into production. This was the first time he ever saw a case like this, but he apologized for alarming me with his diagnosis.

"Thank you, Lord," I exclaimed with tears running down my smiling face.

"Well, I know you don't want to hear this, Regina, and right about now, I know you're probably sick of seeing my face and coming into this office – "

I laughed. "Maybe."

"But I need to meet with you so we can discuss your treatment options."

"I understand."

"How about we get together sometime early next week?"

"Sure."

Dr. Fitzpatrick put me on hold and transferred me to his receptionist who informed me he had an opening on Tuesday at eleven thirty. I asked if I could meet with him tomorrow instead. I wanted to get this over with ASAP. She said she could squeeze me in. After thanking her, I hung up the phone and filled out my vacation request form. Marcia was going to be pissed that I was taking the day off at the last minute, but she'd get over it.

After my heart to heart with both April and Kiya, there were two individuals I planned to meet with tomorrow besides Dr.

Fitzpatrick to bring closure to certain matters in my life: Cami and Leon.

Chapter Twenty-Two
Regina

Leon was twenty minutes late as I took another sip of my café latte and stared through the silver beaded curtain of the Crimson Moon Coffeehouse. Listening to Common's *The Light*, I watched the last remnants of drizzle fall from the gray sky. I was in awe of the rain's ability to make the afternoon rush hour in Center City appear so tranquil.

A white guy wearing a faded blue t-shirt and torn jeans sat his drink on my table. "Ah, excuse me, Miss," he said, pulling the zebra print chair towards him and gawking at my breasts. "Is anyone sitting here?"

"Actually, I'm waiting for my boyfriend to join me," I replied dryly.

"No problem," he said, picking up his drink and sitting down on the tan sofa across the room.

I shook my head and checked my cell phone for any messages. Nothing. Considering how excited Leon was when I called him last night and asked if we could meet after work, I was surprised he didn't arrive before me. Actually, his tardiness was a blessing in disguise. It gave me the chance to think about my decision to have thyroid surgery. Reaching into my purse, I pulled out a hand held mirror and ran my index finger across my throat. Although Dr. Fitzpatrick assured me there would only be a slight change in my voice, the prospects of having a permanent scar across my neck as a reminder didn't sit too well with me. Still, it was better than the alternative to undergo the radioactive iodine.

Koko, the owner of the coffeehouse, walked over to my table and placed my empty glass on a serving tray. "Can I get you anything else, Gigi?"

"I'm cool," I replied, putting my mirror away. "That's a sharp dress you got on tonight, girlfriend." I nodded, admiring her scarlet ensemble.

"Thanks," she said, wiping down the table. "Speaking of girlfriends, how's Ms. Cami doin'? I haven't seen her in a minute."

Nonchalantly, I crossed my arms and said, "Cami's Cami. That's all I can say."

She laughed. "You ain't lyin'. Next time you see her, tell her I said hey!"

"Sure." I nodded, pressing my lips. My chest rose and fell thinking about her. I planned to visit Camille's after I met with Leon.

Sensing the attitude in my voice and body language, Koko gave me a puzzled look. Rather than ask, she went back to the counter to wait on another customer.

Several years ago, Cami worked at a salon on Chestnut Street that was right around the corner. We hung out at the Crimson Moon after she'd finish doing my hair or if we needed to talk after work. I chuckled at the thought of the good stories we shared, and now, those days seemed like a lifetime ago considering all that we recently said to each other. What the hell was I thinking when I called her last night? She wanted to talk right then and there, but I wasn't in the mood to do so. I told her I'd speak with her the next day. She wasn't the only person who had something to say and whatever needed to be discussed, I wanted it to be face to face or she could forget it. After hemming and hawing for a few minutes, Cami conceded.

I picked up my cell phone and checked my messages at home. Still no word from Leon. Shaking my head, I decided enough was enough. I would have to cut my losses. He knew I had a fifteen-minute waiting limit. I'd have to deal with him another time.

I paid for my café latte, said goodbye to Koko and picked up a blue flyer from the counter. The headline in bold print caught my attention: ONE NITE! ONE MIC! ONE LOVE! It was an advertisement for a new poetry venue that Gene was hosting three weeks from this Thursday at Lockette's. I nearly tripped walking down 20th Street when I saw Chris's name as one of the featured performers. I'd called him the previous night, but he apparently wasn't there. I knew I should have left a message, but I didn't and I couldn't understand why. I gave Chris every reason not to ever speak with me again. Cursing myself for being stupid, I placed the flyer in my purse as I waited for the next SEPTA bus to arrive at the corner of 20th and Chestnut.

Since Leon no-showed for our meeting, I had an extra half hour to kill. The sky was changing from overcast gray to lavender. I spent most of the time gathering my thoughts while walking through Lord & Taylor's.

Confused couldn't describe the way I felt about seeing Cami again. We both were in the wrong for what we said, but I didn't know where our friendship would go from here. It wouldn't be easy for me to move on with our lives after what she said. I didn't know how she truly felt about me. Did Cami want to remain friends or not? Walking down 13th Street, I'd soon find out.

Hmmm, I could have sworn that was April I saw walking upstairs into the salon. Well, it certainly looked like her with an up-do hairstyle. It was bad enough Cami dragged her into this mess, but why would she involve her tonight? When the front door was buzzed to let me in, my fear was confirmed. It was definitely April. I recognized her voice when she spoke with Cami in a hushed tone. Pausing midway up the stairs, I leaned against the wall and eavesdropped on their conversation.

"I don't think this is a good idea," April whispered. "You and Gigi need to work this out yourselves."

"April, I need you to be here for me. Please don't go," Cami pleaded. "You didn't see the look on her face that night. She was ready to kill me."

"Hell, I would too if you told me off like that. I'm surprised she agreed to speak with you."

"Well, you're here and she's coming upstairs. Wait a minute. She should have been here by now. I don't hear anything. Oh, fuck!"

"Unbelievable," I muttered. Did Cami think we couldn't have a civilized discussion without needing April as a referee? Although, that might have been a good idea since I felt like breaking her neck last week. Shaking my head, I slowly walked up the remaining stairs to the second floor. Part of me was already pissed at Cami for dragging April into our fight and now they were talking about me behind my back. My hostility towards Cami intensified when I saw her sitting behind the receptionist's counter. She stood up from the chair and closed the appointment book, her eyes never leaving the counter.

April attempted to break the awkward tension in the air. "Hey, Gigi."

"Ladies," I returned, never taking my eyes off Cami. "I hope I'm not interrupting anything." I felt bile rising to my throat as I pressed my lips. I heard Cami's words echo inside my head loud and clear: *You know somethin', Gigi, I don't feel any sympathy for you either since there's a strong chance you might not be able to get pregnant 'cause of your fucked up thyroid!*

"Um, no, you didn't," April answered. "I was about to leave to give you two some privacy."

"No," I said, raising my hand. "You don't need to go anywhere. You should stick around, girl. Right, Cami?"

Cami closed her eyes and sucked her teeth. "April, maybe you should give Gigi and I some privacy like you said."

I crossed my arms. "Oh, hell no! Let her stay in case you need a witness since you thought I was ready to kill you last week."

She walked towards me, raised her hand and said, "If you came here for a fight, Gigi, I ain't the one! Okay?"

I gritted my teeth. "If you don't get your hand out of my face, there will be one tonight!"

She put her hands on her hips. "Look, this has been a rough week for me, and – "

"And?" I interrupted, hunching my shoulders.

"And don't go there with me, hussy!"

"And if you don't stop calling me a hussy," I added, pointing my finger. "I won't have a problem being the next person to knock you on your flat ass!"

Before Cami could respond, April interjected herself between us. "Okay, both of you, time out! I didn't come here for this high school shit. Gigi, have a seat and chill! Cami, you go to our office for a few minutes and calm down!"

"Who the fuck do you think you are, April, givin' me orders in my salon?" Cami asked, patting her chest.

"Quit trippin', Tony Montana, because I'm not one of your employees," April returned. "Could you please do what I said and check yourself?"

Cami pointed her finger. "But she started with me first!"

"Does it really matter?" April asked, crossing her arms, tapping her foot and glancing at Cami's office.

Cami pouted her lips as she walked into her office and slammed the door. I shook my head and chuckled.

April pointed at Cami's station. "Have a seat, Gigi."

"I don't feel like sitting down."

"Could you please sit down and relax? You're not helping matters, either."

Mumbling underneath my breath, I sat down in the salon chair as April went behind the counter and turned on the salon's stereo system. I let out a sigh of exasperation when I heard Johnny Gill and Stacy Lattisaw singing *Where Do We Go From Here.* April sat down on the black sofa across from me and made a comment about the song. Pretending to hear her, I nodded.

Cami opened the door, marched out of her office and turned off the radio. "Excuse me, but only employees of Camille's are allowed to touch the stereo! Thank you!" she yelled, enunciating every syllable.

April shook her head. "Would you please knock it off?"

"Also, only customers are allowed to sit at an employee's station when being serviced!" Cami hissed, gazing at me with anger in her eyes.

I stood up. "That's it! I'm out of here!"

April rose to her feet, touched my shoulders and begged me to stay.

"I'm sorry," I said, removing April's hands. "But I don't know why I even bothered to speak with her again."

"Then, why did you call me, Gigi?" Cami asked. "Did you come here to pick shit with me tonight?"

"No, I didn't. However," I said, glancing at April and Cami. "You two were talking about me as I came upstairs."

"We weren't saying anything derogatory about you," Cami added.

"Regardless if you did or didn't, you should know how rude that is."

Closing her eyes, Cami sucked her teeth. April apologized for her behavior.

"I came here tonight because apparently you wanted to talk with me."

"Yeah, I did," Cami replied. "But we could have done that last night."

"We could have," I said, combing my fingers through my hair. "But I wanted to see you face to face."

"Why? After all, ain't you got somethin' to get off your chest?"

"Touché." I nodded.

"Thought so," Cami muttered. We knew each other too well.

She sat down at her workstation and I sat down on the sofa and crossed my leg. April started to excuse herself, but we asked her to have a seat. There was no sense in her leaving now and having to hear two separate versions of our conversation. Reluctantly, she did so.

Resting her forearms on the chair, Cami sighed and closed her eyes. "Last week, I was very shocked and hurt by your comments about my marriage and dilemma with Derrick. I felt you were out of line, Gigi. You're my girl and I couldn't believe you didn't have my back. I was so pissed off that I couldn't wait to get it over with just to spite you."

Raising my eyebrows, I sat back and stared at her.

"However," Cami cleared her throat. "There was one thing I do regret saying and...um...that was the remark about you not being able to have children."

I sucked my teeth and crossed my arms.

"I didn't realize how wrong it was for me to say what I did...um...until they were about to go through with the abortion."

April closed her eyes, clasped her hands and leaned forward. Cami and I watched her stand up and excused herself as she went to the bathroom. Cami furrowed her brow while I pressed my lips. April's behavior confirmed my suspicions she withheld something from our conversation the day before. Maybe she or someone she knew had an abortion. That would explain why she chose my side of the argument.

Cami and I sat in silence for a few seconds until I asked, "So, I guess you really felt remorseful afterwards?"

"I didn't have the abortion, Gigi," she replied, closing her eyes.

I raised my eyebrows inquisitively. "You didn't?"

Cami shook her head. "I couldn't do it, regardless of who's the father."

"What made you change your mind?"

"You did."

"Huh?" I inquired, hunching my shoulders.

"While I was waiting, I remembered everything you shared with me about yours. How you felt before, during and after. And when you stayed with Damon and me for the weekend, I heard you crying in your sleep. When I came to check in on you the next morning, you were lying in bed with that distant, blank look on your face. It was like someone shattered your heart. As hard as I tried, I couldn't get that sight out of my mind."

My body cringed as her words brought back my memories from that experience. I recalled how horrible I felt prior to and during the operation. The anesthesia they gave me couldn't numb my regret or my sadness for what I did. For the next three days, I paid the price from the pain of the cramping, the bleeding and the vomiting. Afterwards, I had to seek counseling for a few months to deal with the emotional repercussions.

"There was no way I could do that to myself or my baby," she said, rubbing her belly. "I know I can't take back what I said, Gigi, but I'm sorry. Y'all know sometimes I don't think before I speak, but I'm…um…not gonna use that as an excuse to justify myself."

"Hmmm," I sighed while leaning forward, placing my elbows on my thighs and resting my chin on my clasped hands. Damn, I couldn't believe Cami didn't have the abortion. What really blew my mind was that she recalled everything from that weekend.

"I don't know what else to say," she added nonchalantly.

I sighed and then sat up straight. "You said plenty. I owe you an apology, too, Cami."

"Say what?"

"I allowed my emotions to overrule my judgment, like I did when I overreacted about your conversation with April."

She nodded. "Okay."

"Maybe I had too much to drink last week. You were right when you said I brought my hang-ups into your situation. And I was also in the wrong for the nasty comment I made."

"Mm hmmm," Cami mumbled, leaning back in her chair.

"At the time, I didn't agree with you, but I never said I didn't have your back. I didn't approve of your affair with Derrick and the way you played Damon dirty, but – "

"Hold up, Gigi, you – " Cami interrupted.

"No, Cami, you hold up," I interjected, leaning forward and raising my hand. "I let you have your say and now it's my turn!"

She sighed and fidgeted in her seat.

"As I was saying, I didn't like what went down between you and Derrick, but I never said I didn't have your back. Did I?"

Cami stared at the ground and ran her fingers through her braids.

"You're the one who reminded me several weeks ago how close we were when I withheld information from you about my thyroid. You said yourself we've known each other for half of our lives. You've always been there for me, so what makes you think I wouldn't do the same for you?"

She cleared her throat. "So, what's your point, Gigi?"

"My point is if we're best friends, how could you say something so vicious?" I asked, hunching my shoulders.

"Like I said," Cami hemmed, twisting her chair. "I was pissed off and sometimes I say things out of my mouth before I think. Shit, Gigi, was your drunk ass thinking clearly when you told me how much I enjoy getting pregnant by my male customers?"

"No, I wasn't."

"Alright then. Don't come at me with that hypocritical bullshit!"

"Regardless if we weren't thinking straight, there are some lines you don't cross. Do you know how difficult it was for me to come here tonight, much less speak to you again?"

"And you think I didn't feel the same way about you after you insulted me?"

"Touché," I said. "But let me ask you this, Cami. Would you have said something like that to your worst enemy?"

"Hell, yeah!" Cami responded, slapping the arms of her chair.

"So, is that what I am to you? "

She rose to her feet. "And what are you getting at, Gigi?"

"Don't answer a question with a question."

"Look, we were both pissed at each other," Cami repeated, waving her hands. "We both said some things we regretted that night. How many times do I have to apologize?" she pleaded.

I nodded, rising to my feet. "Okay." There was no use in pressing the issue any further. What was done was done. "You're right again. I've nothing else to say."

"Can I ask you a question?"

"Go ahead."

"Are we still gonna be friends?"

I closed my eyes. In light of Cami's revelation tonight, this wasn't going to be an easy question to answer. However, it weighed heavily on our minds.

Cami hunched her shoulders and searched my face for a response.

"I don't know," I whispered.

"You don't know? What the fuck kind of answer is that?" Cami asked.

"It's not that simple and you know it."

"It's pretty cut and dry to me."

"You can do us both a favor," I said, crossing my arms. "And knock off that Betty Bad Ass routine. Okay? In case you forgot, I know you well enough to tell when you're putting on a show."

"Is that what you think?" she hissed.

"Yes," I replied, cocking my eyebrow.

She rolled her eyes and twisted her lips.

"You couldn't look me in the eye when I arrived here tonight until I upset you. That's the way you act whenever something troubles you."

She stared at the ground and sighed.

"Outside of your mother and my grandparents, we're the only children who don't have close ties to our immediate families. Hell, we're closer than sisters. I'm Duane's godmother and your sons regard me as their aunt. Earlier tonight, you said this has been a rough week for you. I know you had to deal with Damon and his reaction to everything. I heard the stress and the apprehension in your voice when you were speaking to April alone."

Cami's eyes began dampening.

I pulled a Kleenex from my purse and handed it to her. "Do you honestly believe that we could pretend that night never happened and move on with our lives?"

She shook her head. "I know we can't change the past, Gigi, but...um...I know we can move on even though it may be rough for both of us."

"And believe me, part of me wants to do so." I paused, clearing my throat. "But another part of me has a hard time getting over what you said."

She opened her mouth to speak, but her tears prevented her from responding.

"Someday, Cami, I may find the strength to forgive you, but I will never forget what happened."

She rested her elbows on the receptionist's counter and lowered her head. I stared at her, wiping the tears from my cheeks. "Tell April I said goodnight."

"No problem," she sobbed.

"Take care," I said, walking towards the stairs.

"You, too."

When I got home, there was a message from Leon on my answering machine.

"Hey, Gigi, it's me, Leon. I got caught in traffic and didn't have my cell phone on me. By the time I got there, the hostess told me you had left. Baby, I fucked up big time. I'm so sorry. Please don't hate on a brotha because I was really lookin' forward to seein' you again. When you get a chance, call me so we can talk. Peace."

Rolling my eyes, I cursed a few obscenities under my breath and sat down on my sofa. Assuming Leon was telling me the truth, I wasn't in the mood to deal with him tonight. For that matter, maybe never again. I lit frankincense crystals in my incense holder and turned on my CD player to unwind. I pulled out the flyer from my purse, unfolded it and stared at Chris's name. A wave of guilt splashed my face as Jill Scott's *Can't Explain* shuffled into rotation. Taking another sip of Merlot, I closed my eyes and sighed. The doorbell rang, pulling me out of my funk. Who could have been at my front door at this hour?

Peeking through the Venetian blinds on the side window, I saw April standing on my doorstep. What was she doing here?

"Hey," I greeted after unlocking the door.

"Hey, Gigi. I hope I'm not disturbing you."

I shook my head. "Come in. Have a seat."

April walked in and sat down on my sofa. "Your living room looks lovely."

"Thanks," I replied, locking the door. "Can I get you anything?"

She shook her head. "I'm sorry for coming over unannounced. I don't usually do that, but I wanted to talk with you, if you don't mind?"

I sat down and crossed my leg. "Sure."

"I dropped Cami off a few minutes ago. She told me what happened."

I leaned back against the arm of my sofa.

"Are you okay?" she asked.

I released a sigh. "Well, I guess I will be." I took another sip of my drink. "How's she doing?"

"She took it harder than she let on."

I nodded, staring into space. "So did I."

"I'm sorry things had to end that way."

I ran my fingers through my hair. "No need to apologize."

April nodded. She clasped her hands and pressed her lips in a nervous manner.

"Are you okay?"

She nodded. "I'm dandy."

I poured myself another drink. "I know you didn't come over here to just ask me about my well-being or to talk about Cami?"

"It's nothing, Gigi," she dismissed, waving her hand.

I took another sip. "No, it's something. What's up?"

"When Cami called and told me what happened last week, I didn't know about your problems with your thyroid."

"There are some things about me that are private, you know?"

"I understand," she replied. "Are you going to be okay?"

"I'll be fine."

She smiled. "That's good to know. Um, I also didn't know you had an abortion."

"Well, that's something else I don't like to talk about too much," I responded.

She cracked a half smile and lowered her head. "Most women don't. It must have been painful for you."

"At the time, it was, but it's something I dealt with through counseling and prayer."

She nodded and stared at the coffee table.

I touched her forearm. "When did you have yours?"

"Last winter," she mumbled. She raised her head and stared into my eyes. "You knew?"

"I wasn't sure, but I didn't want to pry."

She nodded and crossed her arms.

"Did you ever tell Cami?"

"Not until tonight. Two weeks from tomorrow would have been the baby's delivery date. Sometimes I ask myself how my life would be different today if I had kept my baby."

I nodded. "I asked myself the exact same thing too, sweetie." I cleared my throat. "Did you ever have counseling?"

"A little bit. I thought about it again, but I'm not too crazy about therapists."

I cocked my eyebrow. "How come?"

"If you divide the word therapist, what do you get?"

"The rapist." I chuckled. "That's a good one."

"Yeah, it is. I'm not going to take up too much of your time, Gigi," she said, rising to her feet. "Thanks for talking with me."

"No problem, April," I said, standing up. "If you decide to seek counseling, please let me know. I don't mind being there, if you need a friend."

"You would?"

I smiled warmly. "Sure."

Before she left for the evening, I hugged April and thanked her for coming over. I was grateful for her friendship throughout this mess. She asked me to call her if I needed to talk, and I promised her I'd do so.

No matter how many times I told myself time will heal all wounds, it wouldn't be easy for me to deal with the loss of Cami's friendship. We were more than best friends; we were family. And I would miss her dearly.

Chapter Twenty-Three
Chris

The open mic was underway in the Mahogany Room by the time I arrived at Lockette's. As the host, Gene kept the show flowing smoothly. I had mixed emotions about being there. Two days after I visited him, Dad passed away from complications that arose while recovering from his bypass surgery. His death caught everybody off guard. If I knew my visit would have been the last time we'd ever see and speak to each other, maybe I would have patched things up between us. Part of me felt guilty I hadn't done so. Though I was excited about the show, I couldn't shake that feeling.

I rested my backpack against the bar, sat down on an empty stool and ordered a Heineken. It was almost eight thirty and the lounge was nearly standing room only. From the scented candles to the venue's name, One Love, I was digging the vibe! It brought back memories from the Buttamilk days: artists coming together in respect, unity and cooperation. I didn't expect the premiere show turnout to be so strong. Considering the short time that was spent finding the location and promoting the event, Gene did one hell of a job getting the word out.

After introducing the next poet, Gene walked off stage and came over to the bar.

"Yo, Cool C, wassup, man?" he asked, giving me some dap. "I'm glad you came out tonight."

"Thanks, brah," I replied.

He put his hand on my shoulder. "I'm sorry to hear about your dad. How are you doin'?"

I sighed. "I'll be alright."

"Look, man, if you feel like sittin' back tonight to watch, it's aight.

I shook my head. "Just let me know when it's show time."

He nodded. "Okay. In a few minutes, I'm gonna bring you up and then The Twin Poets."

I nodded and scanned the room for Twin Poets.

The Twins were a set of identical brothers with a unique look and socially conscious words. They always delivered inspiring, breathtaking performances. What really impressed me about them was their onstage synergy and flow. They moved in perfect harmony and their brotherly love was quite evident onstage through their mannerisms.

I spotted them sitting at a table near the stage. Watching them sitting back and nibbling away on chew sticks, I thought about my own brother.

"You okay, Cool C?" Gene inquired.

"Mm hmmm," I answered, but my thoughts were somewhere else.

Sam had become sullen and withdrawn since Dad's death. I was surprised he didn't lose it at the funeral like Evelyn did that afternoon. He barely said a word or shed a tear. Afterwards, I'd tried to reach out to him at home or work, but he never returned any of my calls. Just last night, I left a message inviting him to the show. I didn't expect him to show up, but I was concerned about his well-being and just wanted to hear from him.

As Gene made his way back to the stage, I took another sip of beer and pulled the stool a few inches from the bar. Just when I closed my eyes and began to silently recite my lines in preparation for the stage, I felt two fingers tap my left shoulder. I was pleasantly surprised to find it was April standing behind me wearing a big ole smile.

I smiled back and stood up to hug her. "Hey, you." April looked much more relaxed since the last time I had seen her. I was digging her new hairstyle.

"Hey yourself, Chris," she replied. "It's good to see you."

"You, too. What's been goin' on?" I asked, offering her my seat.

"Besides hunting for a job, not too much." April sighed, sitting down. She waved to get the bartender's attention and ordered an apple martini.

"I hear you." I took a drink of my Heineken. "So, what brings you out?"

"Well, I heard you were going to be here and I wanted to see you again," she answered, paying for her drink.

I smiled. "I appreciate that."

April glanced at her cell phone. "Gigi was supposed to meet me here at eight thirty, but she's running late."

I coughed, nearly choking on my beer. "No shit?"

"Mm hmmm," she murmured.

I chuckled, stroking my goatee. I couldn't believe Gigi was coming to Lockette's. Damn, I had forgotten our second date, inclusive of the Leon run-in, had been here. That's when things between us took a turn for the worse.

"What's up?" April inquired.

I shook my head. "It's nothing."

"You sure?"

"Yeah," I lied. "Just getting myself ready."

Tilting her head, April crossed her arms and nodded. I wasn't certain if she believed me, but it was best to keep my thoughts to myself. Besides, I didn't know if Gigi had shared with April everything that happened between us.

Excusing myself, I went to the men's room and handled my business. I needed a minute to gather my thoughts. I remembered how Gigi played me like a chump several weeks ago when I tried to speak with her. It was also the same day Dad had his heart attack. I saw her phone number on my Caller ID a few days later, but she didn't leave a message. I thought about calling her, but I didn't. After Gene told me he saw her give Leon her phone number, it wasn't worth it. Well, that's what my mind kept saying, but my heart had a different story. Yeah, I wanted to see Gigi again, but I didn't know what I'd say to her. Maybe she felt the same way, too. If she did, girlfriend definitely had some explaining to do for her behavior. My cell phone rang as I finished drying my hands.

"Hello?"

"Wassup, Chris?" Sam asked.

"Hey!" I shouted. "Wassup with you?"

"Not much," he replied. The reception was poor and I could barely hear his voice.

"Hold on for a second," I said, leaving the bathroom. "Hello?"

"I'm here."

"That's better. So, how you've been?"

"I'm hangin' in there." His voice sounded so empty. "How about you?"

"The same," I answered, walking towards the front door.

"Yeah," Sam mumbled.

I stood in the foyer. "So…um…how's your mom?"

"Mom's okay. She's been kinda out of it, ya know?"

"Hmmm," I mumbled, shrugging my shoulders.

"Everybody's helpin' her out the best they can." Sam paused. "It…um…hasn't been easy for us, I mean, for her to adjust now that Dad's gone."

Leaning against the wall, I closed my eyes and sighed.

"Hello, Chris?"

I moved out of the way for a couple coming inside. "I'm here, brah. I was thinkin' about what you said."

"Yeah?"

"Yeah. This hasn't been easy for any of us."

"True that. Um, I appreciate you checkin' up on me and all, Chris. Sorry I'm just now gettin' back to you."

"It's cool," I said, walking across the bar and towards the lounge.

"I appreciate the invite for your show, but…um…I'm not up to it."

I glanced inside the lounge. "Well, it's only the first show. There'll be others."

"Mm hmmm."

"Hold on again," I said, sticking my head inside the lounge. Gene was onstage searching the crowd for me. I stood in the doorway and waved to get his attention. I held my hand in the air asking for five minutes. He nodded his head and introduced another poet. "Sorry about that."

"Look, I'ma let you go, but…um…I'll get back to you."

"Sam?"

"Yeah?"

I closed my eyes and sighed. "Um, you know if you…um…need or want to talk, I'm here for you, man."

I stood there for a minute waiting for his response. Prior to Dad's death, I promised myself I would make an attempt to build a better and stronger relationship with Sam. I didn't want to harbor any bitterness towards him the way Dad had done with his brothers and sisters.

"Yeah, that's cool."

"Okay," I murmured. "Have a good one."

"Later," my brother said, hanging up the phone.

I felt a little hurt by Sam's nonchalant response, but given our history and the times he reached out to me urging me to make amends with Dad – to no avail, I couldn't blame him for feeling that way. Putting my phone away, I walked back into the lounge to rejoin April. She was nodding her head in agreement while listening to the poet onstage. Bending over to open my backpack, I pulled out my notebook, turned my back towards the stage and flipped through the pages. *Get it together, Chris,* I kept telling myself, *get it together.* I was too wrapped up in conflicting thoughts about Sam and Gigi when someone accidentally bumped into me, making their way across the aisle.

"Yo," I exclaimed, looking up from my notebook.

April and a few patrons turned toward us when they heard my voice.

The guy turned around and apologized. "My bad, homie."

"Man, watch where you're – " I paused, getting a good look at the clumsy fool who had bumped into me. Leon.

He sighed and shook his head in total surprise and disgust. We kept staring at each other until Leon cleared his throat and extended his hand. "Wassup?"

"Nothin'," I replied, shaking his hand. His grip felt tighter than the first time we met. Neither of us said a word as we sized up each other from head to toe.

April touched my shoulder. "You okay, Chris?"

"Cool," I said, setting my notebook on the bar.

April made her way to intercede between us, but I waved her off. She tilted her head, stood on her toes and motioned her hand towards someone standing outside the lounge. I broke eye contact with Leon and my heart sank when I saw Gigi standing frozen in her tracks by the entrance, her mouth wide open and shock in her eyes. She looked so sexy wearing a short black dress with a matching scarf that concealed her hair. Her chest rose and fell quickly, and I wondered what she was thinking.

Leon turned around and his eyes bulged when he saw her. He glanced back and forth between the two of us, wondering what to make of this situation. Hell, so was I.

"What's goin' on?" April asked, standing there in total confusion.

The sound of Gene's voice introducing me and several claps from the audience pulled me out of my daze. Reluctantly, I picked up my notebook and made my way to the stage. Although I did my best to get myself together, I couldn't take my eyes off Gigi. Neither could Leon as he stood there like a horny fool. Gigi inhaled deeply, cracked a half smile and waved at me. Leon glared at me and then turned his head towards Gigi. Next, he walked towards her. I started reciting my first poem and watched them exchange a few words before I saw her roll her eyes and head towards the front door with Leon in hot pursuit. Damn, what was up with that shit? Maybe I was wrong about Gigi having unresolved issues with homeboy after all.

Chapter Twenty-Four

Regina

Searching for a place to park, I saw Chris standing towards the front of the line to enter Lockette's. It had almost been a month since I last saw him. Damn! He looked good in that pink Polo shirt and denim jeans. Making a left turn onto Walnut Street and another onto 12th Street, I found an empty parking space and hurried out of the car. I wanted to talk with Chris, but I wasn't sure how that would go. So much had transpired between us.

As I locked my car, it occurred to me that Leon might be there also. He had a knack for showing up at the most inopportune times, like the time we ran into each other during my second date with Chris. That had been a debacle. And as if that hadn't been enough, there was the subsequent date with Leon that turned into yet another problem. After he'd stood me up at the Crimson Moon, I'd left him a message explaining how unacceptable his behavior had been. Of course, I didn't hear anything from him until last week when he left a message for me at work rambling about Kiya going into premature labor, someone named Malik coming back into the picture and he needed me now more than ever. Needless to say, I didn't and wasn't going to return his call.

The line into Lockette's snaked around the front of the building. I took my place in the rear and quietly resolved myself to set thoughts of Leon aside. I also decided to shake off my anxiety about my upcoming operation. It was going to take place two weeks from tomorrow. April, who I had grown closer to in the last month, promised to stay with me during my recovery. I shared my feelings for Chris with her and everything that had happened between us. She encouraged me to call him to set things right, but I didn't heed her advice. I wanted to have a face to face conversation with him. I owed Chris that much. She promised to accompany me to the show, but I called her a few hours before we were scheduled to meet and told her to go without me. I was running painfully late.

Butterflies had been swarming inside my stomach all day, making it almost impossible to do anything decent with my hair. Once I finally got it to cooperate, thanks to the scarf on my head, I found myself tossing aside every outfit I tried on. Nothing seemed quite right or quite enough or too much. I needed to look just right. After several hours, I'd finally managed to achieve the look I needed.

I stood outside the entrance to the Mahogany Room and glanced around the crowded room. April was sitting at the bar and engrossed by the show. Chris was standing beside her, looking through his notebook. It appeared he was getting ready to perform soon. I was glad I hadn't missed his performance. I spotted Gene near the stage holding some papers in his hands. From the dark corner to the right, I saw someone walking past him and around the bar. Unfortunately, it was Leon! He wasn't paying attention to where he was going when he bumped into Chris, causing the two to stare each other down. Lord, please don't let them go at it.

April attempted to intervene, but Chris dismissed her. Upon seeing me, she waved her hand. Chris's eyes widened when he noticed me. Leon turned around and began gawking at Chris and myself. I heard April ask Chris, "What's goin' on?" However, before Chris could answer, Gene called him onstage. Sighing aloud, Chris made his way to the stage, but kept looking at me. I smiled gingerly and waved to him. The whole time, I could see Leon studying the both of us. Then, mumbling something under his breath, he came to me. I could tell he was angry.

"Wassup, Gigi?" he asked.

I sucked my teeth. "Hello."

"How you been, girl?"

"Fine."

"How come you ain't returned my phone calls?"

"You and I have nothing to say to each other. Excuse me," I said, walking around him.

Leon cut in front of me and outstretched his arms. "Hold up! What's with the attitude? I think we need to talk, babe."

I crossed my arms. "I don't think so."

He pointed at Chris. "What the fuck is goin' on with you and that dude?"

"I don't think that's any of your business."

"Chill, babe," he replied, reaching out to touch me.

I rolled my eyes. "Don't tell me to chill."

"Why you trippin'?"

A small crowd was starting to gather around us. I was already pissed off that I was missing Chris's performance.

I sighed. "Let's finish this conversation outside."

I marched out the front door with Leon walking two steps behind me. What the hell was he doing here tonight? I should have known our paths would eventually cross. He wasn't the type to take no for an answer.

Standing near the front door, I asked, "What do you want from me, Leon?"

"I'm sorry about being out of touch these past few weeks, Gigi. Things have been hectic for me with the baby's birth and dealing with Kiya's moody ass."

"Congratulations," I returned.

"Well, you might want to hold off on the celebration just yet."

I cocked my eyebrow. "Why do you say that?"

"I'm not so sure I'm the daddy."

"Oh, really," I teased.

"Yep! All of a sudden, this fuckin' Malik dude started coming around," he complained, hunching his shoulders. "Kiya told me they dated a while ago and they ran into each other again last month. I know she told the brotha all our business. He's been hangin' around, helpin' her out and talkin' shit about how much he cares for Kiya and how he'll be there to support her and the baby. Did you know she had the fuckin' nerve to tell me she ain't ever got over him?"

I chuckled. *Well, Leon,* I thought, *that's karma for you.*

"For all I know, they coulda been messin' around while we were dating. How do I know he ain't the daddy? She insisted that ain't the case and I should quit trippin' and face up to my responsibilities. That's why I need you, Gigi," he added, rubbing my arm.

I cleared my throat. "Do you mind?" I asked.

He withdrew his arm, shook his head and finished pleading his case. "I can't deal with all this bullshit alone. You were good to me, babe, and I didn't realize that until it was too late."

"Mm hmmm," I murmured.

"I'm man enough to admit my mistakes."

"So, I'm supposed to welcome you back with open arms and forgive you?"

"I know you got a right to be angry at me and all, but shit, girl, you and I had something special."

"What about Kiya and your child?"

"Fuck Kiya! Until I see the results of a paternity test, I ain't claimin' shit. You know how those bitches be runnin' their baby daddy games on us brothas."

I sucked my teeth and took two steps backward. "Okay, Leon, you just went too far."

He hunched his shoulders. "Wassup?"

"Think about what you just said and to whom you've been talking to."

He ran his fingers through his cornrows. "Shit. I'm sorry."

"Damn right, you're sorry as hell. I may not like Kiya personally, but she's not a bitch. That's the most degrading thing you can say about a woman. And she's a lot smarter than you give her credit for. Regardless of whether you want to believe her, she's the mother of your child."

"We don't know that yet."

"No, I think you do, so don't go using Malik or a paternity test to avoid your responsibilities."

Leon shrugged his shoulders and murmured, "Here you go."

"You got that right. Speaking of responsibilities, I can't believe you had the audacity to say half the things you did to me. In case you forgot, you and I went down this road. Do you remember what you said when I told you I was pregnant?"

"Gigi, that was a long time ago."

"Do you remember what you said, Leon?" I asked, raising my voice.

He stared at the sidewalk and scratched the back of his neck. "Yeah, I remember."

"What did you say?" I asked calmly.

He mumbled those words that ripped into my heart six years ago. "How do I know it's mine?"

I nodded. "Mm hmmm. Do you know how hurtful that was for me to hear that from your lips?"

"I guess it…um…sounds pretty fucked up."

"Fucked up doesn't begin to describe the way you made me feel!"

"Well, I was a different person back then."

I laughed. "Is that what you think? From where I'm standing, you're still the same self-centered, irresponsible jackass that I knew. You don't give a damn about anybody except yourself."

He rolled his eyes. "If I didn't give a damn about you, Gigi, why the fuck am I here? Hell, why the fuck are you here?"

"The reason why I'm here is to let you know, Leon, that it's over between us. Don't try to play me for a fool thinking you care about me. You didn't give a damn about me then or now. Just like you didn't give a damn about the fate of our child."

He sucked his teeth and sighed. "Don't you think you need to stop being bitter and let that shit go?"

"No, you didn't," I murmured, inhaling a deep breath. "Any bitterness I had towards you or myself I resolved a long time ago. Okay? I made my mistakes, accepted them for what they were and moved on with my life. Don't you think it's about time you did the same and grow the hell up?"

"You know somethin', Gigi – " he gritted his teeth while glaring at me.

Before he could finish, the front door of the restaurant opened and a couple excused themselves for walking between us.

I crossed my arms, leaned forward and maintained eye contact. "Yes?" I asked.

If Leon thought his performance was supposed to intimidate me or win a Best Acting Academy Award, he had another thing coming. He took a few deliberately slow steps back, spat on the sidewalk and said, "Fuck you, bitch!"

"No, Leon, fuck you!" I snapped.

Before I returned inside, I watched that trifling Negro walk away. I should have felt hurt by Leon's comment, but I wasn't. He had shown his true colors before in the past and I knew what to expect. If anything, I felt somewhat vindicated since he was no longer an issue in my life. I vowed not to let that argument ruin the rest of my evening.

Chris was in the middle of reciting a poem when I returned to the lounge. He was on fire with his delivery and the audience was in the palm of his hand. I gently tapped April on her shoulder. She turned around and hugged me.

"Are you okay?"

I nodded.

"No, you're not," she replied, offering me her seat. "Who was the brotha with the cornrows?"

I sat down and rolled my eyes. "Long story."

April nodded and massaged my shoulder. The audience clapped as Chris finished his poem. He briefly glanced over towards us, scanned the room and spoke into the mic.

"Thank you so much. Um, I wasn't sure if I was going to be here tonight because this has been a difficult time for me and my family."

I looked at April and raised my eyebrows. She shook her head and hunched her shoulders.

"Several weeks ago," Chris continued. "My father passed away."

I put my hand to my lips. *Oh, Chris,* I thought, *I'm so sorry.*

A few individuals sighed and Chris waited until the crowd grew silent before he continued speaking.

"We didn't have the best relationship as I grew older, and for a long while, um... we weren't on speaking terms. I saw him a few days before he died for the first time in almost fourteen years. There were some things I did and didn't have the chance to say to him."

I pressed my lips and placed my hands on my lap.

"Someone once told me," he said, staring at me, "It's never too late to tell someone you love them, and you shouldn't wait until tragedy strikes."

As I closed my eyes and sighed, Chris opened his notebook and recited a poem dedicated to his father. My heart felt the pain, the forgiveness, the love and the regret in Chris's voice. Several people, including April, were crying. When he finished, he thanked the audience and made his way offstage.

April sighed. "That was beautiful."

I reached into my purse and handed her a Kleenex. "Yes, it was."

Gene hugged Chris and called him back onstage, thanking Chris for coming out tonight and finding the strength to read that piece. He also announced they were taking a break and afterwards, would come back with the Twin Poets.

Several people got up from their seats and left the lounge. Chris started to make his way towards us, but a female sitting near the stage grabbed his forearm. He turned around and she pulled him to the side. She stood about five feet tall and her skin complexion was the same as mine. I watched her grab Chris's hands and they started talking. I rose to my feet and cleared my throat when they embraced.

"Excuse me, April, but I'll be right back."

"Where are you going?" she asked, raising her eyebrows.

"To the bathroom," I replied, leaving the bar.

I turned around and saw April watch me walk inside the ladies' room. Two patrons were talking about Chris's performance and checking themselves over. I inhaled deeply when I overheard the heavyset one wearing a halter top comment about Chris being cute. Her pudgy, diminutive girlfriend with cornrows and facial hair across her chin mentioned she saw him come here alone. The heavy one said she was going to get his phone number before they left the room. The door opened and the person who cornered Chris went into an empty stall. I waited until she was finished to get another look at her. She had a cute face with pretty slanted eyes that were accentuated by her light brown braids. She reminded me of a young Alice Walker. While washing her hands, she turned towards me and said hello. I cracked a half smile and said hi before she went about her business. Staring into the mirror, I felt ashamed of my behavior. I had no right to act jealous. How could I be so selfish about my feelings when Chris recently lost his father?

I went to rejoin April and Chris, but I didn't see either of them in the lounge. Instead, someone else was sitting in April's seat. Where the hell did they go? Suddenly, my cell phone began vibrating inside my purse. Cocking my eyebrow, I read a text message from April.

Gigi,

Hate to run but you know two's company...Please talk to Chris. Okay?

Love ya,

April

I laughed. "Ooh, I'll get you, April," I vowed. I stuck around and waited for Gene to start the second half of the show. The Twins recited two poems and whipped the crowd into a hysterical frenzy with their poignant words. I desperately wanted to get into their performance, but my heart wasn't there. I kept praying Chris would come back. He didn't. However, I saw all of his admirers in attendance.

I decided to head home and chalk up my losses. I wasn't ten steps away from Lockette's when I heard someone say, "Hey, you." Turning around, I saw Chris standing behind me with his backpack strung over his broad shoulders.

I rubbed my arms. "Hey," I responded, walking towards him.

Chris stepped closer. "I hope you weren't leaving just yet."

"Um, no, I wasn't. I was...um...getting ready to...um – " I paused, snapping my fingers and trying to think of an excuse.

"Getting ready to?" he inquired.

"Um, to go put some change in the parking meter," I lied.

"Oh," he nodded. "Isn't there free parking after a certain hour?"

"Well, most meters don't need change, but you never know."

Chris glanced at his watch. "I think you're pretty safe. It's almost nine thirty."

"Maybe you're right. But anyway, it's getting late. I think I should call it a night."

"Okay. Um, if you don't mind, I'd like to walk you to your car. Just to make sure you get there safe."

I pressed my index finger against my chin. "Well, if you'd like to?"

"I don't mind."

I nodded. "Okay." *Thank you, Lord,* I thought.

As we walked towards Walnut Street, Chris cleared his throat and asked, "So, how've you been?"

"Fine. How about you, Kid?"

He shrugged his shoulders. "I'm cool."

"Um, I'm sorry to hear about your father," I offered.

He nodded. "His heart attack was so sudden." Chris paused, staring across the street. "I thought...um...he would pull through and make a full recovery from surgery. I didn't expect him to have complications. Nobody did."

"Mmmm," I murmured. "How's your family?" I asked.

"They're coping. I'm concerned about my brother, Sam, though. He and Dad were real close."

I nodded. "That's very admirable of you."

"Mm hmmm."

"That took a lot of strength for you to recite that poem," I added.

Chris cracked a half smile.

"I'm sorry I missed your performance," I continued. "But I had to address a personal matter tonight."

He nodded. As we made our way around 12th Street, Chris asked, "How's your thyroid?"

I rubbed my forearms. "In a few weeks, I'll be having surgery."

"Oh. Are you okay?"

I hunched my shoulders. "I'll be fine. God willing, of course."

"Amen to that."

I smiled, appreciating his sentiment and concern for my well-being.

Chris clasped his hands when we arrived at my car. "Here we are," he announced.

I smiled. "Thanks for the escort and the conversation." I grazed his forearm. "Um, Chris, there's something I wanted to talk to you about."

He stroked his goatee. "Yes?"

I coughed. "A few weeks ago, I was very cold and insensitive to you the last time we saw each other. I wanted to apologize for my behavior. It was wrong of me to act the way I did when you were only trying to reach out to me."

He put his arms behind his back.

"For the past month, I've been dealing with some things that I did share with you and some that I didn't. Everything came to a head tonight when I confronted Leon."

Chris bit on his bottom lip and nodded.

"I wished I had the strength and the common sense to share with you earlier what I was thinking and feeling. When you came over to my house, I meant everything I said about being attracted to you and wanting to get to know you. I don't know what you think of me, Chris, but I really do care for you. I would understand if you didn't feel the same."

With his eyes closed and remaining silent, Chris stood there taking in my words.

"I'm sorry if this is too much for you right now. I know you have other things on your mind." I wanted to be straightforward and honest.

He opened his eyes, rubbed his head and said dryly, "Hey, it's cool, Gigi."

I inhaled deeply and closed my eyes. *Hey, it's cool, Gigi,* I repeated to myself. Not the answer I expected, but he had every right to feel reluctant to share his feelings.

Chris glanced at his watch. "Um, I hate to be a party pooper, but it's getting late."

I pulled my keys from my purse and dropped my head. "Yeah, it is." I opened my door. "Where are you parked? Do you need a lift?"

"I'll be alright."

I cocked my eyebrow. "Don't be crazy."

"Well," he said, walking around to the passenger side. "If you insist."

Although Chris was parked two blocks away from my car, the drive felt like an eternity. Neither one of us said a word. His silence was killing me. It didn't help matters either that Aaliyah's *I Care For You* was playing on WRNB. I imagined the cute female at Lockette's giving Chris a full body massage and serenading him with her soft voice. Sucking my teeth, I told myself to stop being foolish.

"Everything okay?"

"Yeah," I said, parking my car and turning on my blinkers.

He raised his eyebrows. "Okay. Thanks a lot, Gigi, for sharing with me."

"No problem," I reached out, touching his forearm. "Thanks for listening."

He stared at my hand and then at my face. I curled my bottom lip and did my best not to blush.

"Take care of yourself," he said, climbing out of my Galant.

I sighed. "You, too."

Throwing his backpack over his shoulder, Chris walked to his car and activated his keyless remote. Staring into space, I shouldn't have felt disappointed, but I did. I was so deep into my thoughts I didn't notice him tap on my window.

I rolled down my window. "Yes?"

He tapped his fingers on my roof. "Can I ask you a favor?"

I nodded.

"Can you give me a call after you get settled in so I know you got home safely?"

I laughed. "Sure."

"Promise?" he asked, tilting his head.

I raised my hand. "I promise."

He smiled. "Cool."

Before he walked away, I saw a glow in his eyes. I had only seen that look once before and the last time I did, there was something on his mind. I waited for him to start his car before I took off for I-95.

Chapter Twenty-Five
Chris

By the time I came home and collapsed on my living room sofa after shooting hoops, my muscles were aching. I felt like knocking off a Heineken or two to ease the pain. After patting the spare tire that was developing around my waist, I nixed that idea. I couldn't believe I was slacking off and getting out of shape. I hadn't done pretty much anything since losing my job. I've spent most of the time lounging around my apartment, watching summer reruns and writing sporadically. With the money I saved and was receiving from unemployment, I could get by until the end of the year without working, and that was fine by me.

Yesterday, Sam caught me by surprise when he called me around noon. I didn't expect to hear from him so soon, but he appreciated my offer to talk. We chatted briefly about Dad and our relationship with one another. Although our conversation was short, I suggested we get together on Saturday to talk some more and to run some ball. He agreed, and now, I was paying the price for opening my big ass mouth. The telephone rang, interrupting my thoughts.

"Hello?"

"So, how did it feel to get your ass smoked by your baby brother?" Sam asked.

"Ha! Ha! Very funny."

He laughed. "I know it's been a minute, but I can't remember the last time I put a whippin' on you like I did today."

I nodded. "Go 'head and keep talkin' shit. Give me a few weeks and we'll see who's gonna get their ass spanked."

"Yeah, right," Sam gloated. "Anyway, I wanted to check up on you to make sure you're okay."

"I'm cool. Matter of fact," I paused, rubbing my hamstrings and checking the time on my watch. "I need to get movin' anyway before I lose track of time."

"Aight. I'll talk to you later."

"Peace."

Before hanging up the phone, Sam called my name. "Chris?"

"Yeah?"

"Thanks, man, for reaching out and all."

"Mm hmmm. Peace," I said, hanging up the phone.

I rose to my feet gingerly so I could take a shower and a quick nap. As I laid across my bed, I kept thinking about Gigi. Two days ago, we ran into each other at the premiere show for One Love. She looked well, and in spite of the appearance of her ex, I was glad we talked afterwards. Later that night, she called me to let me know she made it home safe and sound. She also invited me over to her place tonight for dinner. At first, I thought it wasn't a good idea. I suspected Gigi wanted to know how I felt about her. That was my impression from Thursday night when she apologized for her actions and revealed her feelings for me.

Yeah, I forgave her and I still cared for her, but I had a few concerns, especially when it came to Leon. Ever since she told me their history, I've felt like she was withholding something from me. I didn't notice it before, but it had been so obvious in her body language and voice whenever she saw Leon. Also, was homeboy completely out of the picture? If she wanted me to come clean with my feelings, she also had some confessing to do.

"Hi, Kid," Gigi said, opening her front door.

"Hey, you," I returned, walking inside the living room.

She looked fantastic tonight from the peach blouse that fit her body snuggly to the soft curls in her medium-length hair that were accentuated by golden highlights.

"How are you this evening, Sir?"

"I'm cool." The aroma of grilled chicken smacked me in the face. "Mmmmm," I murmured. "Something smells good."

She smiled. "Thanks. Would you care for something to drink?"

I shook my head. "I'm fine."

"Make yourself at home," Gigi suggested as she went to the kitchen.

I sat down on the living room sofa and surveyed the room. A vase of tulips was displayed at the center of the coffee table with two long single candles burning at the opposite ends. The scent of frankincense danced from the small incense holder and into the air of the dimly lit room.

She returned to the living room with a glass of Merlot and sat beside me. "Dinner will be in a few minutes. So, how was your day?"

I rubbed my hamstring. "Not too bad. My legs are a little tender after running ball with my brother earlier this afternoon."

"How's Sam doing?"

I nodded. "He's alright. In fact, he's much better than I originally thought."

Gigi nodded and sipped her wine.

"So, how've you been?" I asked.

"Copasetic," she answered, teasing a strand of her hair.

"I see somebody's letting her hair grow out again."

She smiled. "A little bit. I'm experimenting with a new look."

"It looks nice. Cami did a wonderful job."

Gigi raised her eyebrows and glanced at the floor.

"How's she doing?" I asked.

"Who?" Gigi replied.

"Cami," I said.

She inhaled deeply. "I haven't spoken to her in a minute. We had a disagreement not too long ago."

"Is everything okay?"

"Dandy," she replied nonchalantly.

I stroked my goatee. "Are you sure?"

"Positive. Why do you ask?"

"Well, it's just that – never mind."

"It's just what?" she asked, crossing her legs.

I waved my hand. "It's nothing."

"No, it's something," she added. "Please don't play with me like that, Chris? If there's something you want to ask, feel free."

"Well, I didn't want to pry, but it sounds like something's bothering you."

"What gave you that impression?"

"The way you hesitated when you spoke."

"Hmmm," she murmured, sipping her drink.

I sighed. "I'm sorry."

"For what?"

"For upsetting you."

"You didn't upset me."

"If I had known, I wouldn't have said anything."

She touched my hand. "But you didn't know, so how could you? It's alright." She clasped her hands and closed her eyes. "To make a long story short, Cami and I had a nasty argument and some things were said we both regretted. Afterwards," she paused and stared across the living room. "We had a falling out."

"Maybe it's something that can work itself out in the long run, you know?"

"I don't think so," Gigi responded, rolling her eyes.

Whoa, I thought, *what the hell was that all about?* Gigi told me they were best friends and I couldn't imagine one disagreement could provoke dissention between them. Whatever went down must have been real deep. I ran my finger along the collar of my shirt and said, "Um, maybe I could use a drink after all."

Gigi stood up and went to the kitchen. I could hear her fidgeting with her cabinets before she rejoined me. "Here you go," she said, handing me my glass.

"Thanks," I replied, sipping my drink.

She sat down and reclined against the sofa. Crossing her arms, she curled her bottom lip and stared at me.

I sat my drink on the coffee table. "So…um…is dinner ready?"

"It's finished. I want to let things cool down a little before we eat."

"Okay."

She refilled her glass. "Can I ask you a question?"

I shrugged my shoulders. "Sure."

"Are you okay?" she asked.

"Yeah."

"Well, you don't look it," she commented, taking another sip.

"What makes you say that?"

"I can see it in your brow. You also had that same look the other night at Lockette's."

"Oh," I said nonchalantly.

"Have I said or did something to upset you?"

I shook my head. "I'm fine."

"If you weren't fine, Chris, would you tell me you were just to pacify me?"

Leaning back against the arm of the sofa, I crossed my arms and asked, "Wassup with the third degree?"

She rested her hands on her lap. "You didn't answer my question."

I sighed. "Look, Gigi, I didn't mean to upset you."

"You didn't, so there's no need to apologize again."

"If I weren't feeling fine, I wouldn't say so just to pacify you. Okay?"

"So, why are you acting defensive?"

"I'm acting defensive?" I asked, touching my chest.

"Yes, you are," she answered.

"No, I'm not."

"Yes, you are," she repeated.

"If that's the case," I paused, inhaling deeply. "Don't I have every right to feel defensive considering the way you dissed me?"

"Are you angry with me, Chris?" she asked, shrugging her shoulders.

"No, I'm not," I half-lied.

"So, what's your problem?"

"What the hell is yours?"

Gigi crossed her arms and snapped, "Excuse me, but who do you think you're talking to? Let's get one thing straight, don't you ever take that tone of voice with me in my house again!"

"Sorry," I mumbled.

"It's obvious there's something bothering you and I want to get to the root of the matter."

I rolled my eyes and bit my bottom lip.

"Why can't you be honest with me?"

"Because you're not being honest with me," I blurted.

She widened her eyes. "And what's that supposed to imply?"

"What's goin' on with you and Leon?"

Gigi cocked her eyebrow. "Why are you bringing up his name?"

"You told me how much you really cared about me, but you can't be straightforward with me about him."

"Absolutely nothing is going on between Leon and me."

"Yeah, right! It seems too coincidental that you keep runnin' into him accidentally at poetry venues and having conversations."

She nodded. "So, Gene told you about my encounter at the 2nd Street Soul Café?"

Shit. I didn't mean to let that slip out, but it was too late.

"And now you suspect there's something going on between us since Leon and I crossed paths again?"

I fidgeted in my seat and cleared my throat.

Gigi reclined against the sofa and smiled. "Interesting."

"What's so interesting?"

"You're jealous," she responded, taking another sip.

I sighed. "You're crazy."

"I'm sorry, honey, but you're the one who needs some couch time."

"You've got a lot of nerve telling somebody they need couch time."

Gigi tilted her head and chuckled. "Oh, really?"

"Yeah," I replied angrily. "In case you forgot, weren't you the one who went bananas several weeks ago and gave me the cold shoulder when I tried to reach out to you?"

She sucked her teeth and nodded.

"And another thing, Gigi, you are such a hypocrite. Who do you think you are telling me there's something bothering me when you got upset when I brought up Cami's name? I don't know what you two argued about, but it wouldn't surprise me if you started it."

Rubbing the bridge of her nose, Gigi closed her eyes and shook her head.

"You know something else, you talked a real good game the other night telling me how you wished you had the strength and the common sense to share your thoughts and feelings, but when the opportunity presents itself, you don't."

She opened her eyes and asked, "Are you finished?"

"I'm outta here," I said, rising to my feet.

She rested her hands on her lap. "Do you really want to know what happened between Leon and me?"

"I don't give a damn what's goin' on between you and him."

"No, Chris, before you leave, I'll let you know what's really goin' on. Okay?"

Finally, I thought as I sat back down on the sofa. "Okay," I said.

She nodded. "When Leon and I were dating, I got pregnant. When I told him, he denied being the father and treated me like crap. I ended up having an abortion."

"Damn."

"Oh, it gets better," she continued. "I run into Leon again six years later. He's doing the same thing again to his current girlfriend. He tells me he doesn't care for her or his child, but he's still in love with me and expects me to forgive his sorry ass. I tell him it's over and to get a life. He disrespects me by calling me out of my name. I tell him to go fuck himself. End of story."

No wonder Gigi was furious and upset the night she met Leon's girlfriend.

"And since you're in such an inquisitive mood, Chris, let me give you the 4-1-1 on what happened between me and Cami. My best friend told me she's been cheating on her husband, got herself pregnant and wanted to get an abortion. I disagreed with her decision and insulted her with a nasty remark about her being promiscuous. She insulted me about the possibility of not being able to conceive. Our friendship was history. End of story."

I opened my mouth to say something, but I couldn't. This was deeper than I expected. Instead, I stared at Gigi's face. The lovely smile that greeted me at the front door earlier was replaced with a twisted grimace. Sadness and anger were flaring inside her pupils.

"Is there something else you'd like to know?"

"I didn't know," I said, touching her hand.

Gigi withdrew her hand. "Well, now you do," she mumbled. She tapped her fingers on her thighs, then rose to her feet and opened the front door.

I stood up. "I'm sorry."

"Save your apologies, Chris. I don't want any sympathy from you, okay?" She rolled her eyes and chuckled. "Maybe you were right after all. I'm the one who wasn't straightforward with you from the beginning. I'm the one who opened her big ass mouth and lost her best friend. What difference does it make now? I'm the crazy hypocrite."

I shook my head. "You're being ridiculous."

Gigi nodded. "Yep, that's me...the ridiculous, crazy hypocrite," she said sarcastically.

I touched her shoulder. "Gigi, don't."

She lowered her head, closed her eyes, and whispered, "Please, just go."

I withdrew my hand and walked out the front door. When I first arrived at Gigi's home, the sky was overcast and drizzle fell from the clouds. Raindrops were now flooding the ground as I made my way to my Explorer. Gigi stood at her front door and waited for me to start the engine. After I pulled away from the curb, she finally closed her door.

During the entire ride home, I took into consideration everything that transpired. Maybe it wasn't to be between Gigi and myself, and it was better to move on. She had some serious issues and it wasn't my problem. Yeah, that's what I kept telling myself repeatedly as I sat in the parking lot of my apartment building, but once again, my heart had a different story. I couldn't shake the distant look on her face from my mind.

Gripping my steering wheel, I closed my eyes. "Leave it alone." Five minutes passed before I shook my head and drove back to Gigi's.

Chapter Twenty-Six
Regina

This was not the way I expected my evening to end. I was looking forward to spending a nice, romantic dinner with Chris. I anticipated our budding relationship would finally blossom into something special and he would reveal his feelings for me. Any problems or concerns that were on our minds would be resolved through friendly conversation. Unfortunately, that wasn't the case. Chris and I argued, and I asked him to leave.

The grilled lemon chicken, brown rice and steamed vegetables I prepared were cooling in my refrigerator. I didn't have the stomach to eat anything. Instead, I drowned my sorrows with one glass of wine after another. Staring outside the living room window, I searched for tranquility in the raindrops rejuvenating the earth with their splendid simplicity. I hoped their magic could heal my wounded heart. Rene and Angela couldn't lift my spirits either as they sang the chorus to *You Don't Have To Cry* in perfect harmony on the stereo. Resting on the sofa, I touched the spot where Chris sat, seeking the warmth of his body. However, it was nowhere to be found. I knew I screwed up big time.

"How could I have been so stupid?" I asked aloud.

I pondered everything that had happened. Chris had valid concerns about my history with Leon. I knew it weighed heavily on his mind, and if positions were reversed, I would have felt the same way. He was also right about me not being honest. What made matters worse was the way I disrespected his suspicions and feelings and laughed in his face. I shouldn't have gone there. The only reason I did so was because he inquired about my problems with Cami. My behavior was inexcusable and hypocritical. The other day, when talking on the phone with April, she nonchalantly brought up her name. I forgot Cami's birthday was the following week. Ironically, it was two days after my surgery. I lost count how many times I picked up the telephone to call Cami. Maybe it was because of my guilt when I had the opportunity to make amends the night of our last conversation. Sure, I was bitter and hurt by what she said. But regardless of her remarks and our fight, deep down inside my heart, I missed my best friend.

I rose to my feet and dialed Cami's phone number, holding the receiver tightly and staring at the floor. I said a prayer asking the Lord to give me the strength to find the words to express my feelings. I listened to Cami's voice instructing the caller to leave a message after the beep. I opened my mouth to speak, but hung up the phone. Sitting down on the sofa, I poured myself another glass.

Brian McKnight started crooning *Anytime* as I propped my head against the pillow and closed my eyes. Drifting asleep, I asked myself why I continued hurting the people I loved and cared for by making stupid mistakes. The sound of the telephone ringing startled me from my thoughts.

"Hello?" I asked.

"Hey," Chris answered.

I lowered my head and sighed. I didn't expect to ever hear from him again.

"Hello?"

"I'm here," I replied.

"Um, did I catch you at a bad time?"

"No," I said nonchalantly.

"I need to ask you something, Gigi."

I sucked my teeth. "I don't think it's a good idea."

He sighed. "There's something I need to know and also tell you."

I closed my eyes. "I don't think there's anything else we have to say."

"This will only take a few minutes," he pleaded.

I held the receiver against my breasts. *Please, Chris,* I thought, *why can't you leave well enough alone?*

"Gigi?"

"Chris, I can't – "

"Look, Gigi," he interrupted. "All I want is a few minutes of your time. That's all."

I rubbed the bridge of my nose. "What do you want to talk about?"

"Um, I need to see your face, if you don't mind?"

I cocked my eyebrow. "Huh? Where are you?"

"Outside," he responded.

I peaked outside my Venetian blind. Sure enough, Chris was sitting in his SUV across the street from my house and talking on his cell phone. "I don't believe you," I replied, walking away from the window. "Are you crazy?"

"Maybe," he answered.

I chuckled. "There is no maybe about it."

"Gigi, can I see you?"

"Okay," I said, hanging up the phone and unlocking the front door. Chris crossed the street swiftly and almost tripped climbing up the doorstep. Once inside, I closed the door, leaned against the window sill and crossed my arms. He stood a few steps away from me. His clothes were soaked from head to toe.

"Thanks," he said, rubbing his forehead. "Um, I wanted to ask you why you invited me over for dinner."

I shook my head. "It doesn't matter at this point."

"Yes, it does."

I lowered my head and rubbed my temples. "Please, Chris, it wasn't meant to be."

He took a step forward and raised my chin with his index finger. Looking into my eyes, Chris said, "You didn't answer my question."

I studied Chris's wet face to the rhythm of Lisa Fischer's *How Can I Ease The Pain.* Damn, he looked so sexy. "I invited you over to talk with you," I answered.

He crossed his arm. "About?"

I sighed. "Whatever was troubling you, Chris."

"Mm hmmm."

"Didn't we already have this conversation?"

He nodded. "We did."

"Then why are you doing this to me, Chris?" I begged, shrugging my shoulders. "Why are you putting me through this again? We don't have anything else to say," I repeated.

"I think we do."

"What makes you think that?"

"The look on your face tonight. You had that same look when you asked me to leave the last time I was here."

I ran my fingers through my hair. "What look?"

"You had apprehension in your eyes. Although you said you wanted me to leave, it appeared that wasn't the case."

I chuckled. "Is that what you think?"

"Yeah."

"Well, correct me if I'm wrong," I said, clearing my throat. "But you were the one who wanted to leave this time around."

He nodded. "I did, but…um…sometimes we say and do things –"

"Then don't go there," I interjected, waving my hand.

"And don't you go there, either."

"Excuse me?" I asked, tilting my head.

"Why do you always push me away whenever you're hurting?"

"You don't know me, Chris, so don't judge me!"

"Can you honestly tell me, Gigi, that you're not hurting now?"

I sat down on the sofa, crossed my legs and sipped my Merlot. He furrowed his brow, waiting for my response. Inhaling deeply, I closed my eyes and shook my head.

"Look, Gigi," Chris continued, kneeling down beside me, "I apologize for the comment I made about Cami. I shouldn't have gone there. Before you cut me off, I tried to tell you that sometimes we say or do things that hurt the people we care for."

"Yes, we do," I whispered, resting my hands on my thigh.

He nodded and bit his bottom lip. "I shouldn't have lost my cool tonight. I'm not ashamed to admit my jealousy about your past with Leon. I didn't know if you still had feelings for him."

"I understand," I murmured. Reclining against the sofa, I stared across the living room. "I want to apologize to you for the way I behaved tonight."

"Oh?"

I nodded. "It was wrong for me to take out my frustrations on you about Cami. Truthfully speaking, I was the one acting defensive. Lately, I've been thinking about her so much. Before you returned, I called her to say hi."

"What did she say?"

"Nothing. She didn't answer the phone and I didn't bother leaving her a message."

"Well, you were the one who told me don't wait until tragedy strikes to tell someone that you love them."

I chuckled. "You're too attentive."

"Maybe so, but things might not be as bad as you think."

I sighed. "I don't know."

"Do you mind if I ask you a question?"

I shrugged my shoulders. "Go ahead."

"Are you having a thyroidectomy?"

I cocked my eyebrow. "Yes, I am. Why do you ask?"

"Well, unless you were having radioactive iodine treatment, I don't think there's any danger of not being able to have children."

"No, there isn't," I said, curling my bottom lip.

Chris nodded and shrugged his shoulders.

I crossed my arms. "How did you know about the treatment options?"

"I looked it up the other night on the Internet."

Oh my God, I thought, *I don't believe he did that!* I stared at Chris's face as my thoughts hung onto the lyrics of Bobby Caldwell's *What You Won't Do For Love*. Placing my hands on my lap, I inhaled deeply and asked, "How can you still care for me, Chris, after the way I've treated you?"

"Because I do," he answered, rubbing my hand with his thumb. "Everybody has issues and we're all human. You and I deeply care for each other, don't you agree?"

I nodded and cracked a half smile.

"And if that's the case," Chris paused, clearing his throat. "I'd be a damn fool if I let you walk out of my life tonight."

My heart tingled and I felt the goosebumps dancing on my forearms and the back of my neck. I lowered my head and blushed.

He rubbed my cheek and that beautiful smile danced across his handsome face along with that glow in his eyes.

I tilted my head. "Can I ask you another question?"

"Sure," he answered.

"I've noticed whenever you're thinking about something, you have this glow in your eyes."

He chuckled. "I do?"

I giggled. "Yes, you do. And I'm curious to know what's on your mind."

"It's nothing," he replied, shaking his head.

I touched his arm, letting him know it was okay to share his thoughts. "No, please tell me."

"Every time you smile or blush, I think about the poem I wrote when I first met you."

"What was it called?" I asked aloud, snapping my fingers twice. "Oh, I remember now. It was *Miracle*."

He shook his head.

I cocked my eyebrow. "Huh?" Now, I was totally confused.

"The one aboard the R3 train that you made me freestyle about azaleas."

My eyes widened in total surprise. I had completely forgotten about that one.

"I was thinking about you a few weeks ago and the first stanza popped into my head. I had a creative moment and finished writing the poem."

My mouth fell open. "I don't believe you, Chris. You are too much."

He raised his eyebrows. "Would you like to hear it?"

"Yes," I whispered, nodding. My eyes were dampening as Chris held my hand and recited his verses with his sensual voice.

Azaleas bloom
beneath the sunrise
that welcomes the arrival
and the promise of a new day
when divine intervention flows
from the tree of Life
into the ties that bind us
in the joy of friendship.

I discover inspiration
in the comfort of your smile:
an amalgamation
of brilliance, diligence, and patience
that mirrors your genuine spirit
like the pride that blazes
from your bronze skin;
skin that simply expresses
the imperial elegance
of its African heritage
and the strength of a queen
chasing her dreams
in the pursuit of excellence.

To know you
is an honor and a blessing
for you are my sister,
you are my friend.
And I wish you
nothing but the best
in everything you do,
because the Creator's love
is shining upon you.

I blushed, putting my hands over my mouth. "Chris, that was so beautiful."

He leaned forward and kissed my cheek. "A beautiful poem for a beautiful lady."

I slid over and Chris sat beside me. I closed my eyes and tilted my head as Chris kissed me. His lips and tongue felt so sweet and juicy. They tasted and smelled like peppermints.

I held his hand and whispered, "I love you."

He waved his hand. "I could have told you that."

Ooh, no he didn't, I thought. I punched his arm.

"Damn," he replied, rubbing his biceps. "Girl, you throw a wicked right. Did you knock Leon on his ass with that haymaker?"

I laughed. "Almost. But if you ever joke like that again, you'll find out."

We laughed simultaneously and stared at each other. I couldn't stop blushing as I started crying again and Chris wiped the tears from my cheeks with his fingers. He leaned over and kissed me once more. My heart was bouncing sporadically to Kem's *I Can't Stop Loving You*. It felt so good the way Chris rocked my body and danced his fingers across the small of my back.

I rested my head on his lap and stretched my legs across the sofa. My fingers stroked the landscape of his torso. His muscles felt so firm, yet soothing. I found myself in ecstasy with a smile written across my face, hypnotized by his passionate eyes.

Chris combed his fingers through my hair and whispered, "I love you, too, Gigi."

I inhaled deeply and allowed my soul to descend into the rapture of the moment.

Chapter Twenty-Seven
Regina

I slowly opened my eyes to the sound of two females talking and moving around me. My vision was distorted by the light of the room and everything was a complete blur. If I wasn't mistaken, there was a faint beeping noise to my left. I tried turning my head, but the pain was too unbearable.

"Uhhh," I groaned.

"Relax, Ms. Simmons," a female voice said above me. Slowly but surely, I began to decipher the features on her light-skinned face. She was dressed in pink scrubs. "Your operation went well," she added.

"Her blood pressure is normal," the other nurse replied with her deep voice. "I'll let her family know she's awake."

"Everything will be fine," the light-skinned one said before she followed her colleague.

Closing my eyes, I begged to differ, considering the soreness in my neck and the scratchy feeling of the tube inserted down my throat. My entire body felt heavy and numb. Whatever the hospitals were using for anesthesia these days kicked my ass. Drifting back to sleep, I didn't hear or notice that someone had came into my room until I felt their hand grazing my forearm. Their fingers felt warm along with the soft kiss that touched my cheek. I opened my eyes and saw Chris standing there with a beautiful bouquet of red roses.

He smiled and held my hand. "Hey, you. How're you feeling?"

"Hmmm," I purred, flashing a half smile.

Chris sat the flowers on the table to my right. "Dr. Fitzpatrick had to leave early, but he'll be back tomorrow to check on your progress. He said you did great. I'm proud of you, honey."

I squeezed his fingers to let him know how much I appreciated his kindness and affection. I smiled with thoughts of the time we spent together the past week: going to dinner at Savannah's; watching DVDs over at my house; hanging out at the Crimson Moon; and most importantly, making love for the first time. It felt so wonderful the way he rejuvenated my body and spirit when he rocked my world the other night. There was no greater joy than waking up in his arms with the bed sheets entangled around our bodies and watching slivers of sunlight shine on our brown skin.

He tapped a yellow envelope against the bed's rail. "Gene sends you all the best from his family. He wants you to heal up those vocal chords, Flipper, so he can have one of his favorite Buttacups back on the mic."

I coughed and waved my hand in the air. *Please, Chris, don't joke with me like that,* I thought. It was too painful for me to laugh.

I heard the sound of a female clearing her throat from behind Chris. He stepped aside so I could see April, who approached my bedside and held my hand.

"Oh, Gigi, how are you?" she asked.

I rubbed her hand to let her know I was fine.

"You know Chris and I are going to take good care of you while you're recovering," she said, touching his shoulder.

Chris nodded. "That's right," he added, smoothing my hair with his fingers.

I started crying and couldn't believe how blessed I was to have a good man and a dear friend like each of them in my life.

"Excuse me, Ms. Simmons," the voice of the light-skinned nurse called from behind. "This special delivery just came for you."

Chris and April turned their heads and stepped aside so I could see her holding a fruit basket in her hands with a small card attached to the plastic wrapping. She sat them on the table beside the flowers and left us alone.

Opening the card, Chris read the message aloud. "Regina, best wishes on a speedy recovery. Love, your co-workers in Accounting."

"That was sweet," April replied.

I rolled my eyes and imagined how overjoyed Marcia would be when I returned back to work six weeks from now.

"Girl, you ain't right," she said, cutting her eyes and pressing her lips.

I coughed, cracking myself up. Chris couldn't help laughing either and neither could April.

After getting herself together, April stared at the floor and touched my forearm. "Gigi, I'll be right back. I want to run down the hallway and get something to snack on from the vending machine."

I cocked my eyebrow and watched her leave the room. April's behavior seemed real odd since I knew firsthand she was a fitness nut and ate healthy. *What was that all about?* I thought.

Chris smiled half-heartedly and held my hand. "Um, Gigi," he paused, clearing his throat. "There's somebody here who'd like to see you. She came about an hour ago while you were resting."

Inhaling deeply, I squeezed his hand and knew who my visitor was. I couldn't believe she was here.

Three days earlier, I came home from dinner with Chris and there was a message on my answering machine. The caller didn't say a word, but I heard them breathing. Checking my Caller ID, my suspicions were confirmed when I saw Cami's cell phone number displayed on the screen. Mulling for a good ten minutes, I picked up the phone and called her. The answering machine clicked on and I spoke into the receiver.

"Hey, Cami. It's me, Gigi. Um, I was thinking about you and wanted to call to say hi. I hope all is well with you and the boys. Give your mom all my love. Take care, sweetie."

The next day, Cami left a message on my answering service when I went to the supermarket.

"Hey, Gigi. How ya doin'? Um, April mentioned that you are havin' surgery on Friday. I'll keep you in my prayers and all. Ma told me to tell you she says hello. The boys are doin' fine as can be expected, given the circumstances with me and Damon. They miss their Aunt Gigi, especially Duane. Maybe April can bring them by to see you. You hang in there and I'll talk to ya soon."

I didn't expect Cami to return my call. I was happy to hear her voice again and that she was doing well. I wanted to respond back, but the dry tone in her voice and her suggestion about April bringing her sons by to see me convinced me maybe she wasn't ready to speak one on one again. Maybe I wasn't ready, either.

"Honey, are you alright?" Chris asked, breaking me out of my trance.

I pulled his finger to let him know I was fine.

"Um, would you like me to stay?" he offered.

I shook his hand. I appreciated his concern, but this was something I needed to work out alone.

Chris kissed me on my cheek and whispered in my ear, "Don't curse her out too much!"

"Uhhh," I moaned, laughing at his joke. I closed my eyes and listened to Chris's footsteps disappear from my room. The blood pressure machine was the only sound I heard for a few moments until the heels of a woman's boots clicked slowly across the floor. Her footsteps grew closer and came to a stop at my bedside. I felt the person gripping the metal rail. Opening my eyes, I inhaled deeply when I saw Cami standing over me. It was almost a month since I'd last seen her, but she looked well. Apparently, girlfriend gained some weight as her cheeks and breasts appeared fuller. Clasping her hands in prayers, Cami's bottom lip quivered as she bawled uncontrollably. Setting her purse on the floor, she wiped her tears with the back of her hand.

Cami gripped the rail and inhaled deeply. "I have s-s-something I want to s-s-say to you," she stammered, clearing her throat. "No matter whatever direction our lives will take or whatever we say in anger, I will always love you, Regina Simmons."

I nodded, lifting my trembling hand to reach out to her.

She held my wrist. "You are my best friend and my sister, and," she paused, squeezing my fingers. "You will always be my lil' hussy."

"Uhhhh," I moaned. *I love you, too, Cami,* I thought.

She rested my hand on the bed and hung her head. "When you're able to speak and you're feeling better," she paused, clearing her throat. "We'll sit down and talk. Okay?"

I nodded.

Cami stared at me and her eyes began watering. "Oh, Gigi," she wept. "I am so sorry for what happened."

I pulled her wrist towards my face and kissed her hand. *I'm sorry, too, sweetie,* I thought.

She smiled. Resting my hand on the bed, Cami said, "I brought the boys to see you. They're waiting outside."

I smiled, happy that Cami did so, but also glad she came to see me.

She kissed my cheek. "I see you've been quite busy and all. Got yourself a new man," she said, smiling and widening her eyes.

I blushed. *Yeah, girl,* I thought, *he's all mine.*

"Between you and me, Chris is a good catch." Running her fingers gently through my hair, Cami whispered, "Can I ask you a question, Gigi?"

"Mm hmmm," I mumbled.

"Did you let 'em spank that ass before you had surgery?"

"Uhhhh," I moaned. *No, she didn't,* I thought. I couldn't help myself from laughing, in spite of the pain.

She winked and patted my hand. "That's my hussy. Mama taught you well."

I blushed and cracked a half smile.

Cami turned around when we heard someone knocking at the door. She stepped aside and I saw Chris standing in the doorway.

We stared at each other and started giggling.

"I hope I'm not interrupting. Is everything alright?" he asked.

"We're fine," Cami answered, squeezing my hand.

I glanced back and forth between Chris and Cami and smiled in agreement.

Yes, I thought, *everything is alright.*

Share your thoughts with Bill Holmes
Bill@BillHolmes.com

Visit Bill Holmes' Web site
www.billholmes.com

XpressYourself Novels

QTY

____ *Anything Goes* by Jessica Tilles ISBN: 0-9722990-0-9; $15.00

____ *In My Sisters' Corner* by Jessica Tilles ISBN: 0-9722990-1-7; $15.00

___ *Apple Tree* by Jessica Tilles ISBN: 0-9722990-2-5; $15.00

___ *Sweet Revenge* by Jessica Tilles ISBN: 0-9722990-3-3; $15.00

___ *One Love* by Bill Holmes ISBN: 0-9722990-4-1; $15.00

___ *Fatal Desire* by Jessica Tilles ISBN: 0-9722990-4-1; $15.00

Send to:

Xpress Yourself Publishing, LLC
Attn: Book Orders
P.O. Box 1615
Upper Marlboro, MD 20773

Please send me the books I have checked above. I am enclosing $______ (plus $1.50 per book, shipping and handling). Send check or money order (no cash or C.O.Ds please). Allow up to two weeks for delivery.

Name ______________________________________
Address _____________________________________
City ________________________State/Zip _________

Visit us online at www.xpressyourselfpublishing.org

Printed in the United States
107002LV00002B/523-546/A

9 780972 299046